Also by J.

Girl on the Beach

The Butterfly Trap

Readers' Reviews

A romantic story with some poignant touches - ideal for those lazy afternoons.

A truly moving depiction of wartime in Arnhem and the calm and happiness of a farm after the war. A wonderful and emotional read. A stunning book by author, J.V. Phaure.

Some tales are meant to be written, and this is one of them.

A sensitive and at times poignant tale, cleverly choreographed against a backdrop of post war Devon and war time Holland. An engaging read!

JACK'S STORY

Richard,
Ta da!!
With love and best wishes,

JVPhaure

J. V. PHAURE

Copyright © J.V. Phaure 2021

J.V. Phaure has asserted her right to be identified as the author of this Work in accordance with the Copyright, Designs and Patents Act 1988

A CIP catalogue record for the book is available from the British Library

Cover Design by Robin Freeman

Photography supplied by
the Airborne Assault Museum
www.paradata.org.uk

Paperback ISBN 978-1-914408-62-5

This book is a work of fiction. Names, characters, places and incidents are either a product of the author's imagination or are used fictitiously. Any resemblance to actual people living or dead, events or locales is entirely coincidental.

Typeset, printed and bound in Great Britain by
Biddles Books, King's Lynn, Norfolk

Dedication

To the 1st British Airborne Division and the 1st Polish Independent Parachute Brigade – 17th September 1944.

To all Paratroopers in current and past conflicts,

"Airborne"

And to a paratrooper who served in today's conflicts and lost his young life,

> To Jack

About the Author

J.V. Phaure is a British author, best known for her novels Girl on the Beach and its sequel The Butterfly Trap.

Writing has always been a passion of hers and she takes her inspiration from the people she meets and the countries she has lived in. She loves nothing more than to sit on her village beach and people watch and write. When she's not writing she enjoys windsurfing locally to her.

She lives with her family in North Essex.

To find out more about the author you can visit her website or find her on Instagram, Twitter and Facebook.

www.jvphaure.com

J_V_Phaure

@JvPhaure

Facebook.com/jvphaure

With thanks to all those who have made Jack's Story what it is. But special thanks go to a veteran paratrooper who served alongside Jack in Afghanistan and told me his comrade's story. Who allowed me into his own world as a veteran soldier and allowed me to listen and learn. A very special person who has remained anonymous but knows none of this could have happened without him.

"Do you know what love is?
I'll tell you: it is whatever you can still betray."

John Le Carré

Chapter One

Appledaw Farm, Cowick, Exeter, September, 1946

'Ninety-nine, one hundred, coming ready or not!' Eleanor moved her arm away from her shielded eyes and flashed them open, blinking several times. She turned quickly to see where they might be hiding. The farm seemed quiet; the old Fordson tractor sat close to the track by the paddock where the Red Horn cattle grazed, its plough still caked in dry soil from the field it had crossed the day before. She scanned the yard as the ducks waddled aimlessly across her path, quacking in a babbling chatter to each other, the drake hissing the loudest to keep his girls together as they made their way to the nearby pond. She ran toward the washing line and snatched back a billowing sheet. Turning on her heels, she ran to the weeping willow that rested by the pond. She separated the straggling branches as if parting the curtains on a stage; brushing them away, she peered through their frond-like leaves. Her brows knitted, she stood as quiet as a mouse. She brushed down her dress and bent to tie the lace on her two-toned brown and cream brogues, her eyes sweeping low, looking for small feet tucked behind something on the farm.

'Eleanor, quick come! Quickly, hurry. Look what I've found!'

'Bertie, you're supposed to be hiding.'

'Quick, Eleanor, come, it's urgent!'

Eleanor made her way across the yard to the hay barn, searching each hiding spot for Harry as she went.

'Where are you, Bertie?' She stood in the open space of the hay barn. Particles of dust danced in the air as a beam cast its light through the huge open doors.

'Up here,' Bertie said, his head hanging over the edge. She lifted the skirt of her dress and climbed the wooden ladder to the hayloft. The sunlight peeked through the cracks in the timber frame. Eleanor wasn't expecting to see what Bertie had found. In the corner a girl sat crouched. Her hair was loose and untidy, her eyes hollow, her pretty skirt muddied. Her hands were cut, and her knees were grazed, her white buttoned-down blouse stained with soil. She pulled a light cardigan sweater across, concealing the marks. The buckle on her court shoe was broken. She grappled at what appeared to be a pillowcase and tucked it behind her. Eleanor stood back and gasped. Who was she? She looked weary and frightened.

'I've been hiding forever,' squeaked Harry as he mounted the ladder and crawled onto the hay bales. 'What is it?' He grimaced as he spied the forlorn-looking creature in the corner.

'*It*? Harry. *It* is a girl!' Eleanor snapped disdainfully.

'Ask her name,' Bertie said, pushing Eleanor forward.

Eleanor tugged a little at the cuffs of her cardigan. 'What's your name?'

The girl stared at her, her eyes a deep blank void.

'Your name, what's your name?' she asked again.

The girl's eyes flicked over each peering face that hovered in front of her.

'Where are you from?' Eleanor asked.

Her eyes were a dark brown, as deep as the blackest of holes. She said nothing.

'I'm Eleanor.' She gestured to herself. 'What's your name?'

The girl said nothing. Mute.

'She doesn't understand, she's not from here,' Bertie said, peering at her dirty hands and grimy nails.

'Well, where's she from? How has she come upon our farm?'

'Her hair is tangled! She smells like the pigs!' Harry scoffed, turning up his nose and holding it.

'Stop it, Harry, don't be so mean!' Eleanor spat out.

'How old do you think she is?' Bertie whispered.

'I don't know – she looks a little older than me. Maybe twenty?'

'Twenty, that's just old!' Harry shouted.

'Shhh! Don't be so silly, Harry.'

'Who do we tell?' Bertie asked.

'We tell Aunt Emma,' proclaimed Harry, turning to race back down the ladder.

Eleanor grabbed his arm, 'Nobody, we tell nobody. D'you hear? If you tell a soul I will rip the legs from your toy soldier men and squeeze your nose so tightly, it may even fall off.'

Harry held his nose and pushed his lips together. 'You can't do that! They're mine and Aunt Emma and Uncle Henry will find out.'

'This is our secret, Harry. We must swear to tell nobody,' Eleanor declared. 'Maybe she's a gypsy they passed through a while back, maybe she got left behind?'

'But the gypsies spoke English,' Bertie said.

Eleanor knelt down beside the girl, brushing the sharp ends of hay away from her hands. 'My name's Eleanor, and these are my brothers, Bertie and Harry. Stay here and we'll bring you some food and a blanket and some tea. D'you like tea?'

The girl stared at Eleanor, watching her lips move.

'I don't know why you're bothering – she doesn't understand you!'

Bertie pinched Harry's ear. 'Just be quiet, Harry!' He kept his fingers tight on his younger brother's ear.

Eleanor stayed crouched by her. She touched her hand; it was cold, as cold as ice but as soft as silk. 'Stay here, we'll get you some tea and food and a blanket. Alright?' She squeezed her hand a little as she got up from the hay bale. 'Come on, boys.'

They left the girl in the hayloft and their footsteps were light across the dusty ground of the yard. Eleanor glanced back at the hay barn. Harry kicked a few loose stones as he ambled along behind the others, his hands in the pockets of his flannel shorts. Eleanor tapped her foot on the ground as she waited by the kitchen door, beckoning to her little brother to hurry his way. He moseyed past her and she closed the door with two hands, turning the knob gently to avoid the clicking noise. Standing with her back to it and still holding the doorknob in her hands, she swept her hair away from her face.

'Right, Bertie, have a look in the cupboard for a flask and make some tea. Be sure it's piping hot.' Eleanor teased open the fridge, the milk bottles clinking a little in the door as she did. A large pat of butter sat on a plate wrapped in parchment paper, and she grabbed it along with a lump of hard, crumbly cheese. She closed the door slowly so as to silence the clinking of the milk bottles again. She peered inside the bread bin and took out the farmhouse loaf and carved two slices from it. The hard butter tore at the bread as she tried to smear it in. It would have to do. She wrapped the crudely made sandwich in a clean napkin and left it like a small picnic parcel on the side.

Jack's Story

Bertie placed the copper kettle onto the Aga and waited a while until it let out a squeal. He took it off the heat quickly. He poured the steaming water into the teapot that sat on the kitchen table. Then he plopped two lumps of sugar into the flask and poured the tea through a strainer into the flask, adding a slug of milk.

'What can I do? If I'm to be part of the secret I need a job too?' Harry grumbled.

'Go up to the linen dresser and find an old blanket. If Aunt Emma is there, simply tell her we are making a den, nothing more.' Harry snuck up the stairs to the linen dresser, the floorboards creaking beneath his small footsteps. He peered through the rails of the banister to the hallway below. The sun shone through the large window on the staircase, throwing its beam straight into the hall and upon the old grandfather clock which stood as a gateway to time, its golden pendulum making its steady way back and forth. Harry tilted his head as he peered between the banisters, watching it watch him. Looking both ways and over his shoulder, he stood on his tiptoes and yanked at a cream woollen blanket from the shelf, his breath held, hoping that nothing would topple on to him. With one last tug he grabbed the blanket, falling back. The ornate vase on the round carved table wobbled; he watched it, open-mouthed. He turned and raced back down the stairs, his small hands strumming along the banister's spindles, turning once to look at the face of the grandfather clock watching him. He ran into the kitchen, where Eleanor and Harry were clearing up the evidence of stolen food and hot tea.

'I've got one.' He beamed, waggling it in the air.

'Good, well done, Harry. Come on, let's go.' They ran across the yard and into the hay barn. They stood at the bottom of the ladder for a moment to catch their breath. Then scrambled up it and stood breathless by the girl. She hadn't moved an inch.

'Here.' Eleanor handed her the cheese sandwich wrapped in a red-checked napkin. Bertie thrust his hand out, wiggling the flask at her. Harry stood holding the blanket snugly into his tummy. Taking the blanket from him, Eleanor put it beside the girl.

The girl ripped at the sandwich, stuffing it into her mouth, not pausing for breath as she did. She pushed her straggly hair away from her face, pushing into her mouth the crumbs that caught on her pink lips.

'Poor thing, she must be starving,' Eleanor said, unfolding the blanket and placing it on the girl's knees.

'How long d'you think she's been here?' Bertie whispered.

'I don't know, but she's jolly hungry.' Eleanor took the flask from Bertie and poured the sweet tea into a cup. The girl cupped it in her hands and pressed her lips up against it.

'She can't stay here forever,' Harry said. 'She smells and she eats like a pig.'

'Harry!' Eleanor shoved him. 'I'll have to fetch her some clothes and maybe a flannel so she can wash her face and hands.' Her own clothes, she thought, would be too small, and Aunt Emma's would drown her.

'Do you think she's dying?' Bertie asked as he peered at her soulless eyes.

'I don't think so, but she'll certainly catch her death out here. We need to keep her warm.'

'What's your name?' Harry asked abruptly. He was getting a little impatient with her muteness.

She stared at him.

'Harry, be kind, she's probably frightened,' Eleanor said, pulling him away.

Jack's Story

The shrill sound of Aunt Emma calling disturbed them. 'Eleanor, Bertie, Harry, come inside now to wash your hands and prepare for dinner.' Her voice echoed across the farmyard. 'Uncle Henry will be home soon from the fields.'

'What do we do?' Bertie said. 'We have to go in now and Uncle Henry will be back soon. He can't see us here.'

'I know, come on, we say nothing, not a word,' Eleanor said, her voice hushed. She turned to the girl. 'We'll be back in the morning. We'll bring you some more food then. Understand? We promise not to say a word. I don't know who you are, but you're safe here.' Eleanor ushered the boys away and climbed back down the ladder.

'What have you been up to?' Aunt Emma asked, wiping a strand of hair from her face with the back of her hand as she sat at the table, peeling carrots and swede for the stew. Her hair was clipped at the side and she wore a floral apron.

'Well...' Harry began. Bertie dug his elbow into his side. 'Well, just playing hide and seek mainly, Aunt Emma.'

'That sounds fun. Now, boys, take these peelings out to the pigs and then come back inside as quick as bunnies and wash your hands and set the table. Eleanor, I thought perhaps you could go to the town tomorrow and run a few errands for me. You can take my bicycle.'

'Yes, Aunt Emma, of course.'

Harry and Bertie returned from outside and scurried into the scullery, where Eleanor was already washing her hands.

Eleanor lifted Harry up to the taps and wedged him between herself and the Belfast sink whilst he washed his hands.

'Maybe you could get something in town?' Bertie whispered.

'I was thinking just the same thing myself, only I'm not sure how. I don't have very much money, just the piggy bank from Mother and Father.'

'Why don't we tell Mother and Father – they'd know what to do. They sent us here to be safe. They'd understand.'

'Oh, I don't know, Bertie. No, we mustn't tell a soul. A least not until we know who she is and why she has come upon the farm. She has to be running away from something, but what?'

Aunt Emma poked her head around the door. 'What's all this whispering in here?'

'Oh, nothing, we're just deciding what we might do tomorrow.'

'Right, well, come along now. The table still needs to be laid. Uncle Henry will be back in no time and hungry I daresay.'

The three set the table whilst Aunt Em mashed the boiled swede and carrots. The kitchen door swung open and Uncle Henry stood beaming whilst rubbing his hands together, his nose red and his boots muddy. The kitchen door was like a hug on return from the fields, always giving the emotions of that great sense of homecoming.

'Summit smells good,' he said as he inched his boots off his feet before washing his bear-sized hands at the sink.

'Hungry?' Aunt Em asked.

'Famished.' He rested his hands on her waist, giving her a loving squeeze. 'It's been a long day on the teddie fields, we be nearly finished 'arvesting. Jack will need to 'elp with calvin' – looks like two of the 'eifers be ready to calve. I'll be needing to get 'em settled and warm and get the 'ay down for 'em. The nights be too cold for 'em now. I'll need 'im to 'elp me with the 'ayloft over next few days. He be a good worker, our Jack. You want to 'elp with the calvin', lad?' Uncle Henry said, as tousled Bertie's hair.

Bertie shot a look at Eleanor. She shook her head. *Don't worry,* she telegraphed.

Chapter Two

Appledaw Farm, Cowick, Exeter, late September, 1946

The girl raised her head as the sun glowed like a summer peach in the sky, the red and orange hues throwing it into a liquid gold where the silhouettes of bare trees stood in its glow. The subtlety of its light peeked through the rafters, where the dust from the hay danced with merriment. Only an hour before she'd sat in the darkness, a blackness that was so absolute, hearing only the sounds of scurrying feet from small creatures. The scratching sounds from mice and rats in the rafters. She could see nothing until the sun lifted itself into the sky.

She brushed her fists against her bleary eyes. In the distance the raucous sound of the cockerel declared that a new day had begun. Her tummy gurgled a little. Yesterday she'd eaten nothing but the sandwich; the flask of tea was empty now and cold to the touch. She lay back down and closed her eyes. She pulled the pillowcase closer into her face, the faint scent of fresh meadow flowers still on it. She swallowed and felt the tears sting her eyes. Pulling her arms in closer, she lay like a baby in the womb of its mother. She cradled her head in her hand and let the tears fall. She tried to forget, but it kept coming back. Haunting her thoughts. Why? Did she ever deserve it? She closed her eyes, trying to forget, trying to stop the tears from falling down her cheeks. She buried her head in the crook of her arm.

She needed to run, to never return, to never see again the images behind the door. Had she been heard? All she wanted now was to dispel an unwanted memory. She ran through the darkness, the trees' branches snatching at her legs, coarse ferns grabbing at her as she fell in her tiredness. Scrambling through the undergrowth, she pushed herself away backwards, her hands hiding her face. Red eyes flashed in front of her. She screamed.

Her eyes flashed open. Feeling a tightness in her chest, she lay still, holding her breath as she heard footsteps on the ground below. They stopped. She pushed herself further into the corner; the hay rustled beneath her. She could feel her heart thumping in her chest. The hay's sharp ends dug into the bare skin of her calves as she pushed it away. She darted her eyes toward the ladder as the footsteps shuffled across the ground. She breathed in, her eyes wide, her hands grappling at her skirt. Her eyes stayed fixed on the ladder. Her palms clenched and unclenched. The paralysis crept in on her as the footsteps came nearer.

Eleanor smiled as she pushed herself up into the loft. 'It's me, Eleanor. I've brought you something to eat – it's not much, a scone and jam and some warm milk, here.' She handed her the parcel of food and the warm cup of milk. 'Who are you? D'you understand me?' The girl stared at her as she brushed her hair from her face and pulled away the hay that was stuck in it. Her eyes flickered about the hayloft until they rested on Eleanor. The girl swallowed. 'You look so frightened, bewildered; I wish you could understand me.' Eleanor sighed. 'Did you sleep well? Of course, you didn't. How silly of me to even ask such a question. Why, you must be so frightened out here alone. I wish you could understand me. I'll not tell a soul you're here. You're safe, I promise you that. I have to go now, but I'll be sure to bring you some clothes later and a flannel, to wash your hands and face and make you feel a little better.'

The girl watched her lips and said nothing in response. Eleanor staggered up from the hay and left her alone once more, taking the empty flask with her and the red-checked napkin. The girl watched Eleanor as she climbed down the ladder. Taking the scone from the parchment paper, she noticed it was crumbly and buttery, the jam sweet to taste. The milk was warm inside her. She brushed away the crumbs from her lap and lay back down.

'You're up early, Eleanor,' Aunt Emma said, as she washed out the teapot in the sink, draining the tea leaves into the compost bin.

'Yes, I thought I'd bring the eggs in for you.' Eleanor placed a basketful of eggs on the side, hiding the flask and napkin. 'The hens seem to be slowing down now, Aunt Em.'

'They'll start to do that now the nights are drawing in and the summer skies have left. They need all their energy to keep warm. By the way, I've written a list for the groceries, perhaps you could go after breakfast. Take the cotton bag hanging on the hook in the scullery. As you're passing by Enid Postlethwaite's, I wonder if you could deliver these curtains she asked me to mend – she's not been well at all.'

'Of course, Aunt Em. I'll go wake the boys for breakfast and be sure to go straight after.'

Eleanor left the kitchen and took the stairs two steps at a time. Brushing down her skirt, she flung the door of Bertie's room open; he lay snuggled under the blankets, an open comic by his side.

'Bertie, Bertie.' She pushed his body, shaking it a little. He murmured in his sleep. 'Bertie, wake up, it's breakfast time

Jack's Story

and I need to run some errands for Aunt Em.' Bertie shuffled his body up the bed and yawned.

'What's the time? We need to see the girl, check she's alive,' he said, wiping his tired eyes.

'I've already been out. I snuck out first thing whilst I collected the eggs and let the chickens out. I took her some hot milk and a scone.'

'So, she's still alive then?' Bertie said, his face crumpled with tiredness.

'Yes, of course she is, but you need to make sure you keep an eye on Harry. He's simply too small to keep this a secret; he could blow everything.'

'Righto, I suppose I can play soldiers with him until you get back,' he said, rolling his eyes.

'Good, that's settled then. Up you get and be sure to help Aunt Em whilst I'm gone.' Eleanor patted his toes under the blanket and left him to get washed and dressed.

She pushed open the door to Harry's room; he lay in his bed, one leg hanging over the side, his arm straggled across the pillow, the bedclothes all muddled about him. His teddy bear was under his cheek, a trail of dribble running from his half-open mouth onto the cotton pillowcase. His hair was ruffled, and a toy train was wedged between bear and pillow. Eleanor smiled adoringly at him. *How could he sleep with a wooden toy train?* She tugged softly at his pyjama leg. 'Harry, Harry, wakey, wakey, sleepy head.'

'Mummy...' he said, his eyes shut, still in the land of nod.

'No, it's not Mummy, it's me. Come on, wake up. Aunt Em is downstairs preparing breakfast.' Harry snuggled his bear in tighter and teased open an eye. He blinked a few times before leaving them wide open. 'When are we going to see Mummy again?'

'Soon, very soon, when London is clean and tidy again.'

'I want to see Mummy. I want to show her all my drawings.'

'I know you do, and you will, my sweet Harry. Come on now, up you get.' She pulled the curtains, allowing the morning light to burst through the leaded panes.

Harry swung his legs out of the bed and sat on the edge. Eleanor took his clothes from the chair and helped him dress. She tied his laces and gave his knees a reassuring squeeze. 'Come on,' she said. Together they went downstairs.

Bertie was already at the table, chomping on his marmalade on toast, whilst Aunt Emma, a headscarf tied in her hair, busied herself with the washing. Eleanor pulled out a chair for Harry and fetched the milk jug from the fridge. Harry sat at the table, his legs swinging aimlessly from his chair whilst he waited for Eleanor to spoon him out a bowlful of porridge from the saucepan that rested on the Aga's warming plate.

'Aunt Emma, shall I go now? I've a letter to post to Mother and Father too.'

'Yes, the list is on the side, beside the mended curtains. Be sure to send Enid my best. Tell her when she is feeling a little better, I'd be happy to welcome her back to the sewing class. Oh, and Eleanor dear, if you could also visit the haberdashery department in Colson & Co on the high street. I'm running low on grey and black cotton. One reel of each should be ample. I have a "make and mend" class on Tuesday. If you could get six ounces of tea while you are there, too – we seem to have drunk through it a little quicker than I'd have anticipated.'

Bertie shot a look at Eleanor.

'If you could ask Mr Potter to weigh one shilling and sixpence worth of beef, I thought we could have a roast tomorrow evening and cold meat the following day, and with the leftovers I'll make mince for a pie.'

'I'll be sure to do these things, Aunt Em.'

Eleanor took the list and folded it into four before tucking it into the pocket of her jacket along with the ration coupons ready to be stamped for the beef and tea. She picked up the newly mended curtains for Enid Postlethwaite. Aunt Emma gave her half a crown which she popped into her purse, and she tucked her letter home safely into her pocket. She snatched a piece of Bertie's marmalade on toast before closing the kitchen door behind her and leaving her brothers at the table.

Aunt Emma's bicycle stood propped up against the cow shed. She twizzled it around before placing the cotton bag into its basket and then hitched up her skirt to straddle it. Riding across the yard, she cast a glance over to the hay barn; all was quiet.

The hens darted out of her of way, their feathers fluffing up indignantly as her feet pedalled at speed past them. She passed the young farmhand steering Belle, the farm's working pony, pulling an empty cart behind him. He was dressed in brown slacks held up by braces over a grey flannel shirt. On his head he wore a peaked cap covering a mop of jet-black hair.

'Good day, Miss Eleanor,' he said, tipping his hat. 'How's your day?' he called.

'Morning, Jack, it's a fine day. I'll be sure to say hello when I return. I've a few errands to run first.' She smiled to herself at his silliness in calling her Miss Eleanor.

He smiled as she wheeled freely past him, her hair blowing behind her as the wind raced against her face. She could still hear him playing his harmonica as she reached the end of the farm track, where the farmhand's cottage sat nestled behind a cob wall. Eight churns of fresh milk sat on the stand, waiting to be picked up by Ambrosia Dairy. She rested her foot on the ground by the stone wall of the tied cottages, Garden Cottage and Orchard Cottage. The front gardens and side gardens were filled with cane wigwams and seasonal vegetables. Two small apple trees hung low by the wall. Signalling right, she took the lane towards the town of Exeter.

The cars trundled about the high street as she passed by the Odeon, where *Bambi* was showing in matinées and early evening performances. She freewheeled toward Colson & Co before turning right onto the Cathedral Green, where Exeter Cathedral stood majestic and defiant after the last bombs had been dropped over the city by the Germans, two years before. She slowed down and stood on one pedal before coming to a halt. Propping her bicycle up against the wall of the Old Blacksmith's inn, she made her way with a skip in her step back towards the high street, the cotton bag swinging back and forth as she went.

The great cream canopies overhung the windows of Colson & Co, its windows dressed with beautiful mannequins wearing stylish garments swathed in fur stoles of mink and pointed fox. Exquisite lace and silk of every kind adorned the windows, leaving any woman browsing feeling uniquely glamourous. Churchill had pushed heavily for fashion and make-up still to be used throughout the war. Although clothes and cosmetics were rationed, they were needed to make people feel good and keep morale high.

Three black Colson & Co department store vehicles sat along the front with boxes packed for those who could afford such pleasures. The brass plates of the main door were polished to a high sheen. Eleanor brushed her hands on her skirt before pushing open the door, trying in earnest not to leave a smudge on it. Her reflection looked back at her from the brass hand plate; pushing it open, she breathed in deeply as she took in the sight before her. Milliners, costumers, ladies and children's outfitters, linen, silk and fur surrounded her. Her hand drifted along the softness of the fox that lay draped on the shoulders of a mannequin. It was a contrast to the Exeter of two years prior, when the skies were cold and grey, the sound of whizzing and wheeling as bombs dropped from German planes as they attacked the beautiful city. The fire services had fought against the flames that had engulfed the building from the explosives. Only the four-foot, six-inch cob wall held the flames back and saved Colson & Co. Life was beginning to find its way back, England returning to how it had once been, untouched by war.

Eleanor heard the clipping sounds of heels on the parquet floor: well-turned-out folk perusing the glamour of the shop's interior. Mr Billings, a wealthy businessman and now the proprietor, hurried along the floor with a swathe of suited draughtsmen behind him.

'Come, come, I want every woman to relish the beautiful lace, exquisite downy, delicate linen of which we have such a lavish and splendid display.' His voice was shrill, his arms swaying about him.

She watched as they made their way to the back of the store, which was reaching the end of a refurbishment after the last of the incendiary bombs had been dropped on it. The war had caused much damage to Exeter's high street but for a man with the business acumen of Mr Billings, this only led him on; he had great plans for his store. It would be the pinnacle of fashion and glamour and he would supply everything that his customers wanted, even an Indian elephant should they ask.

A young architect brushed past Eleanor, carrying the draft plans rolled in his arms, trying in vain to keep up with Mr Billings.

'Sorry, miss,' he said as he knocked into her. She smiled politely and let him pass her by.

With her purse in her pocket she made her way towards the sweeping staircase that ran up the centre of the store. Her eyes widened as she spied from each step its vastness. A finely dressed lady in gloves walked past, with a tailored jacket nipped in at the waist and her neatly turned-under hair held with a pretty brooch clip. A handbag was propped over her wrist as she signalled to a rather small man scurrying behind her, laden with boxes and wrapped parcels of goods. Eleanor wondered where she might live, what her life entailed, what it would be like to be dressed so finely and have a servant to scurry behind her with a snap of her gloved fingers. Her hand swept along the veneer of the banister until she reached the second floor. Her eyes spun around it mesmerised by the rolls of fabrics. A gentleman passed her, wearing a tailored waistcoat with a tape measure about his neck.

'Excuse me,' she said. He stopped, his moustache rolling up at each end; a monocle dropped from his eye. 'I wonder if you might tell me where I'd find the cotton,' she said, taking the folded list from her pocket.

'Why yes, cotton to the left of the till, in all colours.' He beetled off towards a waiting gentleman.

'Thank you,' she sighed. She wondered if he'd even heard her gratitude.

Wooden shelves flanked the walls with a myriad of coloured reels of cotton. The tips of her fingers trailed across them until she stopped at grey and black. The cotton reels rattled down the slanted chute as she took one from each slide and then turned to pay at the nearby cash desk.

Jack's Story

The mahogany counter gleamed as she placed the wooden reels on the surface.

'Will that be all, miss?' It was the same portly salesman who she'd stopped earlier, his tape measure still looped about his collar, a pocket watch hanging from his waistcoat. He took up his monocle.

'There's a ha'penny deposit on these reels, miss.'

'Is there? Aunt Emma didn't mention that.'

'Why yes, all the sycamore reels have a deposit; you see they can be rethreaded, miss.'

'Oh, I see. Well, I suppose I should pay then.' Eleanor watched as the salesman pressed down on the keys of the register. Two flag-like numbers popped up above the scrawled inscription in gold: *Sam & Henry Gross, London Manufacturers*.

'That'll be ninepence, and a ha'penny for each will bring it to ten pence, miss.'

Eleanor took out her purse and unclasped the clip. She handed over half a crown and waited patiently whilst the salesman scribbled in black ink a receipt for the cotton reels and a deposit of a penny paid for the pair. He tore the receipt from the pad, which had *Colson & Co* swirled across the top.

'Be sure to bring this receipt with the empty reels, miss,' he said, handing her the receipt along with twenty shiny new pennies change and a brown paper bag with the cotton safely tucked inside.

'I will, thank you and good day.' She folded the receipt and tucked it into her purse along with the change and left the counter. She glided down the stairs, her eyes fixed on the huddle of men still congregating towards the back of the store, the young draughtsman scribbling down on his paper.

She walked past them, her cotton bag brushing against her legs as she breezed by.

The draughtsman looked up as she walked past. 'Miss,' he said. She smiled sweetly and left the store. She'd much to do for Aunt Emma and still needed to get back to check the hayloft of the barn before Uncle Henry emptied it of the hay for the weaning calves.

She moseyed along the high street towards Mary Arches and Deller's Café. The bell tinkled as the door pushed against it. The aromas of loose tea and toasted teacakes wafted through the air, and Eleanor breathed it in. An undertone of cinnamon and sultanas toasting, and loose tea, filled the café. Eleanor's mouth prickled with the divinely sweet bouquet, her eyes widening as she took in the array of pink swirls, the glistening sugar on each cake and the stickiest of ginger cakes that had already had a slice taken from it. Eyeing up the spread of divineness that lay in front of her, she stood patiently behind Mrs Hubbard and Mrs Cooke, who were busy nattering at an audible level.

'Have you heard the news at Parkforton Castle?' Mrs Hubbard said, her triangular handbag perched over her wrist.

'No, why? Do tell.'

'Well, I'm not one to gossip. But the news is the youngest daughter of the Earl and Countess of Devon has run away?' Mrs Hubbard said, shielding her mouth with her gloved hand. Eleanor shuffled forward a little, her body turning in. Mrs Hubbard eyed her sidelong and edged her hand on Mrs Cooke's elbow as she moved her forward in the queue. Eleanor frowned as she stretched her neck a little further out.

'Ooh, run away. What a thing. That must be Lady Constance, surely,' Mrs Cooke said, her brows knitted. Eagerly waiting for more information on the scandalous gossip.

'Yes, young Daisy the chambermaid said that she'd left in the night. There's been no sight of her since. Ran off with a young carpenter, I believe. I mean, I'm not one to speak ill, but the Earl of Devon, I believe, was rather disapproving of the shenanigans and the disgrace it would bring on his family,' Mrs Hubbard continued.

'Well I never. Who would have thought? Wasn't she to be married to that fine young barrister from London – a Viscount or something?'

'Viscount Tarquin Crawford, yes, a fine young man. Educated at Eton or one of the other top schools,' Mrs Hubbard insinuated.

'It was Harrow, my dear. He read Latin with my nephew, Rupert, at Cambridge. Great friends they were. Such an eligible bachelor. Any girl's dream. And she chose a carpenter, saints preserve us.' Her eyes rolled to the ceiling.

'What about her sister, Lady Anastasia – they were close, weren't they? Surely she would have talked her out of it. Benenden girls, weren't they, or was it Roedean?'

Eleanor inched forward. Mrs Hubbard peered over her shoulder and moved closer to Mrs Cooke.

'Benenden, yes, my goodness me. What a to-do. I'm not sure but I believe she may have had some involvement, but who's to know … as I said before, Mary, I'm not one to gossip. The poor Viscount, so humiliating for him. I'm really not one to talk but I believe he came down for a weekend away from London and all the happenings went on. Poor soul. I dare say your nephew will be consoling him. Such a shock and a lady as well.' Mrs Hubbard fanned herself with her coupon card.

'Gracious me. Such humiliation to bring upon his family, too. She always was a bit of a fly-away, that one. Head in the clouds. I won't speak a word of this to anyone.' She smiled wryly behind her gloved hand.

'Will you be at bridge this evening? I couldn't find a fourth player, I thought I might ask young Daisy,' Mrs Hubbard said, a dry smile breaking across her face.

'Oh yes, of course, and I'd love to play bridge with Daisy. I'm sure she has a very clever hand.'

A waitress wearing a black pinafore dress and white apron interrupted the two nattering women.

'May I help you?' she enquired.

'Yes, I'd like to take six iced buns for the church bridge club tonight, if I may. And I'll take a slice of the Jamaican ginger cake, Reverend Holbrooke is rather partial to it.'

'Of course, that'll be sevenpence ha'penny, please.'

Mrs Hubbard thanked the waitress and turned to Mrs Cooke. 'I'll see you this evening, Mary, at the church hall, and remember not a word to anybody.' She bid her a good day and left the café. The waitress then served Mrs Cooke, who left with a wealth of ripe new gossip and three ounces of tea.

Eleanor hadn't meant to eavesdrop, but she wondered if the girl in the hay barn could be from Parkforton Castle? She wasn't dressed like a gypsy and the touch of her hand had felt as soft as silk. *It couldn't be ... she was alone, there was no young carpenter.* The voice of the waitress broke her thoughts.

'May I help you?' she asked with a smile.

'Oh yes, umm, may I have six ounces of tea please, and I'll take an iced bun too. Could I pay for the bun separately, is that alright?'

'Of course, me lover. That'll be ninepence for the tea and a penny for the bun. D'you have your ration card, me lover?'

'Yes, I do.' Eleanor handed her the booklet and waited whilst the waitress stamped the tea coupon with Deller's Café. She took one penny from the inner sleeve of her purse which she'd taken from her piggy bank to pay for the bun. The bell tinkled as she left the café.

As she hurried along the high street, she kept revisiting in her head what she had heard inside Deller's. By all accounts the two women had an insatiable appetite for gossip and the Earl and Countess of Parkforton did have two daughters, and both a few years older than herself, but could the girl in the hayloft be one of them?

She nipped down the cobbled alleyway that led her back to her bicycle. Placing the cotton bag in the basket, she hitched up her skirt and pedalled towards Sidwell Street and the butcher's. She hopped off her bike and bought a shilling and tuppence worth of beef, and then pedalled like lightning towards Newtown and Enid Postlethwaite's. Once the curtains had been safely delivered, along with Aunt Emma's best wishes, she left in haste.

The wind whistled through her hair, snapping at her face, leaving a tinge of red on her cheeks. She sped along the lane; the wheels of her bike rattled over the level crossing, and she lost her footing as she pedalled faster and faster before she turned into the track towards the farm. The dust kicked up in a plume of smoke. The ponies in the paddock grazed on the sweet meadow grass. They lifted their heads as she cycled past, and snorted. She could hear the faint mooing of the cows in the shed as she approached the yard, the chickens hopping out of her way as she whizzed past them. She climbed off her bicycle and propped it against the side of the cowshed, leaving only the iced bun in a brown paper bag in the basket. She poked her head around the cowshed's door.

'Hi Jack!' she said. 'I'll come and help you if you like? I just need to run the tea and bits in for Aunt Emma and see the boys.'

'No worries, Eleanor,' he said with a slight twang to his voice, his hands still gripping the teats of one of the Short Horns who stood placidly grazing on the hay as he yanked down on her.

Eleanor ran across the yard and bustled straight into the kitchen.

'Well, that was an entrance,' Aunt Em said, taking the bag from her. She placed the beef wrapped in paper in the fridge and emptied the tea into its caddy in the pantry.

'Are the boys upstairs?' Eleanor asked as she brushed past the table and towards the hallway.

'Yes. I haven't heard a peep out of them all morning. I think Bertie's been playing soldiers with Harry. Did you remember to post your letter?'

'Oh bother, I forgot, I'll do it tomorrow. Are you playing bridge tonight, Aunt Em?'

'Not tonight, no.' Before her aunt had a chance to ask why she wanted to know, Eleanor had hurtled up the staircase in the direction of the boys' bedrooms. The grandfather clock in the hall ticked as the pendulum swayed back and forth. She burst into Harry's room and found the boys lying on the floor, a battalion of green soldiers in full combat firing from the swirls on the rug or the ridge on the fort that Jack had made from some old wood he'd found in the yard. She sat between them and ruffled Harry's hair.

'Did you get her something?' Bertie said, as he shot down another of Harry's soldiers.

'I got her a bun from Deller's Café.'

'A bun! I thought we agreed she needed clothes.' Bertie exclaimed.

'I know but I only have sixpence in my piggy bank, and Colson's - well, I could never afford it, it's just so grand,' she said. 'I will just have to try and make and mend, there's no other way. But I think I know who she is.'

'She's a gypsy, isn't she?' Harry guffawed. 'I knew it.'

'No, I think she might be special. We need to go to the cowshed.'

'The cowshed?' Bertie questioned, scrunching his face up. 'But she's in the hayloft?'

'Jack's in the cowshed, milking.'

'Right. But what's Jack got to do with it?' Bertie's face took on a completely contorted look.

'I think we should tell Jack,' Eleanor said, her voice a whisper. 'He can help, and we need to get her out of the hayloft. We can trust him, come on.'

The three left the bedroom and the fallen soldiers straggled across the rug and fort. They sped down the stairs, Harry tracking the grandfather clock as he raced past it. He turned back and caught its face watching him, so he gasped and ran even faster. The dirt in the yard flew up from their feet. Eleanor darted first to the bicycle to retrieve the iced bun from its basket and then straight to the cowshed, almost tripping over Patch, the black and white collie who was slumped by the door, napping.

The three bundled into the shed and stood there. Jack was sitting on a small wooden stool, resting his head on the flank of one of the cows. He gave a tentative tug on her udders before looking up. His face bore a grin; his eyes widened and then squinted with a questioning look of curiosity in them.

'You look like you've been up to mischief,' he said, his smile growing even bigger.

'Not so much mischief, but more, well, it's just that ...' Eleanor began.

'We found a girl!' Harry blurted out.

Jack pursed his lips and narrowed his eyes.

'You found a girl?'

The Short Horn stamped her hoof and swished her tail whilst swaying impatiently. 'There, there, easy girl,' he said, patting her rear side before he gently pulled down on her teats. The children could hear the milk hitting the bottom of the metal bucket beneath her.

'Yes, we've found a girl.' Eleanor continued. 'You can't tell a soul, though. Jack, you have to swear on your beret you'll keep this a secret.'

'Swear on my beret. Well, this has to be something of a secret if I'm to swear on my beret. Let me finish milking the cows and then you can swear me in.'

Jack squeezed down on the Short Horn's udders until every last drop had been taken for the morning milking. He tipped the metal bucket of milk into the churn and set it aside with the other pails, ready for the early evening milking. Brushing and patting her rear end, he whistled to Patch, who set to work with Jack leading the cows from the shed and herding them across the yard, down the track. Bertie ran ahead and opened the gate for the cows to file through, their large behinds ambling along, the tail end of the cows' girths heavy and wide as they plodded slowly, some of them ready to calf over the coming days. Jack closed the gate behind them and led Patch back to his kennel.

The children followed Jack back to the cowshed.

Jack's Story

'So, I need to be sworn in?' he said, taking the maroon beret from his pocket and holding it close to his heart.

'Yes, you can't tell a soul. This is serious.' Eleanor's eyes fixed on Jack's.

'Alright, I have my beret, Elle.' He rubbed over the maroon felt. 'I swear on my beret and my brothers in arms who gave the ultimate sacrifice at Arnhem to keep locked your secret.' With his beret still held to his chest, he stood silently for a few seconds; Harry watched him open-mouthed. Jack ruffled his hair. 'Come on, trooper, show me your find.' Harry tucked his hand into Jack's whilst Eleanor, carrying the bag with the bun in it, led the way across the yard, passing the muddy pond with rusty willows growing about it. They stood in the hay barn: the particles of dust catching the light, the scratching sound of mice scurrying about and intricate webs clinging to the lofty beams.

Eleanor's eyes shifted to the ladder. 'She's in the loft. We found her the other day, hiding.' Her voice was a whisper. 'She hasn't said a word since we found her. And today whilst I was running my errands, I overheard Mrs Hubbard and Mrs Cooke saying how the Earl and Countess of Devon's daughter had run away. I mean, it might not be her, but maybe that's who she is?' Her footsteps were light across the ground as she neared the ladder, beckoning to Jack. 'Come, we'll show you.'

Eleanor hitched up her skirt and climbed the ladder to the loft. The sun's rays shone in her eyes as it cut through the cracks in the roof, dazzling her. Bertie and Harry followed behind with Jack bringing up the rear

The girl shifted herself back into the corner, grappling at the blanket and pulling it over her legs, curling its edging in the palm of her hands. She pushed her pillowcase behind her back. Her eyes flicked across them before resting on Jack; he smiled and knelt down nearer to her. She pushed herself further back against the wall. Jack turned to Eleanor, signalling for the bag with the iced bun in it, then took it and gave it to her. The children watched him intently, as if he knew what he was doing. He said nothing to the girl. She opened the brown paper bag; it gave a crinkling sound as she broke into the bun's doughy centre. Her eyes looked empty and carried a fear in them he'd only ever seen once before.

'She needs more water,' Jack said. 'Eleanor, go fill a flask of warmed water and put a little sugar in it. See if you can find an old flannel, too. Her hands and nails are cut and full of dirt. I'll need to clean them, or they'll become infected. Bertie, you go help and bring me a bowl with some warm salty water.' Taking her hands from the blanket, he held them, rubbing away some of the grit that had caught in the edges of her fingers. They were icy cold and shaking. She let him touch her, his hands steadying her trembling. Her eyes dropped as his touch warmed them through, his clasp gentle but firm around them whilst he waited for the other two to return. Harry watched on.

> 'I'm Jack,' he had said. 'Who knows you're here?' She'd sat perfectly still, her uniform that of an SS, with a minuscule alteration to allow the Allies to know she was part of the Resistance. His murky uniform was muddied, bloodstained and carried an odour of sweat and vomit. 'Your name, what is it?' he asked again. 'I'm Private Jack Saunders, 2nd Battalion, the parachute regiment. Why are you alone? We are here to help you.'
>
> She moved her back against the wall of the barn.
>
> 'I am Agathe Lecreux, part of the Resistance. I escaped from the Wehrmacht field brothels. My brother and Frederik are both dead. The SS found us sending messages to your men informing you of the whereabouts of the Germans' locations. My brother was beaten and shackled,

suspended from the ceiling and burnt with a blowtorch. He was tortured to talk. I heard his cries. like an animal he cried; they whipped him until his body could take no more. I watched them lead him to the yard – unbroken. Bruised. Bloody. Defiant in his silence. His face swollen like a punch bag. His back to them as he walked. Bang!'

'Jack, here, I have the water,' Bertie said, breaking his thoughts. He crouched down next to Jack and held the bowl as Jack doused the flannel in the salty water and wrung it out before gently and smoothly brushing it over her hands. He dabbed lightly at the open cuts. She inched back a little from his tender touch. He patted a little more, removing the grit from the open wounds.

'Ow.' She pulled her hand back quickly.

His eyes moved to her face. 'I'm sorry.' His voice low. She offered her hand back tentatively.

'You're English?' He smiled gently, cupping her hands as he dabbed at them. She watched him.

She nodded. Her eyes glazed over with a sheen of tears.

'Where are you from?' Jack said, as he rinsed the flannel and rubbed it over her hand once more.

She shook her head, biting her lip to stop her eyes welling up, though in vain. A tear fell from her face and onto Jack's hand. He looked up at her.

'Don't cry.' His hand moved up to her face and wiped away the sadness that fell. 'You'll be alright.' His voice was low.

'Please don't tell anyone I am here.' Her eyes fell to his hands on hers.

'At least tell me your name. I'm Jack. You can trust me.'

She swallowed and looked up again, her eyes searching his face, before resting on his eyes. She held his gaze. She breathed in and exhaled. 'My name is ...' She stopped. Should she tell them her name? Maybe now she could begin again, forget the past, forget what she had run from. Her eyes searched their faces. They had been kind to her. She swallowed. 'Beth.' Her voice was faint as she cast her glance away from them.

'Here, Beth, drink this water, you must be thirsty.' Eleanor knelt and offered her the sweetened water.

She took the flask and sipped from its spout as four pairs of eyes watched her.

Aunt Emma's calls for lunch disturbed them. Eleanor got up from the floor and beckoned to the boys to come away. Jack took the flannel and bowl. 'I'll come back later,' he said as he got up to leave.

The Standard Fordson tractor growled in the distance as it pulled the harrow, churning up the fields for the next season's harvest. It rumbled through the quietness of the farmland as a sea of birds followed in its tracks.

'So, what do we do?' Eleanor finally asked Jack as they stood in the yard. She knew that the girl couldn't stay in the hay barn for much longer, not if Uncle Henry and Jack were to be clearing the dried hay for calving. She'd be found without a doubt.

'She can't stay in the hayloft, that's for sure.' Jack squeezed Eleanor's arm reassuringly. 'She can stay with me for a while in the cottage. But we need to know who she is. Someone will be worried about her.'

'She can't be from Parkforton Castle, though. Mrs Hubbard said it was Lady Constance, the Earl and Countess's daughter, and that she'd run away with a carpenter. Her name's Beth and there's no carpenter. And, well, she looks like a normal girl.'

'That's if Mrs Hubbard's information is correct. Whatever a normal girl is?' Jack mused.

'Come on you lot,' Aunt Em called from the kitchen door. 'Lunch is ready.'

The three children left Jack and ran in for lunch. As the farmhouse door closed, Jack turned towards his cottage, his thoughts on the girl in the loft. He needed to get her out and he needed to do it quickly.

Chapter Three

Orchard Cottage, Cowick, Exeter, late September, 1946

As the evening drew in and the cold snapped about the stone walls of the tied cottages outside, Jack rested in his chair by the fire. He rocked back and forth, the sound of the blues permeating the room from his harmonica. The lamp on the table beside him cast an amber hue of light across the room and the wooden mantel clock ticked in beat to his rhythm. Every now and again he cast a glance at its hands as they turned.

Through a velvet curtain to one side lay another small room, no bigger than a gabled porch with a low-pitched roof and a single latched window that faced the lane. From the window could be seen a gnarly fruit tree, stunted in growth. A green velvet Queen Anne-style chair sat in the corner, beside a table with a circular top and small drawers following the curve, its elegant legs long and slender. A sewing box rested on the top by a lamp with a cream silk shade. On the floor sat a wooden box with a black handle, the name *Singer* embossed across it. The moon cast a glint of light into the room from the ebony night sky and dotted about the blackness were the whitest of stars, the darkness giving way to the farm's own slumber. Placing his harmonica in the tin, Jack drew the curtains and took his coat from the hook on the door. The chair rocked alone for a short while.

Jack left his cottage and made his way towards the farm. His breath caught in the cold night air, the only sound that of the hooves and heavy breaths of the restless ponies as they galloped across the undulating meadows, the silhouettes of their heads hung low. Towards the end of the track the lights of the farmhouse glowed from behind drawn curtains. Smoke from the coal fire funnelled up the chimney from the room where Aunt Emma and Uncle Henry now rested. The faint firelight, rising to the upstairs landing, threw a safe warmth into the bedrooms where three heads lay in a slumber so deep.

Jack shone his torch along the track, passing the obscure shapes of the cattle lying in their pastures, its beam shining forwards to the outbuildings beyond. The farmhouse was burrowed in the upward land, the ground beyond it sloping westward towards the cowshed and hay barn. Moonlight cast shadows over the murky pond where the ducks lay resting in the reeds, their bills tucked beneath their wings. Jack's feet lightly touched the ground as he made his way towards the barn. The doors were still wide open, pitch black inside. He flashed the torch around it until it rested on the ladder. He stopped. He breathed in deeply. He rested his head on the rung of the ladder, his eyes tightly shut. *Come on, Jack,* he said to himself. His eyes still scrunched closed.

> The wheeling sound of the falling bombs had broken the silence in the dark sky. Aeroplanes' engines had hummed high above as they showered more pain and death on the ground below. The first group of men moved forward on the foreign terrain, their parachutes left in a straggled heap behind them, their purpose served. Around them bodies thumped to the ground, shot down by enemy fire while canopy after canopy landed safely, their comrades desperate to make their way to the next post. Hundreds of soldiers of the 1st British Airborne Division fell through the sky that night on a task never carried out before.
>
> Above, in the aircraft, the rancid smells of vomit and aviation fuel filled the fuselage as the men sat shoulder to

shoulder, packed in together like sardines in a can, ready to jump either to their death or to a death later on. Some of the men made a sign of the cross as they took that leap and floated in the plane's slip stream until their canopies opened. The sound of the men as they hit the ground was clearly audible – grunts and groans from the impact on their bodies. Solitary thuds of the unlucky ones who'd been shot down in mid-air, like falling dandelions, until they rested as crumpled as their parachutes. Three of them made it to safety through the darkness to a nearby farm, where they waited for their comrades in the cold but dry shelter of an outbuilding. Three of them that night met Agathe Lecreux. They sat huddled together for warmth, waiting. He took out his harmonica and began to play it – anything to appease their fear of this wretched war.

Jack brushed his brow as a slight bead of sweat formed on it. He breathed out heavily as he stepped slowly and quietly up each rung of the wooden ladder. He flashed the torch to where she was lying, her head nestling between her arms, the pillowcase wrapped around them bulging a little from the objects inside it, the blanket pulled over her and tucked beneath her chin. He sat by her and brushed the strands of hair from her face. Her skin was soft yet cold. She opened her eyes and gasped, frightened by the figure so close to her.

'Shh – it's me, Jack. I need to get you to safety. Come with me.'

She tried to look at him, her eyes blinded by the brightness of the torch. He turned it away from her and laid it on the hay.

'You'll be found here,' he said. 'We're clearing the hay tomorrow for calving. Come, we must go now.'

She pushed herself up from the hay and brushed her eyes, blinking several times. Taking up her pillowcase, she let Jack

Jack's Story

help her to her feet. She stumbled as she stood; her legs were weak beneath her. She wobbled a little trying to steady herself, but she couldn't.

'Here, put your arm around me, I'll help you.' Slowly, she staggered to the ladder. Jack took each rung first and let the girl follow, his hands steadying her as they descended.

'Take my torch,' he said, turning to her as she reached the last rung and taking her in his arms. He carried her out of the barn and across the yard, down the track, until he reached the cottages at the end. He leant down and wedged himself against the cobbled wall to open the wooden gate.

With her arms still around his neck, he pushed the latch down and nudged the door open with one boot, entering the main room. Its slabbed stone floor was covered in a brown and black mosaic-patterned linoleum. A thick patchwork blanket was draped over a sofa and an enamel range with an open coal fire stood against the wall, a wooden mantelpiece surrounding it, adorned with a small mantel clock, shaped like an arch, that sent out a tinny chime every so often. An oval mirror hung above the range.

Laying her gently on the sofa and tucking the blanket around her, he then knelt by the fire and stoked it. The red-hot coals tumbled between each other as he added a few more lumps from the scuttle before he left her alone in the room.

Her eyes moved around the room: a rocking chair sat in the corner, a cushion resting against the spindles of its arched back. A small nest of tables sat next to it, topped by a lamp and two black and white photos in a silver hinged frame. A picture of a soldier in uniform smiling, and then the same man with a pretty girl by his side, his arm wrapped around her tiny waist. Lying in front of it was an open tobacco tin with a harmonica inside it and a maroon beret. The coals on the fire burned slowly, the embers glowing in the low-lit room, casting a burning red light.

Jack returned after a few minutes, with two mugs in his hand. He poured the warm milk from the pan on the range into them and stirred.

'Here,' he said, handing her the cup of Horlicks. 'It should warm you through, warms your soul and nourishes you – that's what my mother always used to say.'

The girl cupped her hands around its warmth, putting her button nose close to its edge, tingling from the malty aroma.

'My mother said my father drank it when he fought for the British army in the First World War,' he continued. 'He was stationed in India.' Leaving the girl once more, Jack ran up the short flight of stairs up to the landing, where there were three latched doors.

The girl could hear the floorboards creak above her and the sound of water running. Then the creaking of the stairs under his footstep.

'There's a bedroom at the top of the stairs and the bathroom is just along from it. I've put a clean towel in there for you. The bath is running. It might make you feel a little better and warm you up some more.'

The girl placed her half-drunk mug on the floor and pushed herself to the edge of the sofa. Jack helped her stand up, her legs still threatening to buckle beneath her once again.

'Here, wait.' Jack took her into his arms again, taking each step with care. *How long had she been in the hayloft for, without food and water?* He carried her light frame up the wooden stairs. She felt so weak in his arms. Nudging the bathroom door open with his elbow, he set her down on the bare floorboards. An oil lamp burned in the corner on a wooden table and a clean towel hung over the side of the iron roll-top bath. Steam rose up from the hot water gushing from the tap. Jack swished his hands through the water, making sure the temperature wouldn't burn her soft, pale skin, before turning it off. Then he left her alone, closing the bathroom door behind him. He heard the key turn in the lock.

She rested against the bath as she peeled the soiled and grubby clothes off her body, stumbling a little as she did. Her ribcage was visible beneath her skin. Steadily she lifted her bare leg over the edge of the bath; the contact sent a prickle of goosebumps across her soft skin. She wobbled a little as she levered herself up, every inch of her being feeling frail, and slid into the warmth of the water. It cocooned her like the snug warmth of a hot water bottle on the coldest of nights.

She lay in the bath, soaking in the heat, feeling it hug every inch of her skin so gently, so warmly. The cuts on her hands and knees, now below the surface, were being cleansed by the water. Leaning forward, she took the soap from the dish that sat on the metal tidy which spanned the sides of the bath. She let it slip from hand to hand, feeling its soft, waxy silkiness between her palms. She rubbed the creamy lather across her body and let her face slip beneath the water. The sound of it in her ears like the sea in a seashell. A sound reminiscent of her times at the beach in Budleigh Salterton, happier times. A place where she would play for hours as a small child, collecting stones and shells with her sister, chasing waves that rippled between the pebbles. The salty water playing with the stones as they were washed down the beach, rattling, to become part of the seabed. A seabed where her toes would stand, and those stones would scuttle over them with every breaking wave. The laughter that could be heard from the joy it brought for a small girl. The sound of the waves that she'd hear as she rode across the sandy shoreline, where she'd lean across the shoulders of her Silver Sixpence and rub his neck as her head lay low on it. The quiet of the seascape with her on his back. The sound that reminded her of her walks along the parade, older now, a young woman. A place where she'd sit on the edge of the pier that jutted out into the sea. Where she'd watch the swells of the waves with him beside her, his arm around her, just them. The man she loved with every inch of her body. A man she adored. Just sounds now under the water. A memory she didn't want.

She eased herself up, letting out an audible gasp of air. She rubbed more soap into her hands and scrubbed it through her hair, washing away the dust and cold of the barn. Washing away the memories of what she was running from. She held her breath once more and submerged herself until the once-clear water was now a murky grey with a layer of soapy suds resting on the surface. Dirty. Filthy. Unwanted. A little like her memories. Her wet hair straggling down her back, she leant forward and pulled out the plug. The water swirled like a whirlpool, gurgling as it went. She watched it as it twisted through the holes, making sure every last drop of an unwanted memory fell down the drain and washed away, away from her, away from her now cleaned body.

Easing herself out, she placed the tips of her toes over the bath onto the wooden floor and wrapped the towel around her. After picking up her clothes, she walked carefully to the door and unlocked it. As she prised it open, she could hear the melodic tunes – *the blues,* she wondered. Leaning against the banister, she listened intently, her toes curled on the floorboards as she paused, unsure of what to do. She didn't hear the playing stop, nor did she hear Jack's steps on the staircase. As he reached the top, she took in a breath sharply and clasped the towel more tightly around her. He turned his eyes away and headed straight to the door at the top of the stairs. The trickling bathwater from her body pooled around her feet as he disappeared into a room before returning moments later with a bundle of clean clothes.

'Here, take these. I'm afraid they're not for a lady like yourself but they're clean.' He brushed past her, still averting his eyes, and left her alone again.

She stood in the sitting room, clean and warm, dressed, holding only the clothes she had been wearing in the barn. The waist of the baggy brown slacks, cinched in by a thick leather belt, and a loose white cotton shirt, tucked in, hid the smooth lines of the curves beneath. Her feet were still bare. Jack took the harmonica from his mouth and smiled at her.

'I'm sorry about the clothes. Sit by the fire. It'll dry your hair. Here, let me take your clothes.'

She knelt down in front of the fire and let the flames throw their warmth onto her face and hair. Beside her, he began playing his harmonica again. Her eyes watched as the flames thrust themselves up between coals and disappeared again with a sizzling sound. She moved back a little as the heat became too intense against her face.

She smiled faintly. Briefly.

Chapter Four

Orchard Cottage, Cowick, Exeter, late September, 1946

The sound of hooves and the clattering of churns caused the girl to stir. Rubbing her bleary eyes, she lay still. Her eyes shifted to the eiderdown that covered her, and she squinted at its pattern. Her glance then darted around the room, her brow furrowed. She rubbed her brown eyes harder this time and blinked several times. The lane below her window ran past the two tied cottages. As she pushed herself up the bed, the eiderdown dropped; her hand touched the cotton shirt, she pressed it against her skin, smoothing it between her thumb and fingers. She edged the curtain open a little at the side and peered out of the tiny chink she'd made. She caught sight of a man wearing a black peaked cap. He hauled the churns from the milk stand onto the wagon. A bay Shire tossed its head low, snorting. It was coarse in its build, its gait thick with heavy feathering on its legs. It stood calm and friendly, a gentle giant beneath her window. She watched as the Ambrosia Dairy's milk wagon rattled past, the clip-clop of the hooves moved off up the lane and only a heap of fresh manure was left behind.

She opened the curtain a little wider. The sun hung low in the east, just about cresting over the still land. Over the stone wall, a sea of fields with the mist hanging low on the horizon. A tractor moved slowly across the land where a scarecrow stood cold and alone, with only a field mouse for company nesting in its stuffed arms of straw. The rooks cawed in the sky as they swooped down, daring to land on the ploughed fields that flowed over on to the undulating meadowland.

Jack's Story

A tree hunkered low on the brow of the windswept hill, its bough twisted; its arms outstretched as if protecting the very land it stood on. Lifting its branches to the sky, commanding the daylight to fall onto the last of its autumn leaves. Its roots like gnarled, bashed limbs grasping deep into the ground below, anchoring it against the storms and the winds that would ravage the land through the bleak months. Standing, tall, firm. Solitary. Beyond the farmland the fields rolled onto the moors. They were thick and deep with their coarse ferns. Desolate and bleak and unforgiving in the winter months. She stared out towards it, rubbing away the condensation that formed on the pane. A land that was ragged, haunted by screeching sounds in the night. Blood-curdling howls, shadows that lingered in the dark, mists that fell so low obscuring what lay ahead, ferns and thorns snatching and twisting around whatever lay in their path. Grabbing. Taking. Wanting. Her eyes shifted away, her skin prickled, her breath held. The sound of her heartbeat snatching at her throat. She clasped at the eiderdown and pulled it up closer to her.

A five-bar gate broke the line of the stone wall and by it stood a weathered black sign, indicating four directions. To the east was signposted Ottery St Mary, 12 miles; to the south-west, Kenton, 7.5 miles, Bovey Tracey, 11 miles, and to the north-west Crediton, 9 miles away. She crooked her neck to read the sign by the milk stand: *Appledaw Farm*. She let the curtain fall back down and moved back under the covers, tucking her hand under her head on the down-filled pillow. She lay quietly, letting her own thoughts escape. She didn't know the farm; she recognised the signposted places but that was about all. She had to be near Exeter, but where exactly? Where was she? Would she ever be found? Was she really safe?

She reached over and grabbed the brown slacks at the end of her bed. They were scratchy as she pulled them onto her bare skin, her fingers pushed the prong through the furthest hole of the leather belt around her waist, pulling them in tighter. She tucked the shirt in, and it bunched and ballooned over her tiny waist. The draft whipped up through the cracks between the bare floorboards as she pulled the rose-covered eiderdown up and over the pillow. She rested her ear against the door before pushing the latch down. It clinked; she held her breath and pressed a little more. Curling her hand around the edge of the door, she gently teased it open. She swallowed as the hinges squeaked, her eyes creased at the corners, her lips open as she peered around it. The touch of the wall behind her, the floorboards creaking under her footsteps. Her breath ahead of her was caught like a mist. The bathroom door was ajar. The door next to it was closed. The stairs groaned as her toes found each step. Through the banister's spindles, she saw a saucepan of oats warming on the range, beneath it a red glow as the hot coals sizzled; an ornate guard stood in front of the fire. As she stood alone in the room, she recognised the patchwork blanket on the sofa from the night before. Her eyes scanned around it, squinting through the beam of light that drenched the room and lit up dancing particles of dust. The only sounds were the fizzing of the burning red coals and the gentle ticking of the mantel clock.

She stood for a while, not knowing what to do. She felt like an imposter in a house whose owner she didn't know, only that he had treated her with kindness and warmth. Only that he'd brought her in from the cold, protecting her from what she was running from. He knew nothing of her, yet he cared about her enough to help her. Why? He had left her in his cottage, he'd trusted a girl he didn't know. How did he know she wasn't some waif and stray who would rob him? Why did he treat her with such kindness? How could a stranger trust an unknown person? When another person whom she'd known so well, trusted so deeply, had turned out to be false.

Her eyes flicked about the room. The tin and harmonica were missing along with the maroon beret. She turned to the front door: the hook where he'd hung his coat was bare, with only a note pinned to it. She went over to it and took it down
– *Porridge on the range. I hope you slept well. I'll be back at midday. Jack*

She brushed her fingers across it. *Midday,* she said to herself. She went to the range. A bowl and spoon sat beside the pan that was full of oats and milk and gently warming through. The clock on the mantelpiece tinged out eight pretty chimes. She had hours before he'd be back. The creamy oats slipped down her throat, each mouthful warming her through. The spoon's clink against the china resounded as she scraped out every morsel until all that was left was the smoothness of the bowl. Her stomach gurgled with gratification. It was perhaps the most she'd eaten in days.

She made her way to the steps that led down to the back kitchen. There she spied a line of clothes hanging on a wooden rack by a boiler, with a shallow puddle of water below them. A small coal fire was lit and warming the water in the boiler.

She gasped as her toes touched the floor at the bottom of the steps, and quickly she drew her foot back up. She placed it back down and took in a breath, her skin prickling with goosebumps with each step. As the small boiler fire burned gently, she felt the clothes on the rack: they were still damp. She washed out her bowl and the pan in the stone basin and left them on the side to drain.

Back upstairs, she sat on the edge of the bed, the springs below groaning a little, her breath like miniature puffs of smoke floating in the room. Small droplets of condensation trickled down the windowpane. Her eyes moved about the room again. Woodworm lurked hungrily in the darkness of the beams;

dry rot assaulted the timbers; unseen white silverfish darted beneath the cracks in the boards. She snatched up her feet. Lifting the pillow, she took her pillowcase out from beneath it; it was dusty and had strands of broken hay clinging to it. She brushed it down and tipped it up, the contents tumbling haphazardly onto the rose-covered eiderdown. A toothbrush and a book with a leather bookmark toppled out, along with her journal and an ink pen. She sat on the edge of the bed and stared at the contents, brushing her hands across them. That was all she had; that was all that she had grabbed. The corners of the book were creased and curled – *A Tree Grows in Brooklyn*. A cream tassel hung from a page, her toothbrush was dry, and her journal's leather cover was faded, scratched and pawed. Her pen was smooth and black – its gold nib stained with a teardrop of ink. The only possessions she had grabbed in her frenzied escape, the only things she possessed to begin again.

She went to the bathroom and washed her face and brushed her teeth, teasing her fingers through her hair, her reflection staring back at her. The light from the sun pushed through the thin net that hung from a curtain wire line, shielding the inside from prying eyes.

Crouching low, she eased it back gently. Outside, the cows were chomping on the pastures, the grass glistening as each droplet of dew clung to every blade like an iridescent ladybird. Her gaze was caught by a solitary cow who ambled with heaviness away from the herd, finding her own spot. Her girth bulged and her udders hung low. The girl spotted a figure out of the corner of her eye. She spied him at the open gate – the young man whose house she'd stayed in. He wore a cap covering his mop of jet-black hair, his brown slacks muddied, old black boots with the laces tied loosely, leaving them gaping at the top. A woollen tank top to keep off the cold, a jacket thrown over the gate post. He called out over the field. She couldn't make out his words. She watched on as he moved towards the solitary heifer, his feet crushing the blades beneath them; the ground sponge-like underfoot. He eased her in the direction of the open gate. His arms were outstretched as her amble slowed, her udders swollen beneath her; brushing her down as her hooves moved laboriously across the wet ground. Slow. Steady. Weary.

Her head hung low, warm air snorted from the cow's nostrils. The girl from the window watched him rub the animal's side. He seemed to whisper words of inspiration as he led the young heifer away, every movement as slow as the cow's, an unlearned tenderness. The creature traipsed out of the gate. He took up his jacket and led her up the stony track towards the farmyard, passing the pond where the willows wilted and into the warm shelter of the cowshed. Where the sweet smell of hay lured her into an area of quiet and calm.

The girl let the curtain drop and returned to the room where she'd slept. Tucking the journal under her pillow and taking her book, she went to the room below. The fire still glowed. She knelt in front of it and added a couple more lumps of coal to its red glow. She wobbled up and tucked her feet beneath her as she rested on the softness of the patchwork blanket, the whiteness of her breath fading.

'Easy there,' he said. The young heifer moved about the hay-lined floor. Her sides ached, her tail lifted, her sway agitated. 'Easy girl,' he whispered beneath his breath, as she moved to another part of the shed and lay down. Jack looked on. She stood up with laboured movements and walked some more until she lay down again. 'Come on, you're alright, girl.' He rested his leg on the metal bars that kept her in the warm space of the shed.

"Ow she be, young Jack?' came the voice from behind the wheelbarrow, clumps of freshly forked hay toppling over its sides.

'I've brought her in, she's alright, she'd moved out from the herd. She's labouring.'

'Keep an eye on 'er, she'll do well.' Henry turned and left the shed.

Jack whispered to the heifer, who continued walking and lying down as her labour progressed. Six young calves stood in another part of the cowshed, their mothers back in the meadow after being milked earlier. Jack filled the pail with some of the raw milk from that morning's milking for Ambrosia Dairy and let his fingers dip into its creaminess. The first calf dipped his nose into the pail and sucked the milk off Jack's, until it had had his feed. The warmth of each calf as they sucked and tickled Jack's fingers, each of them lapping up their mother's milk, their gentle mouths suckling. Jack would allow them to suck until they had mastered how to drink the milk without his aid – that would be in a couple of days. Until then he let the calves' warm tongues use his fingers to aid them. The labouring heifer mooed softly as she lay down again. 'Come on now, you hungry one, that's enough. I need to help our new mum-to-be.' The days-old calf's huge brown eyes looked up at Jack and stopped sucking from his fingers, the bottom of the pail now visible. He threw some more hay down on the ground for them, keeping them warm in their space. He swilled out the bucket under the tap outside and went back to the heifer. She rubbed herself up against the side of the shed with her tail. Her gait became more laboured – she was getting agitated.

'Henry!' Jack called from the shed.

Henry returned, wheeling in more hay from the barn.

'Be she deliverin'?'

Jack's Story

'Yeah, she is.' Jack climbed over the railing and stood closer to her. Her breathing was heavier and more awkward as she sat down in the hay. She stood again, her frame rocking backwards and forwards. Then he heard the children's footsteps, and their babbling grew as they fell into the shed.

'Jack!'

'Shh, shh.' He winked at them.

They stopped in their tracks. 'Is she having a baby, Uncle Henry?' Harry asked.

'She be dwain that dreckly, and if ye be quiet ye can stay and watch, me lad.'

'Something's happening, girl,' Jack said. A yellowish-white sack began to show from her rear end. 'Come on girl, you're almost there.' His voice a soft whisper as she swayed back and forth, back and forth. She lay back down again on the hay, lifting her back end up and down from the ground as the sack presented more.

'What's that?' Bertie asked as a slimy bubble pushed further out.

'It's the front hooves,' Jack said.

'Eww, it's all slimy,' Harry butted in.

'She's getting tired,' Jack said, turning to Henry.

Henry drew up his lips. 'She be almost there. That she be. Proper job.'

'Come on girl, you're almost there,' Jack said as he rested on the rail. She was oblivious to her audience. The young cow pushed until a sack of sliminess fell from her and plopped onto the hay under her tail. The new young mum stood and then she began to lick the slime from her newly born calf, cleaning it up. It lay in a bundle and was a deep dark brown. It raised its head and its hooves in front of it, unsteady, pushing and wobbling as it tried to stand. The new mum stood over her newborn, still licking it clean and protecting it with the unconditional love that comes with motherhood.

'What is it?' Eleanor asked.

'I can't tell yet, mum's doing a good job cleaning it up. She's a really good mum.' Jack climbed over the rail and left the new mum with her calf.

'We have to name it,' Harry chirped.

Uncle Henry tossed Jack a wink.

'Button,' Jack said, 'I'll call it Button. Right, come on, you three can help me feed the chooks. This mum needs to rest and be with her calf, without your inquisitive eyes peering at her.'

'Well done, son, proper job, me lad.' Henry said as his bear-sized fists squeezed Jack's shoulder, his knuckles chapped and cracked. Jack left the shed with the children. Eleanor and Bertie, their heads together, as thick as thieves, ambled close behind. Harry tucked his hand into Jack's and felt the gentle squeeze of his fingers.

'So, what's going on, scruff?' Jack said as they walked across the yard towards the chickens.

'I've been playing soldiers in my room, I got shot a few times.'

'A few times, and you're still walking?'

'Yes, well, you're still walking, aren't you? I want to be like you, Jack. Brave.'

'I'm one of the lucky ones, scruff,' he said, picking him up and throwing him under his arm like a rugby ball. He plopped Harry on the gate by the hens' coop while he scooped dollops of grain into the bucket before carrying it over to their feeding trough. 'Any eggs, Elle?' he called as the grain rushed into it with a crunching sound.

'I took them inside earlier this morning.'

'Are the trays full yet?'

'Three are, yes.'

'Alright, I'll hang the fresh eggs sign out again.'

'Jack?' Eleanor moved closer as he filled the water bowl.

'Elle ...'

'The girl, she's gone.' Her voice dipped and her eyes had a look of sadness. 'I went to the loft this morning to check on her when I collected the eggs and she wasn't there.'

'That's because she's at the cottage. I got her last night. I knew your uncle would be clearing the hay for calving today. I carried her back late last night.'

'And now, where is she now? I didn't say goodbye to her. I'll never see her again and I wanted to at least wish her luck.'

'You still can – I left her sleeping in this morning. She needed a good night's sleep and rest. She's been in the barn a while.'

'Did she say anything? Who she is, where she's from?'

'No, give her time. For now, she's safe and warm, and when she's ready she'll tell us.'

'I knew you'd know what to do, you're the best, Jack. I'm not sure I ever want to go back to London; I'd miss you way too much and all your stories.' She left Jack and called to her brothers. 'Come on, race you two back. Lunch will be dished up soon.'

Henry passed Jack and slapped him on the shoulders. 'It's been a good mornin', Jack me lad, ye be comin' in for lunch, one of Em's best homemade soups, vegetables from the land, dare I say.' He leant his frame against the farmhouse wall and prised off his muddy boots.

'Sounds tempting. But I best get back.'

Jack passed the cows as he walked down the track, three of them heavy with calf but still with the herd. He watched them awhile as he leant over the five-bar gate. They chomped on the sweet grass, while he took out his harmonica and turned it in his hands.

'Your sister will be back soon; she had a girl – as swee'as.' The twang in his voice heavier. It almost sounded like a melody when he said *as swee'as*. 'I've called her Button, as bright as a button she is,' he said out loud to them. He pushed his foot off the gate and as he walked, he kicked up the stones and dust. His hands cupped his harmonica and, drawing it up to his lips, his eyes danced as he went. He took up the sign that leant on a large stone and hung it on the iron post: *Fresh eggs for sale*. It squeaked as it swung to and fro on its cradle. He opened the door to his cottage and went in.

He hung his cap and jacket on the door's hook and pushed off his boots. Twelve tinny chimes came from the mantel clock, and a coal slipped from below, crumbling into fragments. The floor was hard on his knee as he stoked the fire and pushed a few fresh lumps of coal into the glowing redness. He put his harmonica and tin on the table with his beret. His hand brushed along the wall down the steps. He dipped his head as he reached the bottom step, his woollen socks protecting his feet from the ice-cold floor beneath them. The breakfast bowl and saucepan sat on the drainer, the clothes still on the horse rack, the fine fabrics; even lying over the wooden frame, they were beautiful. He took them and folded them neatly. Dipping his head again, he went back up the steps, stoking the fire once more and setting the guard to one side.

Jack's Story

He knocked lightly on her door. She watched from the other side as the latch pushed down and the door eased open.

'Hello,' Jack said, holding her clothes. 'Here are your clothes, they're dry.'

She took them, holding them pressed up against her chest. 'Thank you.'

'Are you hungry? I'm having some bread and cheese with Emma's homemade apple chutney.'

Her teeth grazed her bottom lip. 'A little,' she lied. She was starving.

'Come on.' He beckoned, tilting his head towards the stairs.

She followed him down to the room below. Its warmth wrapped around her body as she stood, feeling the smoothness of the floor underfoot.

'You should sit down here in the day, it's warmer than your bedroom.'

'I will, thank you.' She sat on the sofa whilst Jack left her briefly, returning with two plates with a hunk of bread, a slab of cheese and a dollop of chutney on each.

'Here.' He handed her the plate of simple food. 'Did you sleep well?'

She nodded, her eyes falling to the plate of cheese and bread. He broke the cheese with his knife, shovelling the chutney onto the hunk of bread. She tilted her head, her eyes crinkling curiously.

'What?' he said, realising he had her gaze on him.

She looked away quickly and broke her bread tidily, slicing a piece of cheese and spreading a layer of chutney on a small morsel. She did it differently to him; he didn't notice, he was too hungry to notice.

'Thank you,' she said, pushing the bread around her plate.

He shook his head, a smile across his face, the sides of his eyes creased.

'I'd like to repay you for your kindness, but I'm not sure how to. I have nothing. I mean, I ...'

He sighed, his eyes smiling, his voice soft. 'You don't need to.' He pushed the last piece of bread about his plate, mopping up every inch of sweet chutney and crumb of cheese. 'Where are you from?'

'I don't know anymore. I thought I knew.' Her words caught in her throat. 'But now ...' She played with the food on her plate and sighed.

'When you're ready you can tell me.' His eyes rested on her. 'But until then, you will be safe here and warm and fed.' She smiled back at him.

'I saw you this morning, with the cows, there was one alone. Was she hurt?'

'No. She was very prignant and ready to calf.'

'You say that word differently to me.'

'Guess I do, miss.'

'How come?'

'How come what, she's prignant or I say it differently to you?'

'Both, I guess.'

'I'm from Christchurch.'

'Christchurch? – I don't know it.'

'Sure, you do, miss. New Zealand, I came over for the war. I was in the 1st British Airborne Division.'

'Oh, I see, of course. I only know Christchurch College.' Her voice trailed off. 'And the cow?'

'She's a mum, with a beautiful curious calf.'

The girl smiled back at Jack.

The clock on the mantelpiece chimed once.

'I'll have to go back now. Will you be alright?'

She nodded.

He rested his arm on the door as he pulled his boots back on and took his cap from the hook and his heavy jacket. The afternoons grew colder on the farm as the sun dipped earlier in the skies now. Before leaving he went to the table and stuffed his beret in his pocket along with his harmonica. 'I'll be back by dusk.'

He left her alone once more. She took the plates down into the kitchen, her toes curled on the stone floor. As she stood at the sink, washing the lunch bits, she could see from the window his figure disappearing into the distance, still with the dulcet tones of *the blues* drifting through the breeze.

The same afternoon, Jack worked the farm with Henry. The cows came in for their evening milking and Jack turned out the churns into the cold store, ready to load them onto the cart. He'd ride it down to the milk stand for collection when the sun rose the following day. He checked in on the newly born calf, who was now standing on its gangly legs by its mother. He poured some fresh milk into the pail, enough to cover his hand, and let the young calves suck one at time at his fingers for their last evening fill. He closed down the coop for the hens, who plumped their feathers and sat side by side on their perch, in their own darkness.

Today had been a good day on the farm, with the arrival of another calf – the first for this heifer. The young calves were feeding well without their mums and would soon learn to feed alone. One would be fattened and taken to market or not; a part Jack always struggled with. It was always the one with hugest eyes, who sucked more heavily on his fingers. Seldom was there a happy ending. A little like war. And now, after his day's work, he'd go back to his cottage where the girl who once hid in the hayloft would be. Now she'd be warm and safe, and she had spoken a little.

Jack bid Henry goodnight and wandered down the track back home. He passed the horses as they took their evening run, their heads hung low, their hooves pounding out divots, disrupting the otherwise smooth contours of the land that enveloped the farmhouse.

He opened the door to his cottage and hung up his coat and cap, taking off his boots. Before he'd reached the fire, he caught from the corner of his eye the figure at the top of the stairs. 'Hello.'

She smiled back down at him. 'Hello,' she said as she descended the stairs and sat perched on the edge of the sofa. 'I can feel the cold around you,' she said moving her hair away from her face. 'Can I do anything to help, maybe help make supper?'

'Sure, that would be grand. I've got sausages in the fridge and potatoes in the sack by the sink.'

'Let me make supper, you sit and rest. You must be tired, and I have nothing to do.'

In the kitchen she found the potatoes and the peeler. As she stood at the sink and peeled them, the melodic tunes of *the blues* floated down to her in the kitchen. She hummed to it as Jack played.

She brought a saucepan of potatoes up to the range along with some sausages.

'You play really well,' she said.

'Yep, my dad taught me, when I was a boy.'

'Is that him in the picture?'

'Yep, with my mum. They looked great together, especially on the dancefloor. Boy they could dance.' He sighed, smiling at the memories.

'That sounds nice.' She offered him a smile back. Jack watched her whilst she stared into the fire. Her hair hung loose about her face, her skin a soft olive hue. Her eyes gazed into the flames; they no longer looked soulless.

He took the harmonica away from his mouth. 'And your family?'

She bit her lip, pushing herself back in the seat. She'd known this question would come and she hadn't time to rehearse her answer. She tucked her hands into the pockets of her slacks to stop them from fidgeting.

'I don't have any family,' she said. Her stare still on the fire.

'I'm sorry.' Jack took up his harmonica and played some more. After a time, the girl got up from the sofa and prodded the potatoes: they were soft in the centre. She took them down to the kitchen and mashed them. Each time she pushed the utensil harder onto the creamed potatoes. Why hadn't she rehearsed her answer? She had no family, so where were they? Was she an orphan, a runaway, was she the survivor of a tragic accident? She pummelled the potatoes more until she stopped, and stood and stared at the saucepan of mash. She brought the now mashed potatoes back up to the range and left it on the top whilst she dished up the sausages and then handed Jack his supper.

As the night drew in and the conversation dwindled, Jack cleared away the plates and stoked the fire, adding some more coals to burn through the night and keep the cottage warm. He placed the guard in front before turning to her.

'I'm going to turn in now. Are you coming?' She nodded as he allowed her to go first before turning out the lamps in the room.

He stopped at his bedroom door, his hand resting on the latch. 'I'll be gone by the time you wake in the morning. Help yourself to oats.'

'I will and thank you, Jack.' She cast him a look before pushing down the latch and closing the door behind her.

She lay in bed, the brown slacks she'd worn that day draped over the brass bedpost. She kept the shirt on for warmth, as her nightdress. She could hear from her bedroom the bath being run, and she listened until the sound of the water stopped. The clock faintly chimed ten, and sometime after the bathroom door unlocked and the door next to it closed. She snuggled down under the covers and let the night steal her away.

Her eyes flashed open. The room was pitch black. It came again – the sound of a man crying out. She lay still in her bed. The pane in her bedroom window frame rattled a little as the wind snapped around the stone walls of the cottage. She lay still, her breath held. It came again, a blood-curdling deep scream, and then it stopped. She inched her way up the bed, her hand fumbling at the curtain as she pushed it open. Her eyes searching in the blackness that hung low outside, wrapping itself around the cottage. Her skin flashed with tiny bumps as the cry came again and the flash of two bright red eyes shone in the moonlight. She held her breath and shot her hand away from the curtain. The beating inside her hammered against her ribcage, her mouth was dry. She swallowed. She lay still, unsure of what she had heard. Maybe her mind was playing tricks on her? She moved the pillow down the bed and folded it closer around her cheeks. It was cold against her face.

Then it came again, the sound of a man in distress. He cried out. *'No! Pull him out. Jesus Christ, hold him.'* She rolled the eiderdown back and pushed the blankets away from her. She fumbled across the room, her arms outstretched, until she felt the door, her breath held as she clicked the latch out of its cradle. She teased open the door a little and stood. She didn't dare move an inch in case a floorboard creaked beneath her footsteps. The clock downstairs chimed one strike. A high-pitched shrieking sound pierced the night and she pelted back across the floor and hid under the covers. There was something out there on the dark moors – she hadn't imagined the sounds or the wail of a man in distress. Her eyes darted around the room, its darkness obscuring her vision. She lay back down and pulled the covers up tightly against her. She waited until her eyes began to close and the tiredness took over her body.

Chapter Five

Operation Market Garden, late August, 1944

In an aircraft hangar somewhere in England, 10,000 men sat, their behinds beginning to lose all feeling, their khaki camouflage thick serge battle dress rubbing shoulder to shoulder.

The brief was precise and simple. They would be dropped into Holland by Dakota C-47s and gliders, their aim to secure the bridges crossing the lower Rhine and hold them intact until relieved. The men were the 1st British Airborne Division and the 1st Polish Independent Parachute Brigade.

The deafening hum of the aeroplanes, towing silent, powerless gliders with huge swathes of rope, menaced the greyness above, the Dakota C-47s like a swarm of unknown giant flying insects ready to invade. The men wore Denison smocks and were encumbered by their parachutes, rucksacks and their weapons held in leg bags. They sat on metal benches, packed in like sardines in a can – shoulder to shoulder in the rough comfort of the fuselage. The air was blue and their banter loud. Their trepidation was hidden. Not one of them letting on about the fear that churned about inside them. Not one of them letting on about their anxiety that bubbled up like a volcano waiting to erupt. Each one afraid, yet each soldier brave – at least that was the face they showed, the bravado they carried. Their shouts were loud above the deafening engines of the planes in the sky.

Jack's Story

'Alright, Joe!' one of the paratroopers shouted above the banter to the young soldier who sat opposite him. He was just a kid, his face green with air sickness, his fists clenched. The blood drained from his white knuckles. His eyes were fixed to the ground. He looked up. He forced a smile. *My name's not Joe,* he thought to himself, *I'm not a Joe any more.* He was wet behind the ears, but not too young to realise that *Joe* was the name given to a new recruit, and he was no longer new. A youngster who they'd mould to be one of them; they'd look after him, they'd become his mother and his brother.

When the red lamp lit up, indicating *ready to go,* and stayed on; it would be the only light in the fuselage. The dispatcher, a flight sergeant in the Royal Airforce, stayed by the door at the tail end of the aircraft, waiting until the time came for the thumbs up and the green light to ignite.

Then they would jump into their drop zone, which was seven miles from their rally point at Arnhem Bridge.

The dispatcher hollered the aircraft drill and each man looked up. Their own thoughts of their families, their loved ones, the war they were jumping into was snatched from their minds. They were soldiers now, their focus needed to change.

'Prepare for action.' The dispatcher shouted up the fuselage. 'Stand and fit equipment.' He shot a look at the young soldier. 'Action stations!' Each soldier from the last stick number checked their comrades, and the tell off came from each soldier until the final OK call came from Number One.

The wind battered around the capsule of fear, howling around their legs, whistling down their necks, battering against their hands which gripped the straps that held their chutes. The engines roared; the pungent smell of aviation fuel swallowed them whole.

It was their time, the tell off had been called. 'Red on!' the dispatcher hollered above the deafening droning of the planes. His unmoved countenance stared out he had become a Sergeant again and needed to reinforce their thoughts as soldiers, to now be unfazed by what the men in this aircraft would be feeling, although deep down he knew their fear he'd jumped out of a plane too, either in the day or the pitch black of night, he had every sympathy for these men. He wasn't a paratrooper. He never would be a paratrooper. But he was one of them, a man with fear.

He attached the static line from their parachutes to the rail in the aircraft, triple-checking the buckles on each, making absolutely damn sure the harnesses were safe and the chutes would open. Churchill hadn't paid for reserves; the cost was deemed a waste of money for the government. The aircraft flew lower over the drop zone. The platoon's commander stood, and his men, each with their own stick number from one to twenty-eight, followed his lead. The rancid smell of vomit filled the fuselage as a paratrooper hurled on the back of his comrade. Another then spewed up a stomach full of the morning's feed. Like a set of dominoes, the platoon's vomit sprayed across the floors and parachutes of the men. The wind sent the rancid smell of sick billowing into their faces like a backdraft.

'Green on! One, go!' the dispatcher bellowed. The commanding officer, Lieutenant Colonel Johnny Frost, jumped. The numbers came loud and clear, the men shuffling up the aircraft, jumping at each stick number as it was called. 'Two go, three go, four go ...'

As each man exited the door and into the plane's slipstream, the wind pushed and shoved them about. Their bodies were thrown and buffeted around the sky until they began to fall in control before the static line performed its function. Their silk canopies opened one by one as another paratrooper fell

Jack's Story

into the sky. A mass of grey mushroom-like shapes falling, following each other in the drift. Then the thump of a soldier hitting the ground feet first, then rolling, before unclipping and gathering up the chute and leaving it discarded on the terrain. Each one made his weapon ready, checked his kit, pulled his compass out of his smock and got his bearings before moving on to his rally point to rendezvous.

'God be with me,' said the paratrooper as he stood on the ledge.

'Twelve go!' hollered the dispatcher. His hand on his back.

'Fuck, sir. I ...'

'Twelve go!' came the command again. He knew the soldier's fear, but he couldn't show him that.

'Twelve go!' His shout came again, this time louder. It felt like a lifetime that Twelve stood by the door, the dispatcher ready to pull him out with immediacy so as not to let a second get in the way of their jump and ruin the sequence of the soldiers as they shuffled forward.

A hand gripped his arm from behind him. 'C'mon buddy, you can do this ... you've done it before ... don't let yourself or your muckas down ... be aggressive and drive out that door.'

'Twelve go! Move it! Don't be a fucking *crow*. Jump or I'll fucking pull you out.' The dispatcher's hand went out to pull him out not wanting to lose a moment of crucial timing.

Twelve's knees buckled beneath him, his feet shuffled forward more, the vomit sprayed. He wiped his sleeve across his chin. He felt the reassuring squeeze on his arm from the soldier behind.

'Go on, buddy, I'm behind you.'

'Twelve go! Thirteen go! Fourteen go! Fifteen go! Sixteen go!'

Like a blind man he plunged out of the plane, falling through the air, the slipstream pushing him, until the brilliant sound of the chute opening above him allowed him to see. Number Thirteen was behind him. The sound of enemy fire permeated the air as the parachutes fell from the sky. Haunting screams surrounded him from those fallen souls. His body was taken by the wind to a point where he would land and then patrol on and later form up with his platoon.

He was no older than seventeen, having worked as an apprentice cobbler in the East End of London before he had been enlisted, with only a few weeks of training with his battalion. His name was Edward Smith, Ted to his family, Private Smith to his regiment, *Joe* to the kind face in the Dakota C47. This would now become his family. The terrain met his body with a cracking pound. There was another thud on the ground behind him.

The machine guns pummelled the air, the cries above, the fallen souls like dandelions drifting in the sky, their bodies hanging, lifeless. Falling, falling, falling. Bones cracking as the ground came up to meet them. The bloodstained, crumpled heaps scattered around; their bodies carried away by the stretcher bearer. A mass of murky-coloured uniforms stained with a shot of liquid redness.

Ted's hands trembled uncontrollably as he tried to unlatch himself from his chute. His eyes darted around the ground, his lips quivering, unstoppable in the motion. His hands like useless tools, unable to do anything, like a blunt knife hacking through bread; he was crumbling with fear. Another body fell and he shook at the sight, his steps stumbling, his heavy black boots glued to the ground as if stuck in a swamp.

'Private!' a paratrooper hollered across the terrain as he unclipped and collapsed his parachute, checked his weapon, sorted his kit, took out his compass from his smock and found

Jack's Story

his bearings. He needed to patrol ahead to his rally point. 'Private!' he bellowed again. It was Number Thirteen.

The paratrooper ran crouched to Private Smith, who was sitting on the ground, his body rigid, his eyes staring into space, his nose a mass of dribbling slime.

'Twelve, what the fuck you playin' at? You'll get yourself shot. Move! You're a fuckin' paratrooper ... now get a grip, sort your kit out and let's get to target.'

The grab of Thirteen's hand on Twelve's arm pushed him up. Each step felt like his boots were stuck in a mud bath. A heaviness that was holding him back. Saliva dribbled from his mouth and slimed across his chin, while tears fell from his eyes, blurring his vision. He smeared his hands across his face, whimpering like a dog. Pictures of his family flooded his mind: his mum, his dad, his younger sister, Penny, and his little brother, Ronnie. The slime from his nose ran over his mouth. Mud and grime were smudged across his face, his tears now like slugs falling down his cheeks. He shoved the cuffs of his uniform across his face. He was a soldier now.

'Come on!' Thirteen shouted again.

Number Twelve scrambled across the ground, his hands shaking as he unclipped himself from the chute and took up his weapon and patrolled on with the paratrooper. Today was the day he would remember Number Thirteen. The day their brotherhood would be formed.

Number Thirteen hailed from Christchurch, New Zealand. He went by the name of Jack – Jack Saunders – and had enlisted at the beginning of the war. He was the son of a soldier: his father had fought in the First World War, met his mum, a sweet English girl, and there they made Jack. He stayed by Twelve's side as they patrolled on, his boots hitting the ground as he marched on to their rendezvous point. He sang *the blues* in his head as he kept his pace up and drove forward, keeping Number Twelve with him, keeping him focused. They'd walked for miles in their platoon, and their bodies soldiered on even though they hadn't eaten since breakfast, most of which was now on the metal floor of the aircraft's fuselage. Their bellies were hungry for nourishment and their bodies fatigued. The fog began to seep in; cold, damp air hung about them, seeping into their uniforms like swamp water.

The sun dipped in the solemn skies, casting little light over the greyness that surrounded them. Boots reverberated as the men marched forward in unison to their rally point. Number Thirteen was part of the anti-tank platoon and was encumbered with his weapon in his webbing bag on his back. The PIAT was his weapon, the Projector Infantry Anti-Tank: it could eliminate a tank at close range. He shifted the straps to stop them digging into his shoulders. It weighed him down more than he cared for. Number Twelve carried the ammo for the PIAT. Each of them held a rifle against their chests, fully loaded, ready to fire. The two soldiers carried on them six grenades each: three were to kill and the other three to cause a smokescreen.

As if a pin from a grenade could be heard dropping on the ground, the birds fell silent in the trees. An eeriness engulfed the air and an uncertain stillness loomed around them. The commander raised his arm – slowly, the troops fell silent. Their boots stopped, dead still. A bird flew from a spinney ahead, soaring alone into the sky. Metal glinted, caught by the sun as she dropped low in the west.

'Take cover, keep your heads down, German rifle men in the spinney!' hollered the commander.

The firing of mortar shells from enemy fire ricocheted within the trees. Number Thirteen fell to the ground and pulled Twelve down with him. Together they scrambled to a nearby stone outbuilding and hid in it. Thirteen crawled up against the wall and cocked his PIAT whilst Twelve sat with his back up against the wall, his knees bent up to his torso below an open window – open in that it was simply a hole in the wall. Twelve spied an upturned wooden bottle crate on the opposite wall. He scrambled over and knocked off a chicken that perched on it. She clucked indignantly and ruffled her feathers. He drew the crate up below the window. On the side of it in red ink was printed Bier von Wiel. What he would give to be someplace else with a beer in his hand. Number Thirteen balanced the weapon on it and pushed himself up to take his view from his cover. Twelve passed him a shell from his patrol sack. Thirteen loaded it into the PIAT. He waited. His target was in sight, about 30 yards from him. The firing of weapons from his platoon penetrated the air. He waited until the firing lessened and the swathe of men groaned as enemy fire pummelled their bodies. Perforating them like human colanders. Some of them baptised by fire. Thirteen's hands shook as he went to fire: he had to be right, his aim precise. He viewed the tanks' turrets from where he knelt behind his weapon. He could see two tanks in their netted camouflage and low-lying branches hanging over them. There were no other immediate obstacles. Thirteen squatted down low, his eye spying through the sight of the PIAT, and then he opened it up and let it fire. He blasted the first tank's turret. His aim was on the money. He high-fived Number Twelve.

'Fucking ammo, buddy.'

Twelve swiftly passed him another shell. Slug after slug was passed until the tank was incapacitated. Thirteen moved his aim onto the second tank until the Germans' armour was blasted out of all recognition. Annihilated. An enemy soldier bailed from the second tank. The platoon on the ground fired at him as he ran, trying to scrabble to safety. Three, four, five rounds discharged from an automatic. His body was hammered with bullets, shaking violently, like a man having 1,000 volts passed through him before falling to the ground. His mouth open, blood trickling from it. His limbs smashed. Half his skull was missing. Fragments of bone, brain, flesh, innards sprayed across the terrain. A bloodiness seeping through his blasted uniform, his back showing his inside riddled with discharged bullets. The ground was drenched in a redness. A body of a young SS soldier killed, lying still, his cheek smothered on the ground, his eyes staring ahead – he was frozen in time.

Through the firing, any surviving enemy soldiers bailed out and found a momentary safety. The platoon opened fire on the ground and took them out like a turkey shoot.

The smell of spent cartridges mingled with the acrid smell of burnt-out bodies from where the fuel had ignited in the tanks and burned them alive. The dank, dark, gruesome smell of death. A soldier rifled through the pockets of a fallen soldier for information. He took a bar of chocolate. Thirteen and Twelve watched before they packed up their weapons to move on.

The paratroopers formed up again and marched on; they had five more miles to cover before they reached Arnhem Bridge.

'So, Twelve, what's ya name?' Thirteen asked.

'Private Ted Smith,' he replied, gasping for breath between the words. 'And you?'

'Private Jack Saunders, pleased to make your acquaintance,' he said and winked.

'You're not from around here, I mean England, like me.'

'Nope, from Christchurch, New Zealand.'

Jack's Story

'You ever killed a man before?' Smith steamed ahead, his mind going back to the dead soldiers.

'Only in this war. It's been a long one, I can tell you that much. Too fucking long. Right, come on, we're almost there.'

'I've never seen a dead man before.'

'Think about it as the enemy – they're not men. They're the enemy.'

'I've still never seen a dead man before, until now.'

Jack cast him a look. He knew what he meant, he knew that feeling too.

Ted and Jack traipsed the terrain with their rally point at the forefront of their minds, where their bellies would be filled with grub from the camp's canteen. Two men who had been numbers in a Dakota would now become like brothers in arms. A friendship forged like no other.

Chapter Six

Orchard Cottage, Cowick, Exeter, early October, 1946

The coal fire sizzled gently in the room. He stood by the front door pulling on his winter jacket when Beth appeared at the top of the stairs. She was dressed in her skirt and blouse, her cardigan draped over her shoulders. He reached out to open the door, not noticing her presence.

'Jack …' Her voice trailed off. His hand left the latch as he turned and saw her standing at the top of the staircase, lit by the sun's rays which slanted through her bedroom doorway and caught the strands of her hair. There was a warmth that its hazelnut brown tones brought to her features, a simple frame for her smile and eyes that held more love in them than she could ever admit to. Only her journal would know of that, her thoughts untold just on a page for her and only her. Her blouse fell against the smooth lines of her curves, giving the faintest silhouette of her femininity. The hue of her strands altered as the sun's rays shifted across the small landing where she stood.

'Are you going to the farm?' Her hand touched the softness of her neck, then strayed back down, her glance catching his but only briefly.

'Yep, I have to go to work. I'm sorry, did I wake you?'

'No.' Her hand went back to her neck. 'You didn't.' Jack went to turn away, his fingers pushing down the latch on the door.

'It's just – I wondered, is there any work? I mean on the farm. I've never worked anywhere before. But I can learn, and I can help with the ponies, maybe? I know a bit about horses. Maybe I could help with the small animals, chickens, maybe collect the eggs. Anything really.' She felt like she was babbling.

'I can ask. Who should I say you are, or at least where you're from?'

'Beth?'

'And your surname, Beth?'

She hadn't thought it through; people would ask.

'Brooklyn?'

'Beth Brooklyn, that's your name?'

She nodded.

'Alright, I can ask for you.' He moved back to the door and opened it.

'Jack?'

He turned back to her, his eyes searching her face.

'Are you alright?' she asked.

'Yep, why?'

'Oh nothing.' She hesitated. 'It's just I heard some noises in the night. They seemed quite near.'

'Probably the foxes screeching. Or maybe the beast of the moor.' A smile cracked across his face.

'The beast? There's a beast on the moor?' He waited in that fraction of a moment when her eyes smiled, and her mouth followed. In a split second, every nerve in his body and brain was electrified. His answering smile caught her unaware.

'No, I'm teasing you.' He placed his cap over his mop of hair.

'It sounded like a person,' she said, her head tilted to one side.

'Slept through it. Didn't hear a thing. I'll be back at midday for lunch and I'll ask about any work too.'

'Thank you,' she said.

Jack closed the door behind him and left Beth at the top of the stairs. She went back to her room and took out her journal and pen and scribbled on a clean page.

Dear Diary,

I'm not sure what day it is but I am safe, you'll be pleased to know. Today, I am starting again. One day, one breath and one step at a time. Three children found me where I was hiding in the hayloft and they have protected me, and also a boy, well, a young man really. He's kind and caring and he has a way that makes me feel safe. How I feel a little with you, you're my safe space. But after running from those memories I feel it's time to find me and tell you.

Today, I asked if there was any work I might be able to do on the farm, to earn my keep at least. He said he'd ask. He, he is Jack and he has a tenderness that makes me feel like, well, makes me feel like I will be alright. And if perchance I feel like I might fail then I will just keep trying, until I succeed. I feel like I've failed already or maybe I'm just learning. It seems a cruel way to learn and one I wish I hadn't learnt.

I feel safe here, although I don't know where here actually is. I feel lost in my head. Yet here I am, in a farm cottage tucked away from prying eyes – away from a life I don't want to be part of. D'you know what I mean, dear diary? I know my thoughts are safe and you will just listen to me. That I can write freely, and you will listen to me patiently without judgement, knowing my words, knowing my thoughts. I feel like I am escaping from this labyrinth of a mess and for days I have seen nothing but their faces in my head. When I close my eyes to it all, the picture becomes clearer. And I want to scream and cry, and yet when I do, nothing comes out, like my sounds are as empty as my feelings. Like my feelings are as empty as my sounds. Lost.

I thought I would miss that life, but I don't. I thought I would miss them, but I don't. I thought I loved him, but now I don't even know what love is. Just a word, meaningless. I don't ever want to be found; I just want to start again. That's what I want to do. That's what I need to do. And I will.

The lid of her ink pen clicked shut as she finished writing the new entry in her diary. She closed the page and held it for a moment before she placed both pen and journal inside her pillowcase and slipped it under the feather-down pillow. She took up her book – *A Tree Grows in Brooklyn* – and left the bedroom.

The fire burned with a red glow in the room downstairs, and, as he had done so the mornings before, Jack had left a pot of oats warming on the range. She poured herself a bowl and found some honey in the kitchen, which she drizzled on top, adding a little sweetness to the creamy oats before sitting on the sofa and taking the bookmark from the last page she had read. Legs drawn up, she balanced the bowl on her lap, letting each mouthful slip down her throat and warm her through. She turned each page as she fell deeper and deeper into the storytelling. A story that told of the coming of age of a young girl, with a poignancy that made her feel as though she was reading a reflection of her own life. If she looked in a mirror, what she saw reflected back was a life that came with struggles and yet shouldn't. She felt like a hand trying to put on a glove that wants to fit but simply won't pass over the fingers. Too small. Too wrong. A misfit.

As she sat with her feet tucked beneath the blanket, the wind whistled through the canes in the garden, the clock ticked on the mantelpiece and the fire fizzed. She'd look up from her reading as another piece of molten coal tumbled down and got caught at the grate. She drew the blanket closer onto her legs, tucking it under her toes. She needed some warmer clothes but had no way of buying anything. She needed the simple things like toiletries, too, but until she had a job, how could she ever afford it? How could she ever start again?

Placing the book on the sofa, she went to the window, which overlooked the lane. The sign still with its directions pointing toward the nearby villages. The sun slanted in the sky above, throwing a bleak shaft of light onto the gnarly tree that stood in the front garden, its branches resting a little tiredly on the stone wall. Its growth seemed stunted. She gazed again at the signpost. *Maybe I could get a job in the town ...* but then she would no longer be hidden. She crossed her arms and tucked her hands under as she stared out onto the bleak land. She smiled as she spotted the scarecrow alone, the wind rattling about its straw arms. Was that what she'd made out in the obscurity of the night? Perhaps the cries were just as Jack had said, a screeching fox.

She took her bowl and the empty saucepan from the range and went down to the kitchen, the stone floor still cold but less so now she was wearing her socks. She could see from the window that two of the cows had been taken to the cowshed. Now she knew that they weren't ill but were in calf. She was learning things about a farm that she'd never known before; she'd led a life that she simply took for granted. She'd wanted for nothing – or had she? If she had, it had been a want for something that was different.

The clock in the room tinged ten strokes. Jack would be back in a couple of hours. There was little she could do other than read. She settled back down on the sofa and opened her book once more. Every now and again her concentration was taken from the words on the page to the outside world – which seemed to have stood still for her. She hadn't seen it for days and wondered if she ever would again. She didn't even know what day it was. Her nights in the barn seemed like a distant memory. She had been there for days before the children had found her.

A young girl on horseback rode past the window, her seat straight, the sound of the horse's hooves familiar to Beth. She got up from the sofa once more and watched a while at the window, her glance on the rider as she rose and fell in the saddle. She yearned to be outside, but she had no real idea of where she was or even how to find her way back to Jack's cottage should she leave. Yet the outside was calling her, the sound of the horse's hooves pushing her to go beyond the front door and follow. Her fingertips stretched out to the windowpane. But if she left, she would be alone again – she would be lost once more and then maybe she would be found and sent back to where she had run from. She pressed her hands against the pane, and the condensation trickled down and between her fingers, catching in them and forming a small pool of cold water in the groove between each finger. She leaned in, pressing her cheek on the glass so as to gaze a little longer at the rider, until the sound of the hooves had gone and the figure was no more in view, and Beth's pang for the outside world had diminished – for a while.

She sighed as she waited. That was the last of the horses or any life that she'd see until Jack returned. Her thoughts caught in her head as she looked out over the land, her hand still pressed up against the pane as if longing to touch the horse that had ridden past. A memory of Silver Sixpence flashed into her mind. A beautiful creature of power and strength, he had meant everything to her. His soft brown eyes and the reassuring nod of his head when her words reached him. Memories of him flooded her mind: the way her head would rest against his as she brushed him down in the stables, the sweat on his neck that glistened on his velvet coat after their hack on the moors. She'd whisper into his ear of how she would always ride him and never let him go. And yet that wasn't true. In the stables he would stand faithfully and powerfully. She'd brush him down and tell him her troubles and doubts, and he would toss his head as if he was listening to her and knowing exactly how she was feeling. The rides they would take over the bracken and ferns, his head tossed high as he powered on, holding her, the strength of his body keeping her safe as they travelled across the rugged lands together, her legs clenched to his sides, her feet tight in the stirrups, knowing he was hers. She would cast away all her sadness at not being the person she wanted to be.

She'd been given Silver Sixpence on her 18th birthday and she had loved him from the first moment she saw him. He wasn't the colour of a sixpence, but she had found one once and was told it would bring her luck, and what luck he was. Her parents had sought and bought the Arabian horse from one of the country's finest breeders in *Horse and Hound*, and although he was a little frisky Beth had a way with him. She let him run free in his pen until he would stop and then she would pet him with soft body contact. She didn't lean into him with secret words; he was a high-spirited horse who would be forever hers, her companion, her equal. She rode him with the freedom she knew of horses and he let her ride him with the style she had. Daily they would ride out together across the barren moors, or over the sandy dunes of the nearby beaches, across the rugged coastlines of Devon. With the wind whistling past their faces, his head hung low, her body forward in her saddle. And then they'd stop at the top of the cliff's edge and watch the waves and the sea crash against the rocks. Watching the swell of water, the clouds fall from the sky's horizon into the greyness of the water, until she'd lean down to him, her hand on his neck and her soft words in his ear. 'Come on boy,' she'd whisper. The air snorted from his nostrils as he carried her across the grassy edges of the cliff, the sweat on his back as he carried her forward. Homeward bound.

Jack's Story

'Who would be brushing him down?' she murmured under her breath. She hadn't told him she was leaving. He wouldn't ride with anybody else, and then what – had she made way for his own fate? He was her Silver Sixpence. But nobody else would ride him and neither would he let them.

The clock chimed twelve, and as it did the front door of the cottage opened. Jack took off his boots and coat and left them at the door.

'Beth,' he said. She didn't turn from the window, as if in her own trance. 'Beth,' he said again as he came a little closer to her. She jumped, startled by his presence. 'Sorry, I didn't mean to make you jump.'

'That's alright – I was just watching the outside world.' Her eyes were still on the fields and the lane.

'I asked at the farm if there was any work.'

'And ...' She turned, her eyes lit up, waiting for the news she so needed to hear.

'There isn't much. But help is needed with the potato farming. I don't know if that's what you'd want to do?'

'I'll do anything. Do they need to meet me?'

'Come up to the farm with me after lunch and I'll introduce you to Henry.'

'What have you told them, Jack?' Her eyes glanced back to the lane.

'Only that you're looking for work. I don't know you to tell them anything else. Is there something I should know?'

She shook her head without looking at him.

'We'll go after lunch then.' He smiled and left her whilst he went to the kitchen to prepare lunch.

Chapter Seven

Appledaw Farm, Cowick, Exeter, early October, 1946

'Young Jack tells me ye be looking for work, dreckly,' Henry said, taking up the pitchfork and shovelling a load of hay into the barrow.

'I am.' She nodded as she tucked her hair behind her ears. He spoke in a dialect that was similar to others she'd heard before; she likened it to that of a pirate.

'So, what can ye do, me lover, ye worked a farm before? Beth, ye be? Ye don't look dressed for farm work.'

'Umm, no. And yes, it's Beth.'

'What be dwain then?'

She cocked her head, squinting. 'A little stable work?'

'Where's that to?'

'Okehampton?' Her eyes creased at the sides.

'Okehampton. Umph. Stable work ye say?'

'That's right, mostly stable work. I'm good with horses, mucking out, feeding, exercising, you know that kind of thing.'

'There won't be that down 'ere me lover. It's teddies harvesting, 'ow be you at that?'

'I can learn about potatoes.' She nodded her head eagerly. 'I'm a quick learner.'

Jack's Story

'Proper job, ye start in mornin'.'

'I can start in the morning? Oh my, that's wonderful, thank you, thank you so much. You don't know what this means to me.' She turned to walk away, her mouth drawing a smile that stretched from ear to ear.

He wiped the sweat from his brow. 'Beth,' he called out. She turned back. 'Where be to?'

'I'm staying with Jack, until I find lodgings.'

'Proper job. Ye be 'ere at seven mind. Dreckly.'

'I will. I promise I will. I won't let you down.'

'Proper job.' Henry threw another clump of hay into the barrow whilst Beth walked away. There was a lightness in her step, almost a skip as she passed the cowshed and went on towards the track that led back down to Orchard Cottage. She could see Jack herding the cows through their meadow and Patch, the black and white collie, running to and fro, to and fro, circling behind them while rounding them up. She stopped and watched him until he reached the gate, the herd mooing gently as they waited to be led out and amble along the track they knew so well.

'How did it go?' he asked, leaning over the gate and lifting the latch before swinging the gate towards him.

'I start tomorrow. Potato harvesting – what does that mean?'

'Bringing the potatoes in from the fields and bagging them up, pretty much. Ready to be sold. Although we've harvested already, so you must be sacking them up.'

'Right. I'm actually quite looking forward to it.' The grin on her face made her eyes dazzle and dance in a way Jack had never seen before.

'It'll be hard work,' he said, tipping his cap further onto his head and drawing up his arms to allow the cows to pass through the gate. Patch whizzed around the back of the herd as their hooves kicked up the loose stones on the track.

'I know, but I want to do this. What time are you back this evening?'

'By dusk. Need to do the evening milking before I leave. I'm just heading the cows up now.' He pulled the gate, whistling ahead to Patch and the cows, their udders hanging low and swaying from side to side as they moved on along.

'D'you mind if I cook something for us?' she asked. 'I'm not a great cook, but it'll give me something to do, at least.'

'Sounds pukka, there's mince in the fridge ... maybe a pie?' He pushed his arms forward around the cows.

'Alright, maybe a pie. I think I can do that.' Her eyes shone as she said those words. Gone was the deep soullessness they had carried days before.

She watched awhile. Jack's arms swayed out and the sound of his call to the ambling herd was caught in the breeze as he turned away from her. It was melodic, almost like the mellifluous sound of the pitter-patter of rain falling on a canvas shelter. Different. Nice. When he smiled, she felt a rush of warmth run through her body. She tucked her hair behind her ear and blinked several times as his figure disappeared. She pulled her cardigan around her more tightly; the wind was beginning to pick up and the sun hung low in the west. Clouds passed over the cottage, holding a tinge of grey. The horses in the meadow seemed calm as they chomped on the sweetness of the grass. She rested her arms on the thick stone wall, brushing away the dust and loose earth on it. A bug squirrelled away under a layer of green spongey moss. She made a clicking sound with her mouth, until one of the horses, chestnut in colour, lifted his head from the grass and walked over to her. He tossed his head over the wall and bumped his nose towards her, curious. She stroked his nose.

Jack's Story

His lashes were a deep black, his eyes soft and warm, as deep as liquid treacle.

'Hello boy,' she smiled. The horse moved his head up and down, nudging her. Beth's touch was gentle and intuitive. He bumped his nose each time she rested from petting it, his ears pinned forward, paying attention to what was in front of him. 'You're a beauty, what's your name?' He dropped his head and snorted, pushing his muzzle closer, bumping Beth again and again, still curious. She smiled and gave out a sigh, and rested her face closer to his nose. She wasn't afraid, she had a way. His eyes were soft. The horse swished his tail and his front hooves stamped, irritated by the flies that circled around. He moved closer to her and her touch.

'Who rides you?' Her voice low and quiet. 'D'you gallop on the soft sands of the beaches? Hack through the ferns and brackens of the moors? Along the cliff tops of the coastal path?' Beth's voice was a whisper in his ear. He snorted again and lowered his head. Her eyes danced as she patted the beautiful creature. 'You're funny, you know what I'm saying, don't you.' She sighed softly as she took her hands away from his head. She brushed down the horse's shoulder and he brought his head up and over, nudging her elbow as she let her arm drop away. 'Go on, boy.' He lifted his head away from her touch and walked on, although not away – he walked on along the edge of the meadow's wall until Beth reached the cottage, where the meadow stopped, and the boundary wall began. And then the horse dug its hoof into the ground and reared up onto his hind legs and whinnied. Beth let out a gasp, her eyes welled up and stung with tears.

In a moment she had found a happiness that sang in her heart, reaching down to her gut. a feeling that came from somewhere so deep, where nobody could ever reach. As if in that moment she had intuitively made contact, reading the mind of this beautiful creature. As if in that moment that horse knew everything, from her hands' contact, from her memories of a beach, from her memories of a moor, where the bracken lay crushed beneath the hooves. Was there some kind of kindred spirit where her sadness would give her joy from a horse who reared up, not out of fear but out of solidarity, recognition, faithfulness and loyalty?

As the tears fell down her face, she watched on as he cantered off. Her mind filled with so much pain and yet for a brief moment, she forgot it all. For a brief moment she forgot why she was running, why she hated the life she'd escaped. Why she wanted to harvest potatoes, to talk with a man who had a kindness about him she couldn't let go of. A man who played the harmonica most nights whilst he rocked in his chair. Lived a simple life and yet was happy with the simplicity of it all. A man who took joy in a mince pie, whose call to the herd caught in the wind and sounded like a melody to her ears. Now she was away from the intelligent arrogance of people who couldn't love, who didn't care and who could damage. A man whose smile warmed her. Within these four walls of a farmhand's cottage, she felt protected by him and the four walls that he lived in. Her protection before had only ever come from a beach on horseback with a creature as beautiful as the one in the field, and maybe it understood what she'd left behind and that was her heartbreak. Now, though, he – the man who was protecting her – was swamping her mind and her thoughts. And she allowed it.

She closed the door to the cottage, leaving the wind outside to whistle around the garden canes and through the gnarly, bent branches of the stunted tree. The fire had almost burned out. She knelt down beside it and stoked it a bit, the heat from the red embers throwing a warmth onto her face. She added some more coals, which smoked angrily until a flame licked around one black lump, darting up and then back down until it fizzed and popped – and the flames grew bigger and angrier. The clock on the mantelpiece sang out five pretty chimes as she stood up and made her way down to the kitchen to prepare a simple supper of mince pie. She wasn't entirely sure how to make it, but with a little rummaging around in the cupboards she found some Bisto gravy granules. In the pantry was the mince and, as luck would have it, there was an onion and some muddy potatoes to the side of the sink. As the aromas of a pie sifted through the cottage, Beth went to retrieve her diary.

The sound of the front door stirred her from her writing.

'Hello,' she said as she appeared at the top of the stairs, pulling her cardigan around her smooth lines. 'I've made a pie.' Her voice sounded a little triumphant.

'That's good,' Jack said.

'Is everything alright?' she asked, descending the stairs and standing a little haphazardly in the room. His face was solemn, his eyes seemed dark, a shadow encasing them, and a redness shot through the whites of them. He pushed his hand through his hair and took out his harmonica and slumped into his chair. Taking his beret from his pocket, he held it, grazing his thumb across the felt until he placed it on the side table. He rolled his harmonica a few times in his hands and rubbed his fingers across the edge of it before turning it again.

'Jack?' She stood, her hand on the newel on the banister.

He looked different, tired. Sad. Not the man she'd left on the track with swaying arms and a melodic sound in his voice that stayed in her head. He put the harmonica to his lips and played it. She left him alone.

From her room she could hear the dulcet tones of *the blues* still being played, the tinny chime of the clock as it struck seven and the warming smell of the pie that baked in the range, ready to be eaten. She brushed her fingers along her lips and pushed herself up from the bed to go back downstairs. She stood at the top step and brushed down her skirt, tucked her hair behind her ear and breathed out. She passed by him as he played his harmonica as if not even noticing her. She inched the pie out of the range, the steam hitting her face and making her step back a little.

'Are you hungry?' she asked as she took the pie and placed it on a cast iron mat on the small dining table, two chairs either side. The table and chairs were tucked in the corner of the room. She went to the kitchen and brought back two plates and cutlery and set the table. In a cupboard she found two glasses and filled them with water. Jack still played his harmonica in his chair, which gently rocked back and forth to the sound.

'It's ready,' she said, standing by the laid table. They hadn't sat together to eat like this before, just as she had never eaten on her lap until she'd stayed in the cottage. He put his harmonica on the side table and got up. The rocking chair still rocked until it finally stopped. When he pulled out his chair, it scraped across the floor like chalk on a blackboard. She did the same, although she lifted hers. In silence she mounded the pie onto his plate.

'It looks good,' he said.

'I've never made a pie before.' She smiled curiously as she handed him a plateful.

'Tastes good,' he said, looking up and shovelling a sizeable amount onto his fork, his face low to his plate as he scooped up another mouthful.

'I start tomorrow on the farm,' Beth broke in as she pushed the mince around her plate and watched him as he barely caught his breath eating. She knew she'd already told him

Jack's Story

this but what else was she to say. He looked up from his food momentarily.

'That's good, I'll wake you.' Jack finished his meal and cleared his plate and wandered aimlessly back to his chair. He picked up his harmonica and played the melancholy melodies. The rock of the chair felt as slow and lumbering as the music, a little like the non-existent conversation they'd just had over a dinner table.

'Jack?'

He looked up from his playing.

'Is it me? Have I done something?' She stood holding the empty pie dish and plate.

'No,' he said as he played with the harmonica in his hands, rotating it between his fingers.

She went through to the kitchen and began to fill the sink with warm soapy water, then went back to the table to retrieve the glasses. Jack said nothing to her; she may as well have been invisible. The soapy suds were warm around her hands, and she scrubbed the pie dish until she could see the shine of the enamel. She let the water drain away and stood at the sink. The sky was now dotted with shiny white stars and the moon just a crescent shape, intermittently hidden as the night clouds passed by it as if on a journey to another land. The gurgling of the last remnants of water broke her thoughts.

Standing at the top of the steps, she leant her shoulder against the wall. 'Then what? You've barely said a word to me since you came home. Was it the table? Should I not have laid the table? I won't do it again.' A coal fell from the fire into the grate at the front. Jack watched it.

'No, it wasn't the table. And I'd like you to do it again. It felt good.'

'Then what is it? D'you want me to leave? Is that it?'

There was a silence in the room, the words fell, and she waited for him to catch them and hold them and tell her no. 'Jack? Please, is it me?' She swallowed, waiting for him to answer. And then he did.

'No. It's not you.'

She shook her head whilst playing with the cuffs of her sleeves.

'Then what?' Her voice almost a whisper.

He sank his head into his hands and pushed back his hair. His eyes stared out to an endless nowhere. He exhaled as if releasing some inner kind of pain and his eyes filled with a wash of tears. He rubbed his harmonica on the cloth of his trousers, his eyes narrowing as he looked into hers. 'The knacker man came today.'

'I don't understand,' she said.

'A bullet straight between his eyes. Bang!' Jack's eyes turned away; they still seemed fixed on nothing, his brow furrowed a little and his gaze dropped back to the coals on the fire. His eyes as dark and deep as the blackness of the coal. His cheeks sucked in as if to stop the feeling of sadness pouring down his face. His fist clenched the harmonica. The pointless rocking of his chair as he stared at the red heat of the fire. A sound snorted from his nose before he took up his harmonica again. He blew through the small holes of the mouthpiece, his lips not touching it, just blowing through it as if cleaning out any dust or debris. Like blowing down the barrel of a gun. The sound of a broken noise came through, no melody, just a strange whistling noise. 'The knacker man.' His words caught under his breath. The slow shake of his head, the slow rock of the chair. The slow quietness of his voice. 'Bang!' His hand formed the shape of a gun as two fingers cocked in the air.

Jack's Story

The sound of a gun splitting the silence, echoing through the trees. The birds suddenly flying from what was a peaceful space, their singing ceasing. 'You know what's coming, you know that fear of a sound. That fear of silence before death. It's an animal, yet every time it takes me back there, back to that space where gunshots were all around. The pummelling noise in the skies. The sound of silence, the eeriness it brings. It's deafening. Yet the sounds that then came deafened your ears, where you watched men fall, where you tried to save but couldn't. For what? I hate it. I hate it when the knacker man comes.'

She said nothing as she listened to Jack. She said nothing as she watched him recount his past. She listened as she heard his words fall from his lips, catching every one of them and holding them. She pushed her shoulder away from the wall and moved towards him. Crouching at his feet. she took his hands in hers and held them, rubbing her thumbs along them as he had done to her when he found her. 'Maybe it will be a while before he comes again. That will be better for you.' She understood then in that moment – the knacker man was the man trained to kill and she understood in that moment that Jack, too, was trained to kill. She realised the screams in the night were those of a man haunted by nightmares. She watched him as the chair rocked, her hands rested lightly on his knees and the dulcet tones of the harmonica played. She watched a man who felt.

That night she lay in bed and she heard the cries from that man. She listened to him scream out in anguish until the sounds stopped and all that she could hear was the screeching from the animals on the moor, maybe a beast of the moor, no longer a man's shrieks. His mind now rested.

Chapter Eight

St Lawrence's Church Hall, Cowick, Exeter, late October, 1946

'Ladies, ladies, please could we have a little decorum in the hall. I understand many have a lot to say on the matters this evening, but please, a little polite hush would be greatly appreciated.' Reverend Walter Holbrooke stood at the edge of the church hall as he addressed what seemed to be a congregation of quick-witted minds, assertive tongues and forthright opinions – a hall of women only. He edged his way through the collection of tables filled by church-going ladies who were all a-chatter and a-natter with the news that was filtering around the surrounding villages of Exeter. If a community grapevine could flourish in a bumper few weeks, this certainly would have filled cellars with your finest, juiciest gossip. Mrs Hubbard spoke behind her hand to Mrs Cooke, a wry smile crossing her face as the reverend passed them by, carrying in a tight embrace a small black Bible with a soft leather cover and pale cream leaves inside. A red cord hung along the edge of the spine, ensuring the book would open in the exact place that was required.

Daisy, who worked as a chambermaid during the week at Parkforton Castle, poured tea from behind the trestle table which sat squarely at the front of the hall. It was covered in a chequered tablecloth and hosted a plate of Battenberg cakes kindly baked by one of the ladies from the Women's Institute, along with a Victoria sponge, some slices of lemon drizzle, a Jamaican ginger cake baked by Emma Stephens of Appledaw Farm and eight iced buns kindly donated by Deller's Café.

Jack's Story

Daisy apportioned an assortment of cakes on ten serving plates before dispensing them onto each table of women along with a handful of paper napkins and tea plates. After that she carried a tray and dispensed cups of tea to the thirsty throng.

This evening's church meeting would mainly be about how the WI could manage to grow its members after the fraught relations it had with the Women's Voluntary Service. It was common knowledge within the WI that the WVS had been poaching their members throughout the war years, and numbers had certainly dwindled. Without the likes of Mrs Hubbard and Mrs Cooke, the WI certainly would have become obsolete in the community, and the underhand swiping of its members had ruffled a few feathers.

The two ladies were instrumental in organising the return of the wartime evacuees back to their original cities and towns. Mrs Hubbard had taken on the lead role as billeting officer at the beginning of the war, based in the church hall. She had assigned children from the government's evacuation programme, named Operation Pied Piper, which relocated young people from London. Their country hosts were specific about what qualities they would accept in an evacuee, and those were: polite, sanitised, no worms, no headlice and preferably white. The phrase that rang in the ears of the children was: *'I'll take that one.'* Throughout the war years, the WI had made it their business to expand the workforce. The men had gone to war and now it would fall upon the women's shoulders to tend to the land. Reservists were called in, plus urban volunteers, schoolchildren, evacuees and displaced persons of varying nationalities.

And now, two years post-war these children were clean city wretches without headlice, worms and persistent bedwetting habits. They were sanitised, wholesome and rounded on the edges, filled with country vegetables, even the non-white ones. There had been many fraught moments of families being told by those with more open minds – Emma Stephens, for one, who was a city girl at heart and had found love in the countryside and gone on to marry her farmer – when the meetings had become driven by colour and not by nurture. When some would point-blank refuse to take anyone who didn't meet a tick-list of perfection in their eyes. Emma Stephens would stand her ground and point out that this was what the world was warring against. A war where a man wanted a blue-eyed, blond world. The 'non-white ones', as they had been branded, had the same colour liquid running through their veins, and there was a need to learn how to braid the hair of small girls who could skip and dance too, just like the white girls, or the need to learn how to cut the fuzziness of the boys' hair. To understand that the Christian faith wasn't the only one, and if a child required a praying mat and a room where they could pray facing east, this would be respected. The countryside folk needed to learn these things and their prejudice or judgement would not be tolerated.

To those outside the niche set of the WI members and folks without tunnel vision, the evacuees were quite simply city children, who later in life would lead lives that were rich in culture and kudos. Their lives in the cities and greater towns would give them experiences, advantages and a melting pot of culture that a rural child could only ever dream of. Lives that would in part revolutionise them from being quite simply city urchins with headlice, worms and bedwetting habits. Emma knew that and she would explain it over and over again. The country folk were different to the city folk: they fed from the land, rattled about in their small communities and lived simple yet warm lives. Their grapevines of gossip, should they bear grapes, would keep a country in wine for weeks, months, years in fact. The country folk would look upon the city people as dirty and verminous, their women painted and powdered.

In the cities where these children came from – London, mostly – people lived on streets where houses were joined from beginning to end, even the grand ones. Like a string of brickwork. Like a chain of sticky coloured paper, all looped together, that would adorn trestle tables similar to the one at the front of the hall, to mark the end of a bloody war. A string of bricks that, gelled together, resembled the hands that joined delicately in a chain of fragile paper dolls, cut from a concertina of paper, which, when opened, would bounce joyously together, person after person after person – but when the hold was too tight would tear, fracture and that bond would be broken, like tissue paper ripped. The holding of paper hands, joined, a symbol of unity.

These urchins came from a city that was a good place to lose oneself. Mayfair – where girls wandered the streets in their finery every afternoon and evening, Shepherd's Market to be precise, where there was no shepherd, sheep, lambing, shearing or a market for the farmers to sell their produce. Instead its labyrinth of passageways led to a square where these girls wandered. They charged between ten shillings and one pound for the encounter. Pubs, nightclubs and dance halls were all very popular throughout the war years, and afterwards were open weekly – a stark contrast to the annual farmers' dance in a barn. The city folk would look upon the country folk as posh country people, backward and snobbish. Evacuation was an experience to be recalled with pleasure or erased from the memory in future years. A gentle nudge from Edith, would bring Emma back into the meeting and her unbroken gaze as the light caught on the stained-glass window of the church and a small sigh from Emma to suggest that community life really would never change.

Next on the agenda was how the community would raise funds for the church's roof, which had seen better days, along with the growing need for more volunteers to tend to the allotments. There was also growing demand for the 'make and mend classes' run by Emma Stephens of Appledaw Farm. And last but by no means least was how the WI would organise the summer farmers' dance with the use of Appledaw Farm's barn for the event. The evening's meeting would close with a little light relief of bridge, organised by Mrs Hubbard. The meeting had brought quite a turnout from the church, the village and surrounding villages' WIs, and Mrs Hubbard and Mrs Cooke had also rallied the keen bridge players.

'Ladies... (I believe we have no gentlemen here),' Reverend Holbrooke began with a chortle.

'Oh, he is a one, isn't he?' Mrs Hubbard muttered behind her handkerchief with a lace edging.

'Before we start, ladies, I would like to express my thanks to the Women's Institute and all those present on this rather blustery evening. I would also like to acknowledge all that Mrs Hubbard has done as billeting officer for the evacuees that came to us. And as we go forward in returning them to their now safe homes and the warmth again of their mothers' and fathers' arms.' He cleared his throat and continued. 'I'd like, as always, to begin with a prayer.' The women in the church hall bowed their heads, Reverend Holbrooke scanned the tops of heads in the room. Taking out his Bible, he opened it to Proverbs 26:20. 'Without a wood a fire goes out,' he began. 'Without a gossip a quarrel dies down. In the name of the Father, the Son and the Holy Ghost, Amen.' He closed his Bible and took a cotton handkerchief from his pocket and snuffled his nose into it before taking a cup of tea that Daisy gave him.

'Amen,' came a murmured noise from the dipped heads of the ladies in the hall.

Mrs Hubbard raised her head and drew in her cheeks, her lips pursed. She pulled the plate closer to her and looked around the room indignantly. Enid Postlethwaite, the community's midwife, who had now recovered from her bout of influenza, threw a look across the tables, allowing it to rest on Mrs Cooke and Mrs Hubbard's table and the company they kept. They may well be on the committee for the WI and she may well be the billeting officer for the evacuees, but they also needed to learn how tittle-tattle would not be tolerated within the ladies' circle. Although Enid Postlethwaite was a few years younger, she was bright enough to show her dismay to Reverend Holbrooke. And Reverend Holbrooke was very keen on Enid Postlethwaite. She smiled drily at them before breaking off a piece of Battenberg and popping the crumbly, pink cake into her mouth, then dabbing the corner of her mouth with her paper napkin.

'Well, I never,' muttered Mrs Hubbard under her breath. 'I've never gossiped about a soul in my life.' Her lips still pursed, she sucked in her cheeks as she inched each finger from her gloved hand, and then held the gloves and pulled her hand across the empty fingers tightly before shooting an acidic look back over to Enid Postlethwaite and her table. Enid raised her eyebrows on its receipt and turned to Emma Stephens, a close friend, who sat beside her.

'What a prayer! How very dare the Rev …Oh, Reverend Holbrooke.' A placed smile fell onto Mrs Hubbard's face. 'How lovely you could make bridge and attend this meeting this evening,' she continued, the smile still fixed in place. 'And why, I did like your choice of prayer to start. I was just saying the very same to Mary too. Wasn't I, Mary dear?'

'Absolutely, a fine choice of words, Reverend.'

'Yes, ladies, I believe Proverbs 26 is most befitting, especially at times like this when we have the Earl and Countess of Devon worrying about the whereabouts of their daughter, Lady Constance. I hope you will join me in prayer on Sunday that she returns home fit and well.'

'Why, yes of course, Reverend. We've all been so worried for Lady Constance's safety and obviously the awful uncertainty for the family. Such a worry indeed, I can't begin to imagine,' Mrs Hubbard uttered, taking her cup and saucer and sipping from it. 'Do we know any more of her whereabouts?'

'My dear Mrs Hubbard,' Reverend Holbrooke continued, holding his Bible in two hands close to his black, well-ironed shirt. 'We know that the family are beside themselves with worry and that their anguish at this time should be in our prayers and thoughts.' He sidled away from the ladies and made his way toward the table where Emma Stephens sat discussing the 'make and mend' class with Enid. 'Enid, it's wonderful to see you out and about again.' The Reverend's hand touched her arm with a warm welcome.

'Why thank you, Reverend Holbrooke, it's lovely to be amongst friends again and to be back delivering such little wonders into the world. Emma's been doing such a wonderful job with the 'make and mend' classes with the villagers.'

'That's wonderful, Emma.' Reverend Holbrooke turned to Emma, his hand resting on the back of a chair. 'How are the children? Will they be returning to London soon?'

'They are all well, Reverend. My sister's house in Ealing was bombed and until it's rebuilt to a liveable state, I see the children being with me and Henry for a little while longer. To be honest, it's rather lovely having them and I'm not sure I want them to leave. Although Charlotte misses them dearly and I know Harry needs his mother again. Eleanor has been a great help on the farm and since we've lost the workforce with the war now ended, she's been an absolute Godsend – I can't lie. And the boys simply adore Jack. If Harry could, he'd follow him around all day, like Jack's own shadow. I'm not even sure how we will prise him away when the time comes. Henry has just taken on an extra hand, too, a friend of Jack's.'

'That's wonderful news, Emma, the farm must be thriving for you and Henry to be taking on more hands.'

'It certainly is, Reverend and with the whole 'dig for victory' we just haven't stopped. But there comes a point when we have to look for help and it was almost like a divine piece of luck when Jack asked if there was any extra work going for a friend who needed a job,' Emma continued.

'Our Lord works in mysterious ways and I'm sure your new farmhand will bring much prosperity to your farm. He has landed upon a good farm. You are blessed, Emma.'

Emma twizzled in her chair as she took up the notes she'd made for the 'make and mend' classes and also for the farmers' barn dance. '*She,*' she muttered.

But Reverend Holbrooke had already left the table, and was making his way back to the trestle table where Daisy was topping up the tea.

'Ladies, I see you all have a generous amount of cake on your tables, thank you Daisy. And you are all now with a much-needed cup of tea, so without further ado I would like to commence this evening's meeting. Beginning with, perhaps, the farmers' annual dance. Emma and Henry Stephens have kindly given their barn for the joyous event. I'm sure you would all join with me in thanking them for this wonderful gesture. The dance brings much joy to the surrounding villages and also the donations and ticket sales certainly help with the church and the community. I have it marked down as the 15th of July for the date. Could we perhaps have a show of hands for this date to be added to the community's summer events diary.' A sea of arms waggled in the air.

'That's marvellous,' Reverend Holbrooke continued, jotting down in the church's diary the upcoming event. As the cake plates emptied on each table and the last drops of tea were poured from the pot, each item was ticked off the agenda and the evening drew to a close. The church hall slowly emptied, and Emma and Enid carried the trays of dirty crockery into the kitchen and washed up. Outside the kitchen door Mrs Hubbard and Mrs Cooke pushed in their chairs in readiness to leave the hall.

'A girl, you say, Emma,' Enid said, taking a cup and drying it with the damp tea towel.

'Yes, a friend of Jack's. She's staying with him whilst she finds her own lodgings.'

'Will she be coming to the "make and mend" classes?'

'I don't know, I haven't asked her. I don't really know very much about her other than that she works hard, and she arrives and leaves each day with Jack.'

'Does she have family nearby?' Enid pushed curiously.

'To be honest, I don't know. Henry says she's a pretty maid.' Emma laughed. 'Why d'you ask, Enid?'

'Well, it seems a little coincidental, don't you think?'

From outside the kitchen door the heels of Mrs Hubbard and Mrs Cooke could be heard clipping across the parquet floor as they approached the hall's main door.

'In what way?' Emma stopped, a soapy cup in her hand.

'Lady Con –'

'We'll be off now,' came the high-pitched voice of Prudence Hubbard. 'The hall's perfectly tidy and all the chairs back where they belong. I've made a minute of the evening's meeting and will distribute it, and also pin a copy on the church's noticeboard.'

'That's very kind of you. Thank you, Prue.' Emma turned from the sink.

'No trouble at all, always one to help in the community. I'll see you at the "make and mend" class on Thursday, if I may. I'll bring your minutes then.'

'That would be lovely. I'll look forward to seeing you.'

The two ladies left the hall and the door swished shut behind them.

'D'you think they heard our conversation?' Enid said as she wrung out the sodden tea towel, laid it on the boiler and took a dry one from the linen drawer.

'D'you mean about the new farmhand – who she is?'

'Yes, Emma. Had it not crossed your mind?'

'I daresay it hadn't. To be honest I think it's just as it is.'

'And that is?'

'Jack's friend. Her name's Beth Brooklyn for a start and I just don't think it could even be possible. She's staying with Jack at the cottage, and he doesn't know the Earl or Countess of Devon. I mean, we don't mix in those circles.' She laughed. 'We have a farm, and for Lady Constance to be working on it would be absurd. I think it's simply coincidental, as I've said. She doesn't even dress like a lady.'

Enid shrugged her shoulders. 'And how does a lady dress?' She mused over Emma's defensive response as she stacked the cups and saucers in the cupboard and dried the teapots.

'Well – not like Beth. Really, Enid, remember what Reverend Holbrooke said about gossiping. I think we're finished here in the kitchen, finally.' Emma swished away the dirty water from the sink and wiped down the sides. 'Can I drop you home? It's dark out there now and it's getting rather late.' Locking up the church hall, the two women left.

Emma pulled up outside Enid's house on Victoria Street in Exeter. As Enid opened the door of the Wolseley, she turned to Emma. 'The rumour was she ran off with a carpenter.'

Emma sighed and gave out a laugh of disbelief that Enid would even think like Prudence Hubbard and Mary Cooke. 'Jack's not a carpenter. He's our farmhand, the children love him, and we love him. And I will not encourage this kind of talk. He's a veteran paratrooper, Enid, and not to be part of the gossip for the village. He fought for our country! Now please, I want to hear no more of this. I thought more of you than to join in with the tittle-tattle of the villagers.'

'You're right, I'm sorry, Emma. I spoke out of turn. But you've spoken to her?'

'Yes, briefly.'

'And what does she sound like?' Enid pushed.

'What d'you mean – what is this, Enid? She sounds like a girl, like me.'

'Like you?' Enid raised her eyebrows and looked squarely at Emma. 'Emma, you are not from around here, you've married a farmer and that went with a whole heap of fraught battles between your parents. Have you forgotten that bit of your life? Really, this isn't just coincidence, surely you don't believe that.'

'It's getting late, Enid.' Emma looked dead ahead, refusing to allow herself eye contact with her dearest friend.

'I'll see you at the class. Good night.' Enid pressed her hand on Emma's forearm.

The headlights of the Wolseley lit the roads as Emma took the short drive home. As she crossed the level crossing, she bumped about in the soft squidgy seat of the car, her hands gripping the steering wheel tightly as she trundled along

Jack's Story

the lane. The indicator clicked loudly as she turned into the Appledaw Farm track. She stopped the car just after the track's entrance at Orchard Cottage, where the post for fresh eggs swayed in the darkness. She pushed the latch down on the gate and walked up the path toward the front door. She rapped on it, listening to the wind whistling through the canes and the hoot of an owl overhead. She pulled her headscarf closer over her head, tucking in the wisps of hair that escaped and pulled her long woollen coat in more closely around her body. She shivered in the cold night. Jack opened the door and light from the room inside lit the step where she stood.

From the kitchen, Beth could hear voices. They were muffled as she cleared away the plates and pans. She could make out the voice of Emma . As she let the dirty dish water gurgle down the drain, she heard the front door close and a car pull away. From the kitchen window she could see the red rear lights of a car driving up towards the farm. It was Emma's car, as she'd thought.

Emma sat in her own kitchen whilst she waited for the milk to boil on the Aga's top plate. The evening had been long and drawn out, and Reverend Holbrooke's words played heavily on her mind. She took a cup from the cupboard and spooned in some cocoa powder and poured in the frothy hot milk. The bubbles of caught milk stuck to the bottom of the pan, not wanting to leave. She stirred the cup and turned out the kitchen light. The low glow of the fire in the snug room threw a warm amber light across it. Patch lay close by on the thick Persian-style rug in front of the hearth, his head resting on his paws, his ears flopping over his eyes almost. He lifted his nose as Emma poked her head into the room. 'Night, Patch.'

The face of the grandfather clock watched her as she climbed the stairs.

She stopped at each room along the landing. Eleanor lay fast asleep in her bed, her pillow doubled over and cheeks cushioned into it. Bertie had fallen asleep reading his comic. Emma turned out the light and put his comic on the bedside table next to him. Harry lay straggled in his bed; placing her cocoa on the chest of drawers, she went to his bedside. One leg was hanging out over the side, and his blue and white striped pyjamas were rucked up and ruffled, showing his soft white skin. She tucked his leg back into the bed and removed the wooden train that was wedged between his bear, his cheek and the pillow. She pulled the covers up and kissed his forehead, brushing his blond hair to one side as she did. He looked like his mother, she thought, her sister, her only sister. A sister she missed dearly. She leant over him again and kissed him sweetly.

She took up her cocoa and left him with his dreams. In her room she undressed and climbed beneath the covers of her own bed. Henry was already asleep. She sat with the simple light from her bedside lamp and thought of the evening and Lady Constance and then thought of her own sister. Henry let out a grunt next to her and pulled the eiderdown further over the mound of his body.

'Are you asleep?' Her voice soft and low.

He grunted again and rolled towards her, draping his arm across her stomach as she drank her hot cocoa.

'The girl on the farm, Henry. What d'you know of her?'

'Pretty maid she be.'

She pulled the eiderdown higher up over her. 'Where does she come from?'

'Okehampton, pretty maid she be.' A snore came from him. *Pretty maid.* The low light of her bedside lamp threw a softness across the covers of the bed. The shadows of the trees fell along her walls from the moonlight. Was Beth who she said she was? Emma knew what it was like to escape a middle-class upbringing. Enid was right, her parents had been dead against Henry and farm life: she was a city girl, her father was an accountant, her mother the buyer of elegant buttons in the haberdashery department of Harvey Nichols in Knightsbridge. They'd been less than pleased at her falling in love with a farmer's son. She'd also had no children, children she'd always wanted, and she and Henry had somehow managed to build their lives without the pitter-patter of tiny feet. Although war wasn't what she would want, it gave her three children to care for and when they left, her heart would break. Her mind battled over what she knew in her heart to be true. A missing daughter, the despair and pain her parents would be going through, but also the loyalty to Beth, knowing she must have run for a reason, the same reason she had left her only London living once. To find her own happiness. She drank the last drop of her cocoa and placed it on the table before reaching over to the lamp and turning it off. She closed her eyes to slumber deep.

Chapter Nine

Appledaw Farm, Cowick, Exeter, November, 1946

Jack wandered aimlessly about the yard, carrying buckets filled to the brim with the final feed for the calves in the cowshed. They had grown fast and were now ready to be led out with the cows to graze in the farm's pastures, where the grass was sweeter and more abundant. There were only eight calves; the ninth, which would suck longer on Jack's fingers from the pail of its mother's milk and look up at him with the biggest, brownest eyes, was no longer with the girls. He was no longer with any farm. He was simply no longer. Many days had passed since that time and this farm season was sliding seamlessly into the next, as if the golden hues of autumn would blend into the bare limbs of the trees and that would become the ever-changing, ever-moving farming calendar. Not a calendar of days and numbers but a calendar of seasons, rain, darkness, warmth, yellow sun. The winter months would soon be passing through like the winds that travelled across the bleak lands of the moors and rustled through the heathers and ferns, until the head of white snowdrop would push its pretty petals up and look about as if calling to the blossoms that now it was safe and spring could begin her journey and chase the winds away, and instead invite the breeze to rustle through the reeds of the pond and fronds of the willows that hung about.

The cows had been milked that morning and the churns of fresh creamy milk sat along the edge of the shed, waiting for Jack to carry them out to the cold store where they would rest until the evening's milking was done, when they would be taken down to the milk stand next to the tied cottages for collection by the Ambrosia Dairy cart. After morning tea, he would lead the cows back to the meadow where they chomped on the sweetest and greenest of grass along with the calves. The fields were now almost harvested of their potatoes, which were left to dry in the barn below the hayloft like a mountain of countryside goodness. The earthy smell of rich soil permeated the air. Clumps of thick mud fell on the ground and were packed down underfoot. When the rain came, the mud sludged across the yard and made a squelching noise, clinging to the soles of the farm boots, packed into the grooves and caking the upper toes.

Jack walked past the hayloft, wheeling an empty barrow. He caught a glimpse of Beth struggling as she tried to shift the sack of potatoes she'd filled. He stopped, unnoticed by her. He watched her as she inched the hessian sack across the ground until she almost fell with it, next to a few full sacks, with a sigh. He smiled. And then as she rubbed her muddy hands down the white cotton of her shirt. He watched her as she pushed her hair away from her face and knotted and wrapped it into a makeshift bun at the nape of her neck tucking away the wisps of her hair that clung to her wet lips. The smear of dirt across her cheeks, unbeknown to her. He couldn't help but gaze at the girl who had knelt by his side and cupped his hands in hers as she listened to him recount the story of the knacker man. The same girl he had knelt by, whose hands he had cupped, in the loft of the hay barn where she now worked. Was this his kindred spirit? Was this his compensation for all the memories of loss and death and fear, the unnecessary losses?

The potato wagon had come a few days ago and taken away a truckload of full sacks. And today it would return to collect the sacks that the girl had filled, the girl Jack had never expected to ever see working on the farm. The girl was different to the girl she had been weeks before. There was something about her that hung in his mind all morning, from when they'd left the cottage as the sun began to rise in the sky, throwing a hue of crimson and orange across the skies. From that time in the morning when the skies warned the shepherds, she had stopped as she passed the horses and beckoned to Jack to slow down, and the chestnut stallion had made his way over to her and tossed his nose at her and snorted. From that time in the morning when he watched her as she patted him.

'Hello boy,' she had whispered. The horse, as before, walked alongside the wall as if walking side by side with her. It was as if she had a knowledge or maybe a natural instinct, unlearned like Jack. But was she unlearned, was hers a natural instinct? Jack had said nothing as they walked along the track to the farm. He had stopped at the five-bar gate to lead the cows to the milk shed and Beth had continued to the hayloft, where she would fill the sacks and stack the potatoes ready for the potato wagon that would come again that day.

It was late morning on the farm and the light in the hayloft slanted through the door, particles of dust dancing in it. She was dressed simply in Jack's slacks and his cotton shirt again, and on her feet, she wore her buckled shoes. Jack had fixed the broken buckle.

'Mornin to ye, me lover,' came Henry's welcoming voice as he appeared at the entrance of the barn. 'That we'll be stoppin' for tea. Ye want one, me lover.'

'That would be lovely.' She wiped her forearm across her brow before lugging another filled sack to the side of the barn. She liked the way Henry always called her 'me lover' and never Beth.

Jack's Story

'Proper job ye be dwain with they teddies.'

Her eyes flicked across the monumental mountain that sat in front of her. She'd only filled five sacks that morning and discarded any rotten ones into a barrow for the pigswill. Jack would come and wheel the barrow away for her every now and again. To the side of the barn there was sack upon sack already filled from the day before. They were tied with string, ready to be taken to market or the potato buyer.

Jack poked his head around the barn door. 'Tea's up.'

She turned to him and smiled. 'I'm coming just now.'

She left the sack half-filled and made her way out of the barn towards the farmhouse. Jack was already standing at the kitchen door when he watched her cross the yard. Her aura seeped into the wintry air; she was quietly beautiful, and now that she'd been in his cottage for some time, it was beginning to feel like she was meant to be there. The sun had shifted in the sky and although it was cold, the sky was the bluest of blues, a little like the colour of the mountainous springs that fell into the clearest of pools in Christchurch. Jack would throw himself into the deeper pools from the rugged edges where the waterfalls fell, where he'd swim in a lagoon before the war had torn through the world and left countries bereft of populations and families. Jack had left his native country, New Zealand, to save a world he believed in, like his father had done in the First World War.

His eyes caught on her; trapped, he was unable to move away. The rays of the sun beamed though the strands of Beth's hair that fell loosely about her face, the rest of it still caught up in a knot at the nape of her neck. The sun's ray passed through the cotton shirt like an iridescent light, showing the silhouette of her body beneath. His gaze never left her until the sound of the children's voices came from the farmhouse kitchen as they bustled out of its door. A smile cracked across his face as they tumbled into each other like a deck of cards that had been neatly formed into a towering pyramid and then collapsed in a kamikaze way. Eleanor was the first to utter anything.

'Beth!'

Beth stopped in her tracks and smiled. She loved it when they bounded out of the house to see her. They never spoke a word of the time they had found her – it was as if the secret was theirs to be kept. It was as if that time had never happened, as if all of it was just a figment of their imagination.

From the kitchen window Aunt Emma watched as Beth sat with Eleanor on an old wooden barrel that was turned up on its curved edges. Beth carefully looped her fingers in and took the string that wrapped around Eleanor's fingers and held them in the very same way in between her fingers. Eleanor giggled with laughter as she tried to take the cradle of string back, placing her fingers between Beth's. The smile lit up Beth's face like the moon lights the sky and the stars twinkle about it. That picture of awe that makes you breathe in with sublime happiness. Beth, a girl who made Eleanor laugh from the deepest part of her belly, who helped her grow into a beautiful young girl, who would sometimes sit and read to her from her book – *A Tree Grows in Brooklyn*.

Emma's eyes flicked across the yard to Jack and then back to Beth. In the few weeks she'd been on the farm, there had been a change. Jack stood with his leg bent up and the sole of his boot cocked up against the timber side of the barn's wall. His tea rested on a nearby water barrel, and there he played his harmonica. Every once in a while, his playing stopped as the infectiousness of Beth's laughter fluttered through the air like the wings of butterflies, until those butterflies of laughter rested somewhere near him on the water barrel and their wings flickered gently whilst he played his harmonica. Emma

Jack's Story

watched him as his eyes fell on Beth and his lips formed into a smile and his eyes stayed on her. He too had lost so much in his life, his father, his mother, his comrades at war and now she could see him falling for a beautiful girl who the children adored as much. Esther had been a kind and loving friend and she owed her a loyalty too.

Harry ran over to Jack and he laughed and ruffled his hair and took him under his arms, his legs dangling behind – his fits of giggles as Jack threatened to turn him upside down into the water barrel. His pleading to be freed but wanting more. Emma's lips formed a smile as Bertie tugged at Jack's shirt to free his little brother, whose giggles echoed around the farmyard. She watched her sister's children as they lived, loved and played on her farm. She had watched them and over them now for almost six years.

Emma had no children of her own. She had always wanted children, but she had never carried well and each time when she finally thought it was her time, she would lose her baby before she had reached even eight weeks. Until one day, her calendar was marked eight weeks and five days, and then the marking read nine weeks, ten weeks, eleven weeks, twelve weeks – and the swell of her tummy grew and she would hold it in the yard as she'd talk to Esther, months into her pregnancy.

Esther was Jack's mother and would work as the milkmaid on the farm when the time came. She was also a seamstress in the village; she had started the 'make and mend' classes that Emma was part of. She had watched whilst Emma's bump had grown bigger and bigger and inside grew a baby whose feet kicked and squirmed. A much-longed-for baby. Esther became a friend to Emma and with Jack, her only son, away at war, Appledaw Farm was where she found her life after leaving New Zealand and returning home to Devon. The tied cottages were up for lease and a milkmaid was needed as Emma's pregnancy progressed, so Jack's mother was perfect. She would talk of her fear for him and her pride in him and the letters she would receive, and as she spoke of his return Emma would hold her bump, keeping her wanted baby cocooned and warm inside her. Safe, always safe.

Then one day, when the leaves on the trees turned from a luscious green to golden browns and reds, Esther didn't come to the 'make and mend' class. Neither did she buy her tea from Deller's Café that week or arrive at the farm to help milk the cows, as she had arranged with Emma. Emma had mentioned how her bump seemed to get in the way as she leant forward now on the milking stool, and Henry had voiced his concerns too. Esther had offered her help: she was close, she lived in the cottage and Henry and Emma knew her well. But now for a couple of days she hadn't been seen.

Emma had walked down to the cottage to check on Esther that day. A faint wisp of smoke funnelled up through the chimney, Emma felt relieved to see it. *At least the fire's going – that's a good sign.* The churning in her stomach subsided as she walked up the short pathway to the front door. She pushed the door open and called out her name.

'Esther, it's only me, Emma.' There was no reply. Emma walked into the main room and there the fire just smouldered in warm ash. A pan of stale milk sat on the range top, the candle on the mantelpiece flickering as it grasped at the last remnants of wax to melt and burn. The draft from the open door blew it out. Emma's skin prickled up, she walked forward – and there she was. She found Esther in her sewing chair. She seemed to be asleep; a peaceful kind of sleep, a sleep where your eyes rest closed, forever. On her lap a small patchwork blanket rested in her hands, the crochet needle and thread still almost held between her fingers and the letters *H.S.* beautifully embroidered in the corner. Emma had shared with Esther that if the baby was a girl, she would be Henrietta, and if a boy, Henry.

'Esther,' she remembered saying softly, almost a sound beneath her breath. 'Esther.' The fire still with a layer of warm ash and simple mist of smoke from it. Esther's eyes remained closed and her head tilting to one side. Emma knelt at her feet and cradled her hands in hers. They were soft yet cold. Had she come earlier, might she have prevented this? The smoke from the chimney had funnelled out; there was no reason to think anything was wrong. Yet everything was wrong. She had lost a dear friend and Jack had lost his mother.

The doctor said it was her heart. Maybe her heart was breaking, and nobody had noticed? How would she ever be able to break the news to Jack, caught up in a bloody war? How could she ever tell Esther's only son, who she'd burned with pride for and yet feared for, that his mother had lost her own life?

The doctor made a call to the coroner and Esther's body was taken away from Orchard Cottage. It was empty now, just the furniture remaining. A velvet Queen Anne-style chair rested by the window in the gable end of the cottage, next to it a sewing machine with a wooden lid with the words *SINGER* inscribed across it in black italic letters. A sewing box sat open on a circular table with elegantly carved legs and small drawers around it. Next to the sewing box, a picture of a soldier in uniform, and next to that a picture of Esther with her soldier's arm around her waist. As her body was taken away, Dr Hobson handed the small patchwork blanket to Emma. Emma held it close to her and breathed in the essence of Esther, a wonderful friend, a mother, and now she would rest in peace with the man who caught her heart and gave her Jack.

The following afternoon Emma's waters broke, and Enid Postlethwaite, the village's midwife, was called by the operator to visit Appledaw Farm as a matter of urgency. That evening, as the crimson and golden leaves fell from the trees, and the sun sank in the west, and dusk fell upon the rise and fall of the lands enveloping the farmhouse, Henry paced the floor of the kitchen, his bear-sized hands with cracked knuckles pushing through his hair. His pacing stopped when he rested his hands on the sink. And as he watched the leaves flutter from the trees, the silence around was broken by the periodic screams of his wife as she pushed and breathed, pushed and breathed. He stood at that kitchen sink and listened to the cries of his wife as she laboured. He listened to the strain of her sounds as she pushed her baby into the world. He listened as he heard a hush and then a scream, a scream that pierced the air. A howl that sent prickles up his spine. Dr Hobson stood at the kitchen door and in that moment Henry knew.

He stood at the bedroom door, where he watched Enid swaddle baby, baby who lay still, who lay in the crook of Emma's arm, close to the warmth of his mother. Swaddled in a soft patchwork blanket with the palest blue crochet initials in the corner: *H.S.* Emma rocked the tiny bundle in her arms, her baby. The tears fell silently down her cheeks. Henry rested beside her and kissed the still forehead of his son. His son's eyes closed. The silence, the quiet in the room was grief. Emma's happy ending had turned into a painful nightmare. That day the walls of Emma's home came down around her and the hours passed in a blur.

Emma was jolted out of her thoughts as Henry came in the kitchen door and put down his teacup on the side. Beth returned to the hayloft to continue sacking up the potatoes and Jack went back to the calves with a barrow of fresh hay. Emma took the corner of her apron and dabbed her eyes, then brushed it down flat against her dress, her hand resting on her stomach for a brief moment. A stomach that would never carry a baby again.

Weeks had passed since the meeting in the church hall and Prudence Hubbard had begun the process as billeting officer to send the evacuees safely on their train journeys back to the cities and greater towns. The time had come when a call would be put through from the operator and Emma would hear the sweetest sound of her sister's voice on the telephone. The words that would break her heart into a million pieces: 'Hello darling sister, I have so missed my children and now the time is safe and good for them to board the Great Western Railway and travel back to Paddington, where I can hug them hard for every year they've been away.' Harry had been only two when Emma had agreed that the farm was safest place for the children to be. London was being bombed and Charlotte, Emma's sister, was required to stay in the city as she worked in the Cabinet Office as a secretary and her husband had been enlisted. Handing her children over had broken her heart that day, but it was for the best and they would be safe. And one day they would return, and that day was soon.

Chapter Ten

Arnhem, Holland, mid-September, 1944

The sky in Holland cast a charcoal-grey light around an area that seemed empty of all life. There was a heaviness in the air where the stench was of death, fear and the unknown. The road, which appeared more like an unserved route to nowhere, had trenches dug out along it, where there were mortar pits and the smell of death still clung in the air. Dead bodies lay in those trenches. A battlefield of heavy fighting and lost soldiers, brave soldiers.

The mist began to fall like a smokescreen about the two paratroopers. Visibility was fading, and the sound of the marching boots had diminished. Jack's compass showed they were heading west. Since falling through the skies and landing on the rough unknown terrain, their platoon had been ambushed three times by German enemy fire, in places they weren't expecting. The plans and maps of where they had expected to be met by the Germans didn't tally and their ammo was running low. The need to get to their rally point was vital: once there, as planned in a hangar somewhere in England, the cavalry would arrive, the weapons along with the manpower. Then they could take the bridges and drive forward with a *tour de force* – but now, with the light dropping away, it was too dangerous to continue. The terrain was unfamiliar to them and their vision was becoming ever more hampered by the lack of sunlight and the mist that fell upon them.

Jack's Story

As tiredness began to take over their bodies, and the cold seeped through their skin and into their bones, they realised their comrades were no longer visible. The sunlight had left the sky and the two paratroopers knew they urgently needed to hole up, to sit and wait until the darkness cleared. Every noise made their ears prick up; Ted would turn his head quickly with fear each time a rustle from the wooded areas came too close. His eyes darted from side to side, the sweat on his forehead running down his face. He brushed it away, still holding his rifle ready to fire and to protect him from the fear he was harbouring, the fear in his body running through his veins thicker than the liquid that would spill out if enemy fire should take him.

There was a clicking sound from beneath the hedges. They couldn't see. They stopped and slowly crouched down low until their bellies lay on the ground beneath. The clicking sound came again, and then the firing and the mortaring started again. They couldn't see the direction it came from or even if they were being fired at. Ted scrambled slowly on his belly, following Jack's feet. He wiped the wetness from his face and tried to clear his eyes of the tears that kept coming. The sound of his heart beating as he crawled through the dirt until the firing stopped. Through the trees the ghastly annihilated bodies and the groans of the wounded as they lay. *The stretcher man will come, the stretcher man will come.* And then there, ahead of them, a sight that seemed wondrous. As wondrous as a Christmas tree on the eve of Christmas morning with the joyous sound of laughter and merriment. A wondrous sight that lifted their souls and told them they had not been shot and the firing was on the other side of the track through the trees that shadowed the land. But many poor souls had lost their lives, their chance to ever see a wondrous sight again gone. Jack smeared his hands across his eyes.

A barn was what they could see ahead of them. It would give them shelter and warmth for a few hours, and safety until they would patrol on. As Ted watched Jack lift his body from the ground, he felt a warm fluid run down his leg. His boot began to fill, squelching wetly as he allowed his body to crouch low. His foot slid in the boot as the liquid ran down until it stopped at his toes. He had no pain – he had not been shot. Their bodies were fatigued, and the order had been to patrol until their rendezvous point, but tiredness and hunger were making them disoriented. Unaccounted-for ambushes had taken down too many of their men. Every march forward had weakened them more and their need to drive forward would end here, at least until day broke through again.

The sounds of the mortaring had ceased for now. The door of the barn swung on a hinge in the wind; it was off the road they had followed and in the dark, they could barely see their compasses. Together they stood, the cold rattling down their necks, their stomachs aching from hunger, their uniforms wet and soiled. But there seemed to be a warmth inside the barn.

Jack shone his small torch around the barn. A noise, louder than a scurrying creature, came from behind the bales of hay. The sound of a human body shifting. The two paratroopers took up their weapons and inched slowly forward, their hearts beating louder against their chests and rising up into their throats and staying there. Their breath white in the cold night air.

The shuffling sound came again. The two soldiers stopped. They had seen death today, they had heard death today, but they did not want to share their space with death that night. They could not sit with a German they were about to kill and watch the life drain away from the eyes of the enemy. They were soldiers, but their feelings were those of young men, too, and that was more present in their bodies. They inched their way forward, their guns ready.

Jack's Story

Jack shone his torch directly on the hay bale and the figure that sat cowering in the corner. It dazzled the crouching soldier. An arm went up to his face, a German uniform with SS on the sleeve. The safety catch on Jack's rifle clicked as he levelled it at point-blank range, his finger shaking on the trigger. The soldier was as young as him, maybe younger, and thinner. There was a fear in his eyes. A bullet would kill him, and his fear would end. Jack's finger rattled uncontrollably on the trigger. To fire at a tank, where it was metal and there was nobody to see, was different. To shoot and kill a person whose soul you could see in their eyes wasn't the same. It was somebody's son, somebody's brother, it was somebody's somebody. A human being.

Ted turned away, he held his own breath and closed his eyes and waited for the bang of the rifle from Jack.

'*Nee, alsjeblieft, ik ben niet de vijand,*' the voice came.

The soldier's uniform is the SS, shoot him, Jack kept saying in his head. He held his rifle at the soldier.

'*Nee, alsjeblieft, ik smeek je dat ik niet de vijand ben. Alsjeblieft, ik ben Nederlands.*' The rifle in Jack's hands shook, he took a step forward. '*Nee, alsjeblieft, ik ben ... ik ben ...* I am zee Resistance, come closer you will see.'

Jack allowed his weapon to drop momentarily. He shone the light at the soldier. It was not a young man. She tilted her head away, the beam from the torch dazzling her eyes. Her face was white, as white as snow and her hair dark, darker than the night and short, not a nice kind of short, but a short that had been hacked with a knife or blunt scissors. Uneven. Jagged. Ugly. An ugly frame around a sunken, drawn-in feminine face. It could almost have been a boy; the only sign that it was a girl was her voice, which was soft, as soft as the lullaby that a mother would sing to her baby, her face like a porcelain doll's. Her hair cropped short around it. Her lip was cut and bruised. Her cheek had the imprint of the butt of a rifle where she had taken a forceful blow, and now that imprint remained in black and purple on her china-white skin. Dark shadows hung under her eyes, which were a deep, dark black that stared at the two soldiers like hollow black holes.

'What is your name?' Jack asked. He knelt closer to her.

She swallowed. 'You are British?' She almost smiled with fear and happiness that she was safer now.

'Yes, we are British soldiers. Have you defected?'

She shook her head. *'Nee, ik ben Nederlands.'*

'Dutch? Your uniform, it's German,' Jack said, his eyes creasing at the sides.

'Ja. It is. But I am not.' She nodded her head uncontrollably, acknowledging his words. Her eyes held a sadness and blackness that could only come from loss, from fear, from the unknown torture ahead, from the torture that had been endured. Jack lifted the rifle again.

'But it is not a true uniform. You see.' She lifted her arm and showed a sign that revealed she was only disguised as a member of the *Schutzstaffel,* a code sign that would tell any other Resistance operative that she was friend not foe. 'I am part of the Resistance – please, you have to believe me.' Jack watched as her hands played with each other and then held her bent up knees against her pounding chest. Knees that crushed into her skeletal frame, which had barely any flesh on it, not even enough to cover her ribs. He crouched nearer to her and let his rifle drop from its firing position. He took his water from his canvas backpack. Her lips were dry and cracked, with brown dried blood stuck to them.

'Here.' He handed her his water flask. 'I am Jack. What is your name? We are here to help you.'

Jack's Story

'My name is Agathe Lecreux.' Her bottom lip trembled as she uttered the words. She took a sip from the bottle, the water dribbling down her chin. She hadn't drunk all day. She handed it back. 'I escaped from the *Wehrmacht* field brothels. My brother and Frederik are both dead. The *Schutzstaffel* found us sending messages to your men informing you of the whereabouts of the German's locations. My brother was beaten and shackled, suspended from the ceiling and burnt with a blowtorch. He was tortured to talk. I heard his cries, like an animal he cried; they whipped him until his body could take no more. I watched them lead him to the yard – unbroken. Bruised. Bloody. Defiant in his silence. His back to them as he walked. Bang! We were found when our messages were not being received by your soldiers. There was a problem with communications. I am here alone. I have been here for days. My radio seems to not reach the British soldiers. Please, you have to believe me.'

'I believe you.'

The door of the barn pushed open. Jack flashed his torch onto it and took up his rifle ready to fire, but it was a paratrooper who stood there. 'Fuck,' he said. 'Am I glad to see you boys.' He walked over to Jack and Ted. 'A German?'

'No, she is Dutch, with the Resistance,' replied Jack. 'We'll stay here for the night, until the sun comes up, and then we patrol forward to the bridge.

'Arnhem Bridge?' she said. 'And then what? The Germans are everywhere.'

'Our order is to seize the bridges to allow the armoured Corps to cross into Germany and occupy it. They are on their way.'

'The fucking Jerries are everywhere! I hope they bloody hurry up with more ammo! Where the fuck is the back-up?' the lone paratrooper said as he took his webbing sack from his back and slung it to the ground. His voice was heavy in sound, a northerner. 'They took us out. Mortars firing from every fucking direction. Shot my man, I had to leave him, there was nothing I could do. He was shot in the air as we landed. I felt like an animal, taking his ammo, weapon, his food, his water, and leaving him.'

'The stretcher bearer will get him,' Jack said. 'There was nothing you could have done.'

'That's what makes it so bloody bad, there was nothing I could do. There are bodies everywhere out there. The trenches are like an open grave.' He slumped down next to his sack and took out a can of corned beef. He turned it in his hands. Nobody said anything, but in their minds and thoughts were the groans of the wounded and the bloody bodies of the dead. They sat for maybe a minute in silence until the lone paratrooper peeled open the tin lid with the key that was attached to it. 'You gonna join me? Could be our last supper.'

Jack and Ted took off their backpacks and sat beside him. Jack placed the torch on the ground, still illuminated but shining toward the timber wall.

'What's your name?' the lone paratrooper asked.

'Jack, Private Jack Saunders, and my oppo is Ted, Private Ted Smith. And you?'

'Jim, Private Jim Brown. And the girl?'

'Agathe,' she said. 'Agathe Lecreux.'

'When did you eat last, Agathe?'

'I don't know, a few days ago, maybe a week. I don't remember.' She swallowed. She could feel her mouth salivating at the thought of something.

'Here, take this.' Jim handed her a spoonful of the dead paratrooper's tinned corned beef.

Jack's Story

'Thank you,' she said.

'Where are you from, Jim?' Jack asked.

'Yorkshire. Been in this bloody war since the beginning, 1939. Too many fucking years. The only thing that keeps me sane are letters from home.'

'Letters are good, me too,' Jack said.

'And Ted, what about you?' Jim asked, scooping the corned beef from the tin.

'This is my first time, I've just enlisted. I'm from Bow, London, and I want to go home. I want to go back to my family. To my brother and my sister, to my mum and my dad. I want to just go home. I don't want to be here. I just wanna go home. I don't care that I'm a coward, I don't care. I just wanna see my mum. I just wanna go home.' He rocked himself and the snot dribbled from his nose and down over his mouth.

Jim Brown and Jack Saunders watched Ted as he tried to be a man but broke. He was a boy, he was just a boy, a brave boy, a courageous boy, a scared boy. But just a boy.

'Have you written home, Ted?' Jack asked.

'Can't read or write,' Ted replied, still rocking back and forth, blubbering into his sleeve.

'I'll help you, Ted, and you will,' Jack said. 'I will make sure you do.'

'Promise you will, Jack. Tell me I will go home.'

'You will go home.'

Jim Brown took out a cigarette and lit it. 'Want one?' The three nodded. If a cigarette could be smoked and enjoyed that night, it would be. Jim blew the smoke into the air and took out a picture from his box. He smoothed his thumb across it and smiled. 'I need to get back home for this one.' He sighed.

'I can smell her sweet auburn hair in my sleep. When I close my eyes, I can smell it.'

'May I see?' Agathe asked. Jim handed her the photo. 'She is very pretty. What is her name?'

'Peggy, and when I get back, we'll get married.'

'That is a nice thing, that is beautiful in fact,' Agathe said as she handed the photo back to Jim.

The night fell around them like a thick black cloak. Jack took out his harmonica and began to play it. Anything to appease their fear of this wretched war. Jack let Ted close his eyes and laid his rifle by his side. He pulled Agathe closer to him, he could feel the bones under her uniform. He pulled her closer still so she could feel the heat from his body and there she slept. Jack and Jim slumped against their rucksacks, the rifles ready by their sides. They allowed their eyes to shut for moments but never fully.

The light sneaked through the chinks in the timber frame. Jack shook Ted from his sleep. Jim came back from outside the barn, adjusting the zip on his trousers.

'We need to move on,' Jack said, checking his kit and reading his compass in the dim morning light. 'Agathe, you will have to come with us. You are not safe here alone.'

'D'you know how to use one of these?' Private Jim said, handing her the dead paratrooper's rifle.

'I will learn,' she said, stuffing the ammo into her pockets. As daybreak broke through the clouds lifting the mist that slunk slow across the terrain, they ate a humble breakfast before they pulled their webbing sacks onto their backs and began to patrol forward. Agathe's body was weak but she was strong and determined: she had withstood a brothel, she had withstood rape, she would withstand a journey – a journey to freedom. She also knew the area better than them. She was Dutch, after all, and her uniform could be used to fool the *Schutzstaffel*. They would take cover each time they heard Jeeps coming along the road. The Jeeps were only ever carrying the German soldiers back and forth, back and forth, with a commanding officer always in one. Then the rumble of enemy tanks as they drove along the roads. When the tanks were no longer in sight, the four of them – three paratroopers of the 2nd Battalion and a Dutch Resistance fighter – patrolled on intermittently, taking cover when the mortaring started again. Agathe learnt very quickly how to load and fire a rifle, a dead paratrooper's rifle, but it kept her alive.

After the mortaring had ceased, Agathe told the three paratroopers that the Jeeps were going to a house that the German army had occupied and turned into a kind of base; the Dutch residents had been removed. Ted, in his naivety, had asked where they'd been removed to. '*Hemel*,' she had answered – heaven.

They had three miles before they would reach the bridge. Once there, they could hide, find shelter, occupy a house. Agathe as their translator would explain their needs and they would occupy it as friendly forces, allies not foes. And there they would wait too for back-up. The back-up that was coming from England.

It was early that evening when they reached the town. The sky fell around the buildings and the drone of a plane flew low. The only sound that was recognisable now, and then it came: the whizzing, wheeling noise as bomb after bomb was dropped low from the sky and walls of a building crumbled. In amongst the rubble lay the bodies of children, parents, grandparents, civilians, unarmed innocent people. From another building the brave would run and try in vain to free those crushed bodies. A child's hand reached from beneath the broken stone, its fingers twitching. Jack's hand touched the fingers.

'He's alive,' Private Jack shouted although he didn't know if it was a boy or a girl. 'Agathe, can you talk, let them know we are here.' As the paratroopers moved forward and pulled stone, mortar, timber from the piles of rubble, Agathe held the fingers of the child, rubbing them, warming them, keeping them alive.

'We zijn hier, we zijn hier. De Britse soldaten halen je ecruit. Blijf demen.' As each piece of stone was thrown carefully from the body of the child Agathe spoke in Dutch to the small person. The soldiers could then see her small broken body. She lay under her crushed house, bloody, her legs smashed by the force of the bomb and bricks and mortar that lay across her. By her side, as if shielding her, lay her mother, her arm across her, lifeless. She had taken most of the force. Her eyes as immobile as her limbs. Her soul had long departed and would now walk with her ancestors. Private Jack knelt low and steadily by the small body of the girl, carefully trying not to disturb the rubble and allow it to fall near the face of her young mother. He gently removed her arm from her daughter's chest and laid it by her side. He brushed his fingers along the lids of her eyes so they closed and she slept forever. With gentleness he lifted the small girl up away from her mother. He stumbled a little as his boots fell between the uneven mounds of what used to be their home. He carried her down, her eyes staring into his, frightened, alone, an orphan now. She wore a bow in the side of her hair. It was pink and her hair was blonde with a ringlet running through it. She had a splattering of freckles on her nose and her lashes were thick with creamy white dust. She wore a red cardigan and a blue pinafore dress, and her knees were grazed, bleeding where her socks stopped. Her foot hung from her ankle, the wrong way, broken. His arms were strong around her, his smile reassuring her.

'*Mama,*' she cried. He shook his head in a slow-motion kind of way. '*Mama.*' He laid the small girl gently on the ground. Agathe stayed with her and smoothed her hair and smiled, singing a soft Dutch lullaby to appease her. The paratroopers went back to the rubble and dug with their hands until they found more bodies – the father, a small boy and a doll. Private Ted took the doll and brushed it down, and he realised the power of that doll in that instant. She was not broken, and she would give happiness when all else had been taken.

'Are there any others alive?' Agathe asked. Solemnly the soldiers shook their heads. 'The doctor's house is here on this street. We can take her there.' Private Jack lifted the girl from Agathe's lap and carried her to the doctor's door. Agathe pressed hard on the bell; from the step they could hear it chime inside. In the distance they could hear the heels of boots and an authoritarian voice commanding over the marching.

'*Open de deur haast je de deur open,*' Agathe whispered into the pane of the glass in the door. She could see a door to the right and a staircase that led upstairs from the hallway. She pressed urgently again on the bell. The small girl in Private Jack's arms whimpered, '*Mama.*' Agathe rang the doorbell again with a feeling of urgency bubbling up inside her.

A man hurriedly made his way down the hallway. He was small, with grey hair, wearing a waistcoat and a pair of trousers to match. He opened the door, not fully, enough for him to see the four people and a small child.

'Dr Janssen, ik ben Agathe, onderdeel van het verzet. Dit zijn Britse soldaten, verberg on alsjeblieft en neem net meisje mee. Har ankle is gebrokenen, haar familie is dood.'

He looked at them, his face ashen. He checked the small girl's ankle.

'Quickly, hurry, please, inside, up the stairs. Hurry.' He beckoned them inside and closed the door. The boots of the enemy echoed through the streets. The sound of a German officer's commands and then the gunfire.

The four sat huddled upstairs, the small girl still in Jack's arms, her cries hushed by his finger over her mouth, softly, with no force. She understood.

'Her ankle is broken, and her family is dead. We need to stay here and watch. Agathe is with the Resistance. And we are from the 2nd Battalion,' he said to the doctor.

'You have come to liberate us from Nazi occupation – they have already killed so many, thousands have starved, they have stopped all access on our waterways. Food is running short. We need to be liberated. My wife, Sophie, has a radio. She too is with the Resistance. The attic is the safest place, go there, I will take the child. What is her name, her age?'

'I don't know,' Jack said as he let his arms hand her into the doctor's. He smiled as he let her go. The doctor ushered them up a staircase that was hidden behind a door, disguised as a bookcase.

Standing on the landing and closing the bookcase door tightly, the doctor took the child to his room, where there was a medical bed and a cabinet. He spoke softly to her.

'Marta, ik ben zes,' she said.

Chapter Eleven

Appledaw Farm, Cowick, Exeter, early November, 1946

The wheels of Samson's Food Suppliers' wagon rattled down the track of the farm, leaving a plume of dirt-filled air in their wake. The last of the potatoes had been collected and Henry and Emma would receive a fine cheque for their produce. Beth stood in the barn and looked at the now empty space. A carpet of dried dirt lay on the ground where the potatoes had once been, and a bundle of unused hessian sacks were stacked above an old timber crate. A rat scurried across the dirt and squeezed its way through a chink in the timber frame. It left a minuscule trail of footprints that perhaps only a fairy could follow.

'Proper job, ye be dwain.' Henry stood behind her, smiling.

She turned and smiled at him. 'I guess that's it.' Her voice was tinged with sadness. She'd enjoyed working on the farm more than she could ever imagine, and had been able to pay her way, too. Each week she'd give Jack a little of her earnings for her rent and keep, and in return he would play his harmonica and tell her stories of the farm before she arrived. They never spoke about her time being found by him and the children, and he never asked her how she had come to be in the hayloft, hiding from something or somebody.

She stood a little anyway in the empty barn, a shaft of winter sunlight catching her, not really knowing what she might do now. The winter was beginning to slink in, and the harvesting of winter vegetables had been completed. The fields now empty and ready to be turned once again with the harrow. She didn't think her help would be needed in any other way on the farm.

'Well, thank you for letting me work on your farm,' she said, brushing down her trousers. 'I've learnt so much and you and Emma have been so kind to me.'

'Ye be going some place else, me lover?' Henry said as he took up the hessian sacks from the crate.

'Umm, no, not really. But ...I just thought.'

'Well, me lover, ye be dwain a proper job, Jack 'as the walls to fix. Ye be helping 'im?'

'You mean you'd like me to stay and work?'

'Dreckly I would.'

'Oh my, that would be wonderful. I don't know how to thank you and Emma enough. You've been so good to me, really you have. I'd love to stay and help Jack, as long as I don't get in his way.'

'Dare say you won't be gettin' in 'is way. Mark my words.' He winked at her. 'The cattle will be coming in soon from pastures, the grass be no good in the winter months. Dare say our Jack could use a pair of 'ands with extra feeds. The troughs' water will freeze with the cold winter nights and needs refilling. Horses will be brought int' stables, dare say ye knows about that.' He winked. 'Plenty be dwain about 'ere. If it's good for ye, pretty maid, I'd be offering you a job, dreckly.'

'Oh my, I can't believe it. Yes, yes, I'd love to stay and work here. Thank you, thank you, thank you.' She ran over and hugged him – she hadn't meant to hug him quite so hard or even quite so long, but her body instinctively did. The happiness in her whole being took over and with that she let it bubble over. Henry's arms held her like a father's would as he brushed down her hair. He hadn't been expecting it either, yet the warmth of his arms embraced the happiness of a young woman like a daughter, a daughter he'd never had.

'Proper job, ye be 'ere with Jack in t'mornin'.'

'I will, I will, I promise.' With a lightness in her step she walked out of the hayloft in the direction of the paddock and toward the tied cottages.

'Beth!' The door of the kitchen flew open and Eleanor bundled out of it, running straight across the yard towards Beth, who stopped in her tracks and stood smiling.

'Hello, Eleanor, where are the boys?'

'Oh, they're playing upstairs. Beth, can I walk with you?'

'Of course,' she said, her hands linked behind her back. 'You going to say anything? You seem a little quiet. Did you just want to walk?' She nudged her body into Eleanor's.

Eleanor stopped and took in a deep breath. She scrunched up her nose and lips and then exhaled.

'I think I might be going home soon.'

'Why? What makes you think that?'

'I overheard Aunt Em – she was crying with Uncle Henry the other night. She said something like, *I knew this day would come and now it seems so hard, but they're not mine. I lost mine.*'

'Are your parents in London then?'

'Yes, we came here to be safe when the war broke out. That's when Jack came, or at least when we met him. He came after the war and his mother worked here on the farm. She did the "make and mend" classes until she passed away. And Jack came back, and now I've got so used to seeing him and being here, going back to the city, seems all wrong. I don't think I can.'

They walked on a little more until they reached the paddock where the horses were.

'Come.' Beth took Eleanor by the hand and led her to the wall, making a clicking sound with her mouth. The chestnut stallion lifted his head from grazing and walked over to the stone wall, where the girls now stood.

'How did you do that? Storm never comes to anyone except Jack. Uncle Henry said he was born with an unknown spirit in him. You're like Jack, d'you know that?'

Beth smiled and gave a warm sigh. 'Hello, boy,' she said as he nosed her. 'D'you ride?' she asked Eleanor.

'No.'

'Ever tried?'

'No, never.'

'Maybe you should. It might help you think about everything, just you and a horse and the wind in your hair.'

'Beth?'

'Yes.'

'When we leave, will you promise you'll write to me, you won't forget us.'

'Of course, I'll write, but you don't know you're leaving yet, you might have overheard something entirely different, silly. There will come a time when you'll go home because that's what will happen with all the children who were evacuated. Look at it this way, though: you can always come back and visit because this is your aunt and uncle. Think of all those children who won't return and will find it even harder. Remember that bit, that's the important part to keep, and your heart will grow fond of London again. It might hurt for a while but then it will be alright. I promise you.'

Jack's Story

'I guess so. I'd better go back in, Aunt Em will be wondering where I am.' She turned to leave Beth at the wall. 'Beth.' She took her hand. 'Promise you'll stay on the farm and look after Jack.'

Beth nodded faintly with a glimmer of a smile. 'Go on, in you go.' Her voice was as soft as a whisper. She watched as Eleanor ran up the track toward the farmhouse. 'So,' she said, smiling at the chestnut horse. 'You're Storm and you've an unknown spirit in you, do you.' And she her drew her hand slowly down Storm's nose. He bumped her arm as if telling her not to stop. 'When was the last time you were ridden, boy?' He pushed his nose up and over the wall. His hoof stamped on the ground and he whinnied loud, then he whinnied again, even louder than the first time. Beth stood back and let him make his noise. 'Go on, boy,' she said. He rose up onto his hind legs and whinnied again.

'Easy, bey,' came the voice from behind. 'Don't be scared, 'e be 'avin' 'is say, 'e be.'

'Oh, I'm not scared.'

'Ye know about these creatures?'

'A little, yes.'

'Ye ever ridden one like 'im before?'

'What, you mean spirited?' She sighed. 'Yes.'

'Ye got thrown off.'

'No, I didn't in fact. I think most thought I would.'

'Ye think ye can ride this one? 'E be different t'rest of 'em.'

'He's beautiful, I'd love to ride him. But I don't have any riding clothes.'

'I'll sort it dreckly, they could do with an exercise. Jack will ride with ye after the field walls 'ave been tended to. 'e's like a dragon, 'e be. Won't let anyone near 'im. Dare say ye won't get no closer, me lover.'

'I'll ride with Jack when the walls are mended. I best get back to the cottage and prepare this evening's meal.'

'Saddles in the barn. There be a storm brewin', north wind's blowin' through, she be. Best ye take 'em out in mornin', I'll tell Jack to get saddles down. Right ye are.'

'Alright,' she said.

She left Henry at the gate and carried on back to the cottages. The wind was picking up and the weathervane swung between the north and north-west. The clouds rolled through the skies like a mass of grey; their greyness would make any quarry proud as if pleased to echo the earth. Beth turned back: Henry was nearing the farmhouse and the chestnut horse was bucking in the field as if possessed. The dark clouds lolled over the cottage, chasing the thunderstorm that loomed, the sky cocooned in black.

She pushed the door open and closed it tightly behind her. The sky rumbled in the distance across the moors and a jagged light flew through the sky with a cracking sound. Then the rain came like sheets of glass falling. She stood at the window and watched the tree on the horizon stand firm against the storm. Another strike of lightning lit through the blackness of the clouds.

The latch rattled and Jack bolted through the door, closing it behind him to batten out the lashing rainfall, his cap and clothes drenched through to his skin, the grin on his face embracing the weathers on the moors. She smiled at him as he stood, still grinning, at the door. He took off his cap and hung it on the door and peeled off his sodden boots. He brushed his hands through his hair and wiped them on his trousers to dry them.

Jack's Story

'You're a bit wet,' she said eventually.

'You bet.' Without a thought he untucked his shirt and pulled it in one go over his head, and then walked across the room to hang it on the back of the chair by the hearth. Steam rose up from it as the fire radiated its heat on to it. Beth held her breath for a moment, looking up to the ceiling and then out to the tree that stood firm on the horizon as the rain battered down. She swallowed hard as she brought her look back to the fire, and in that moment her eyes flashed across his bare torso that glistened with the wetness from his shirt. His arms were strong and defined and she could see the definition in his stomach and chest. On his upper right arm there was an inking in black of a lion above the king's crown, and beneath it wings and in Roman numerals the number two. His trousers were held loosely about his waist with a leather belt.

He placed the kettle on the hot plate. Her eyes still on him, the muscle in his arm flexed as he put the kettle down to heat. He then knelt down and placed four lumps of coal onto the hot embers. The inking was almost protruding on his upper arm as he took each coal one by one with the tongs. She watched him as the strength in his shoulder blades rippled each time he placed a lump of coal onto the burning fire. He tucked the tongs back into the coal scuttle and stood up. From the corner of his eye, he caught Beth's gaze on him. She glanced away quickly, a sting of warmth rising into her cheeks, and brushed the back of her hand across her cheek, hoping he hadn't noticed. His eyes, warm and kind, rested on her as he brushed past her and went up the stairs.

She swallowed, knowing he had left the room, knowing he'd seen her gaze on him and perhaps the flush in her olive-toned cheek. Her hand pressed against her neck, she exhaled, biting on the inside of her cheek until she heard the door of his room shut. Her look flashed back to the stairs where she'd watched his half-naked body walk up the stairs. Yet he'd said nothing.

Had he realised her own discomfort and left the room? Her glance went back to his shirt that hung over the chair. It was dirtied from the soil and work on the farm. She went to it, letting her hand glide along it and bit her lip as she stood with her fingertips softly smoothing down the cotton that had the sweat of a man clinging to it. She pushed her hair away from her face, twirling it into a makeshift knot at the nape of her neck, and then went to the kitchen to prepare supper.

She stood at the sink, peeling the potatoes, and every once in a while she'd look out at the sky, now a sheet of blackness with the stars camouflaged by the rain that fell heavily. She opened the drawer and took the cutlery from it to lay the table, taking the water jug and glasses as she went back up to the room and set the table for them both. Jack's shirt still hung on the back of the chair. Taking it up, she brushed it against her cheek and breathed in, allowing the smell of him to reach the depth of her lungs, puncturing them with a feeling of intoxication. Then she folded it and laid it on the arm of the sofa. Hearing his footsteps on the stairs, she went back down to the kitchen, where he came to stand and watch her as she wiped away the mud from the potatoes she'd peeled.

'Your shirt, it's dry,' she said. He smiled at her and she felt the warmth prickle in her cheeks. They spoke not a word over supper and without saying anything she cleared away the plates before retreating to her room. She took out her diary and wrote in it, the sound of his harmonica filtering up the staircase and resting at her closed door.

Dear Diary

I have worked at the farm for six weeks now, and each day I have loved it more than the day before. Today, Henry spoke about Storm. Storm's a beautiful chestnut stallion in the paddock, who has a spirit in him that nobody seems to understand. Yet he is gentle when he noses me at the wall and he walks alongside me when

Jack's Story

I come back to the cottage, like he knows who I am, where I'm from, what I'm running from. He whinnied today and showed his strength of character. Henry said he was different. But he's not. Like Silver Sixpence, he has a way, a way you learn from. I wonder sometimes – well, always, in fact – who will be riding Silver, who will be brushing him down, knowing his whinnying is because of the storm and the cold and the winds just like Storm today. Henry said I could ride him, and I'd like nothing more than to saddle him and ride across the moors, across the foams of the breaking waves on the beaches, but I must ride with Jack. I have only ever ridden alone, you know that, just me and my Silver, and now my life is changing. And Jack, dear diary, is a man who makes me feel a way I don't understand. I'm not sure I'm allowed to feel like that, and I don't know whether I should. I'm running away and now I want to fall. And I want him to pick me up. Why do I feel that way, why do I feel like I can't breathe when he is near me, my lungs fill with a feeling of intoxicating wanting. My heart keeps a steady rhythm until he walks into the room and then the thoughts of him arrive and the tempo rises. It feels like he hears my heart like a drum out of beat crashing against my ribcage, but he says nothing. But he cries in the night and I think he cries for another – I am sure he cries for another. I must sleep now, dear diary. Sleep well.

He pushed the guard in front of the fire and turned out the paraffin lamp. His footsteps were light on the staircase. No light came from under the door of Beth's room. He lay still in his bed as a night moth flitted inside the lamp above him and an owl hooted his calls in the darkness. His eyes stared up at the ceiling as he watched the wings bash gently up against the illumination and get pushed away by the intensity of the bulb's heat, the small fragility of its wings. He pushed his arms behind his head, revealing the inking on his upper arm, the inking of a lion, the crown and the wings, Airborne. His mind taking him back and forth in the day. The way she had walked across the yard, the sunlight behind her passing through the cotton of her shirt, the silhouette of her smooth lines beneath it. The softness of her smile, the mud of potatoes on her cheeks and forehead where she'd wiped her face. Her smile, how could he forget her smile. And today in the room she'd seemed adorably shy around him. She exuded an aura that seeped through his veins – he had found her in a hayloft, damaged from something, yet now she was a woman who showed her confidence on the farm despite retaining the vulnerability and fragility of the moth's iridescent wings. As the sound of the owl lessened in the skies, his eyes began to give way to the night and the moth flitted alone in the shimmering light.

'Hold her, Jim, hold her, don't let her go! I've got you buddy, stay with me Ted, d'you hear me, you stay with me, d'you hear, eyes open buddy, eyes open.' Ted's body was slumped across his shoulder as he ran and stumbled with him across the ground, a ground full of bodies, an open graveyard. He slumped Ted up against the tree, the red liquid seeping through his smock. 'I made you a promise, now you stay with me, d'you hear.' He ran back. Jim's body lay over the weak body of Agathe, blood dribbling from his mouth.

'Take her, rescue her.' Jim pushed her away from him, his body riddled with bullets from enemy fire. 'Take her.' The wet, bloodied soil smeared across his face and hands, Jim handed Jack a photo. 'Tell Peggy Arthur I love her, and we will wander through...' The last of his breath never made it past his lips. His eyes closed in that moment.

Jack gently lifted Jim's arm away from her body, her eyes like a black hole staring back at him, her hand soft against the face of her protection, now another victim of the bloody war. Jack threw Agathe into his arms and stumbled and ran, her arms linked around his neck, her eyes holding a fear that penetrated through to Jack's soul.

Jack's Story

'Don't you go anywhere, d'you hear me, don't you give up on me. I'm not going down, we will reach the other side, d'you hear me Agathe, you stay with me, you fuckin' stay with me.' Every word laboured and breathless as he ran with her. The shells fired, the mortaring pummelled the air, and he ran and stumbled and ran again until he reached the tree and there he sat. Numb. His hands in her hair, smoothing it, her breathing shallow. His wet mouth on her forehead. 'You stay with me, d'you hear,' he said into her skin. She lay against his chest, her eyes slowly closing. Ted slumped against him, his wound bunged by Jack's thumb. 'You stay with me buddy, d'you hear, you stay with me,' he cried.

Beth lay in her bed and listened to him cry out. She tucked her pillow under her cheek, and heard only his cries through the night.

Chapter Twelve

Appledaw Farm, Cowick, Exeter, early December, 1946

Over the weeks working at the farm, Beth had made enough money to pay for her lodgings and put a little aside to save. She had made do with the slacks that Jack had given her for the farm, but the skirt and blouse she had been found in were beginning to look worn and tired. The slacks, although huge around her, had become her staple work clothes. The buckle on her shoe had broken countless times and Jack had fixed it, but now she had decided to take the brave step of venturing into the town of Exeter and purchasing a few bits for her wardrobe. Eleanor had asked if she could join her and so together the two cycled down the lanes in the direction of Exeter. They left their bicycles propped against the wall next to the Old Blacksmith's inn and sauntered down the cobbled alley toward the high street, where a line of black Colson & Co vehicles were parked along the kerbside.

'Here, you'll love this shop, it's so fine and elegant,' Eleanor said, tugging at Beth's arm and dragging her toward the entrance of Colson & Co. Beth took in a breath and wiped her hands on her skirt; they felt clammy and she had a stirring inside her stomach that wouldn't disappear. The door swished open and what greeted her eyes was the magnificence of finery, silk, fur stoles wrapped around mannequins' necks. The parquet floor was polished to a brilliant sheen and the woman at the counters displayed elegant smiles, waiting to bestow their perfumes, cosmetics and fineries on any lady who might stop a little while and browse.

Beth shot her eyes to the floor, not wanting to be drawn in by the beautifully manicured and proficient sales assistants. She felt a flush of warmth run through her spine and up her neck, her throat dry and the hairs on her arms prickling her skin. She swallowed and breathed in, closing her eyes as if she was about to submerge herself beneath the waves of the sea and hold her breath until a time when her lungs would explode, and she would need to come back up for air. The sound of her heart pounding against her ribcage. Her eyes blinked in slow motion and a myriad of colours like a rainbow moved about her. A haze of opulence and unwanted elegance surrounded her.

'Isn't it wonderful,' Eleanor said, twizzling in a small circle so that her skirt billowed out. The young apprentice draughtsman passed her by. 'Miss,' he said, tipping his cap. Eleanor smiled. In that moment Beth noticed the coyness of Eleanor –how perhaps she herself had once been. Her eyes scanned the ground floor of the department store again. Her fingers twitched uncontrollably and fumbled at her skirt.

'Come,' said Eleanor, 'let me show you more.' Beth hesitated. 'Come on, come on.' Eleanor took her hand insistently to lead her past the silks that draped beautifully, past the jewels that glistened and past the sales assistants wafting perfumes in the air that made all the women's feminine instincts tingle until they reached the back of the grand department store. To the left the architects and draughtsmen huddled around Mr Billings, the wealthy proprietor, whilst carpenters and tradesmen busied themselves under the instruction of the architect. Behind Eleanor and Beth was the sweeping staircase that rose like a column up the centre of Colson & Co. To the right of the staircase was a wonderment of women's fashion and a richness of materials and exotic styles. Eleanor's eyes dazzled when she pulled Beth to come with her and explore the exquisiteness of the high-glamour fashion. Sequins and crystals glistened and shone under the chandeliers. Evening gowns swept the floor and hung beautifully on mannequins, their thin hands resting on their perfectly shaped hips, with a cleverly held cigarette holder and black cigarette with a golden filter tip between their spindly fingers. Daringly low fronts of gowns in shimmering shades, mermaid fishtails that swept the ground or high-heeled sparkling evening shoes that glittered in silver and gold.

Eleanor stood by one of the mannequins and struck a *British Vogue* front cover magazine pose.

'Could you ever imagine wearing this, just like a princess, like Princess Elizabeth and Philip Mountbatten. Positively dreamy, don't you think? D'you think the Earl and Countess of Parkforton would have dances with the princess?' She twirled from her pose and peeped around a beautiful ivory dress made in a fabric that hung effortlessly to the floor, its back latticed in silver thread and the neckline scooped into an elegant fall.

Beth smiled uncomfortably as Eleanor floated past the beauty of it all, lapping up the world of high society that she could only ever dream of.

'Come on, Eleanor, I need to buy some clothes and boots. And not from here.' Beth took Eleanor's hand impatiently and dragged her away from the serenity of evening gowns and toward the double doors that would take them back to the high street. Eleanor pushed the doors open and as she did, Mrs Cooke sauntered in with Mrs Hubbard. They were nattering, their heads locked together, too busy gossiping to notice the two girls until they brushed past Beth and knocked into her shoulder as they did.

'Watch where you're going, would you!' Mrs Hubbard tutted loudly.

Jack's Story

'I'm sorry,' Beth said, catching the woman's indignant look. Mrs Hubbard's steely eyes were pinned on her, flashing a look of disdain. Beth darted her eyes away quickly and hurried from the shop. Mrs Hubbard turned back and stopped; her eyes creased as she sliced a sideways glance following Eleanor and the girl she had knocked into, who had now disappeared down the street and out of view. *Surely not,* she thought to herself. She bobbed her hair with her hand and pulled her gloves at the wrist before catching up with Mrs Cooke, who was already admiring the fur stoles. She turned again to the high street: the figure of the girl had gone. She drew in her cheeks and pursed her lips. 'I wonder,' she murmured through sucked-in cheeks.

'You wonder what, Prue dear?'

'Oh, nothing Mary, nothing at all.' Her lips still pursed, her eyes still creased at the sides.

Eleanor and Beth left the high street of Exeter behind them, the basket on the front of Beth's bicycle brimming with her new purchases. She carried a sense of pride because she had saved up and bought them herself, and she had worked the farm to do so. She had stepped away from her norm and just this simple action was a life-affirming moment for her. In the paper bag was a pair of brown ankle boots with laces, simply decorated with small circles cut out. The man in the shop had called them brogues and *en vogue*. She'd also found some ladies' slacks, a jacket, skirt, underwear, a sweater and a blouse, all bought with most of her savings. The bikes rattled along the lanes and as the girls freewheeled down the hills the wind whooshed past their faces, giving each of them a glow to their cheeks. Beth breathed in the feeling of freedom as the breeze swept across her knuckles until they finally reached the track to the farm.

'I had fun with you today, Beth.' Eleanor said, hitching up her skirt and clambering off the bike as she leant it up against the barn's wall.

Beth smiled but said nothing.

'I'll see you later, I better go in and see what the boys are up to.' She left Beth alone. Beth's thoughts went back to Colson & Co and the finery of the shop, and the woman who had knocked her shoulder and stared at her for too long. She took her things from the basket and walked across the yard.

'Horses are saddled for ye, me lover.'

She turned her body slightly to catch Henry hollering across the yard from the cowshed.

'Ye be ridin' out this afternoon with young Jack.' His grin was broad, his gait firm and thick.

'Right,' she said pulling the brown paper bag closer to her chest. Her footsteps slow across the track, her thoughts somewhere else, she glanced over to the paddock: it was empty.

She closed the door of the cottage behind her and stood with her back to it, holding it closed as if she'd been followed and she was hiding behind it, waiting for the hammering on the door and *them* coming to get her, to drag her away. Her thoughts kept returning to the Colson & Co and the woman, her clipped voice, her indignant glare – yet that look had seemed to stare into Beth's eyes, a look of knowing. Beth swallowed and took in a breath big enough to fill the depths of her lungs. She could feel the beat of her heart thumping so hard ... she swallowed again until the room went black and the thumping stopped.

'Beth, Beth, it's Jack, can you hear me?'

Jack's Story

Her eyes flickered open and closed, open and closed, until his blurry face stopped moving. He smiled at her.

'Did they come?' she said, her voice a whimper.

'Who?' He brushed the hair away from her face.

'Where am I?'

'You're at the cottage.'

She began to push herself up from the floor. The brown paper bag on the floor had ripped down the edging and her clothes lay about it.

'Are you alright?' he asked.

'It just went black – I don't remember much. I was standing and then –'

'Shh, shh.' He brushed the back of his hand against her cheek. 'Here, let me.' He helped her up and guided her to the sofa. He placed her bag beside her and left her briefly to make a sweet tea. Then he crouched down by her whilst she cupped the tea in her hands. 'Where have you been today?'

'I went into Exeter, to buy some clothes and boots,' she sighed. 'I'm fine now, really. It was probably the hills, I haven't ridden a bike for a while.'

'We're riding the horses later – are you sure you want to?'

'Yes, I'm sure I want to. I'll be fine, really, I will. Anyway, I bought some new boots, especially.'

Jack grinned as she took out her boots to show him. He grazed his thumb across her hand. 'I'll make a picnic for the ride.' He wobbled up and left her alone on the sofa. She circled her fingers across her hand where Jack had brushed it and smoothed it softly. She listened a while to the sound of him humming as he prepared a simple picnic until she took up her bag and went to her room to change. She left the clothes she'd worn that morning in a crumpled mess on the floor by her feet whilst she stood and gazed at herself in the long mirror in the door of the wardrobe. It had two small drawers with carved patterns on them at the base, and had stood empty for the weeks she'd lived in the cottage. The trousers that she'd bought were slightly tapered at the bottom and nipped in at the waist, with two tucks on the front and slanting pockets where she could just slide her hands in effortlessly. The material was a little softer on her legs than the slacks Jack had given to her for the farm. The blouse had long sleeves and was cut in at the waist, showing the lines of her figure. She wore beneath it a camisole top that fell simply over her curves. She turned slightly and smoothed her hand down the back of the trousers, allowing her foot to almost leave the ground as she did. The brown brogues had that sheen to them which only ever came with new boots or a high polish. She smiled gently at the reflection of herself and let out a sigh as her eyes moved from her reflection to the window, the moors that fell into the horizon and the lone tree that stood firm and strong whilst the sun burned through the wintery clouds. She closed her eyes and let herself imagine the ride and the moors, dispelling the memories of the morning and the woman in the department store.

It was the sound of Jack's calls that stopped her from imagining any more of that morning. She bundled her crumpled clothes onto the bed and quickly folded the new clothes and placed them in the drawers beneath the wardrobe. She brushed her hands over her slight frame and closed the bedroom door behind her.

Jack stood at the bottom of the stairs with a canvas satchel across his body. His eyes caught on the slightness of her figure as she descended the staircase. His gaze staying on her. Her own eyes looking towards the floor, not noticing his look of awe.

Jack's Story

'Let's go,' he said, unlatching the front door. Together they walked up the track towards the yard where Storm and Brandy stood, their heads tossing up and down in their bridles where they were tethered. Jack untied the reins and handed them to Beth. Storm stood back, his hind hooves treading the ground, his head tossing up and down. He moved further backwards, his hooves still stomping at the earth.

'Steady boy,' she whispered into him. She lifted her leg up and hooked it into the stirrup before drawing her weight up and throwing herself over the saddle until her bottom rested on it. Jack watched her agility and capability; she turned down his offer of a helping foot up. Storm moved back again, jumpy, and his hooves stomped into the ground, kicking up small particles of earth.

'This one be seeing the fairies,' Henry said as he held the bridle. 'Ye be sure ye can 'andle a creature like this? 'E'll throw ye, 'e will.'

'He'll be fine, he's just a little frisky, aren't you boy.' She lay closer to him, her breastbone resting on his neck as she smoothed her hands across him. Jack made a clicking noise with his mouth and together they moved out of the yard and down the track.

'Thought we could take them onto the moors? A gentle hack?' Jack said as he rode onto the lane passing the tied cottages. At the signpost they turned off and walked the horses down a bridle path lined with hawthorn and blackberry bushes that weaved between the bare, thorny branches. Beth pushed away the low-hanging branches as they ambled down the pathway until it opened on to the land, where the crows flew low over the ploughed fields and the scarecrow stood alone. There in the distance stood the lone tree on the brow of the undulating land, a landmark to be reached. Storm was uneasy in his walk and tossed his head up and down; Beth pulled in the rein a little to steady his friskiness. 'Ready!' Jack called out as he turned in his saddle. 'Ya,' he said as he dug his stirrups into his horse and rode her out fast ahead of Beth. Beth watched as Jack rode the land, his horse cantering across the open barren terrain, its head low, heels high, divots of earth kicking up as it cantered ahead. Jack's seat was raised from his saddle, his body leaning over the creature's neck.

She leant her body across Storm, his hooves to-ing and fro-ing in their steps.

'Easy boy,' she said, whispering in his ear. 'You ready, let's go.' She dug her stirrups into the stallion's side, and he knew the time had come for him to be ridden. They rode on together over the moors, crushing the bracken beneath his hooves. The horse's breath snorted from his nose. 'Jack!' Beth cried. 'Stop!' He turned back and rode towards her, the wind lashing at his back as his body moved into the horse, pushing the creature ahead. He slowed his canter until he drew up next to Beth. 'What?' he said as he came to her side.

She smiled with a glint in her eye. 'Race you.' Laughing, she dug her heels hard into the stallion's side and lifted herself from the seat of her saddle, her body pushed forward into her ride. She rode him hard and fast, the bracken pushing down beneath the hooves, crushed by the power of the creature as he cantered: an explosive energy that resonated through the happiness of Beth. 'Come on boy,' she said as she pushed her head against his neck and held the reins close to his mane, feeling the frisson of joy that the freedom of the wildness of the moors bestowed upon them both. She cantered across the heath, the wind pushing into her face, biting at her, its sharp cold against her cheeks as she went, knowing she was ahead of Jack, with a horse that nobody else wanted to handle. The man who'd found her, the man who made her heart leap without realising why, who was now behind her chasing her through the bracken and ferns, against the wind that flew through their hair and clothes. She could hear only the sound of the horses snorting and the pummelling of their hooves breaking the bleak ground beneath them. Beth rode Storm knowing she was the closest she ever came to dreaming whilst being perfectly awake and alive – an uncontrollable sensation running through her body.

There were springs meandering through the gorse and thistles; she took the reins and called to Storm to jump, Jack watched from behind as the horse took each leap in a stride above the moorland springs. He watched as the power in her legs held the horse, her body raised above its saddle and over its mane, holding her posture, keeping control, and still she rode him harder. He heard the pummelling of its hooves with a girl on top who rode in a way he'd never seen before. Storm pushed the strength of his magnificent body forward, his mane swept back in the wind, his tail high, his hooves, the sheen of his coat like liquid velvet. The power in his body as he carried the girl with him. The girl who had shown herself to be his companion, not his master, and there he would carry her as a strong spirit and his own force of nature.

'To the tree,' she called back to Jack, her voice carrying in the wind. Her hair tousled and free.

Together they rode, the horses' heads low and their heels up as they rode faster and faster, the sun beating through the wintery clouds until the tree neared and Beth began to slow her speed until she reached the bare branches that stretched out their limbs. There she let Storm whinny with her on his back. There she let him raise his forelegs up into the air in a triumphant union of horse and rider. In a triumphant moment of a stallion and its companion. She knew how to ride a horse like Storm, and it was as if Storm knew how to let her ride him. She laid herself forward in her saddle and whispered into him, and as she did, she turned her head sideways, her hair falling against her face, and there she looked at Jack whose face was wind-beaten and smiling. Her eyes intriguing through the strands of hair caught on her lips. She scrunched her nose.

'I won,' she said, kicking her foot from the stirrup and allowing her body to fall from the horse. Then she led him by the rein to the clear stream so he could drink. She went back to the foot of the tree, where she dropped her body and slunk down, resting her back against its wide girth. 'What?' she said, her eyes quizzical yet playful as Jack looked at her, searching her face for a clue as to why she was who she was. How he had just watched a girl ride a horse that nobody dared to go near. Why every emotion she transcended hit him like a freight train and every micro-movement of hers made his body want to take her. Jack shook his head. He had no answer for her because his answer was his feelings and his need and his desire. He took the satchel from across his body and sat by her, pulling up a thistle from the ground and twizzling it in his fingers.

'Who taught you to ride like that?' he asked finally.

'Me.' She sighed.

'How?' Jack took from the bag the sandwiches he'd made, along with two pickled eggs and a bottle of soda.

'Is it important, Jack?'

'It's not important if you don't want to tell me, but nobody has ridden Storm like that, nobody has been able to.'

'Henry says you ride him.'

'I ride him, but I know him.'

'Maybe I know him too. Maybe because nobody understands how to.'

'And how d'you understand? What is it, Beth, what is it about you?'

She shrugged. 'That he's a horse, a creature of power and spirit, and that I'm not his master. But I'm one with him, to keep him company – to be like him, not ahead of him. And you? Who taught you to ride or to feel the way you feel?'

'War. War taught me. Being 2 PARA, it taught me humility, compassion, bravery, death. War taught me, Beth.' He unwrapped the parchment paper and handed Beth half of the sandwich he'd made. 'Today, you seemed frightened again. Yet you rode a horse with every emotion in your body that I could read, because I can read it in me. What are you running from?'

She sighed, and it sounded almost like a cry – but not a cry, more a sound that comes from confusion and not knowing and not understanding and trying hard to unscramble it all, and yet it's damage. A damage that tangles your mind into knots that are so snarled they just stay there in a mess until somebody reaches out to them and tries to untangle them, and if she let them be untangled, she would lose what she craved. Her freedom.

She stared into the distance, holding the sandwich between her fingers. Her eyes fixed ahead of her, unblinking.

'What are you running from?' he asked again.

She bit her lip and breathed out, turning her head to him and looking into his eyes. Her eyes flickered as she stared into his – she swallowed, she felt her heart beating. *Could he hear it too?*

'I'm not running,' she said. Her eyes dropped and the brightness that was there when she'd climbed down from Storm's back turned to a look of loss and emptiness. He lifted her chin with his finger. Her mouth opened slightly. The warmth of his eyes smiled at her.

'Betrayal,' she said under her breath. Her eyes dropped away from his and she bit at the inside of her cheek, trying to stop the tears that were forming in her eyes. A single tear trickled down her cheek, and in that moment, Jack saw once more the girl he'd found in the hayloft, the girl who reminded him of Arnhem and Agathe. With his thumb he brushed away the tear.

The wind rippled through the ferns and the sun moved around the sky to the west. They said very little that afternoon as they sat beneath the tree whose root spread low beneath them, anchoring itself to the ground. Perhaps that time on the moors and the silence was the beginning of their understanding of each other, with unspoken words but a deep feeling of unity. The clouds began to drop low as the mists moved in low onto the moors, seeping up the ferns and bracken in its path. Storm began to stomp his hooves.

'We'd best get back, the weather is changing,' Jack said eventually as he pushed himself up from the ground. He put his hand out and pulled Beth up. His grip, strong and firm, brought her close into his body. She put her hand up to stop herself from falling into his chest. Her hand touched his shirt and his chest below. Her eyes caught his, and she took in a breath as their faces were inches apart – she could feel his breath on her face and his gaze on her. She glanced down to her hand, which was still on his shirt, and drew it away, closing her fingers into her palm. He bent his head down and found her eyes as she looked away.

Turning away from him, she took the reins and mounted Storm. She let out a sound and Storm lifted his head and took speed across the moors, as the mist fell low and the chill in the air snapped at their bodies. They rode the ferns and bracken, leaving the barest of trees alone on the moor, where it held only their feelings beneath its outstretched limbs.

Chapter Thirteen

Arnhem, Holland, mid-September, 1944

The man rapped on the door with urgency, his body pushing against his vigorous rapping in order to shield and cushion the noise. His knocks became more acute and desperate as his knuckles rapped again, his ear close to the wooden panelling. Hurried footsteps sounded on the other side, across a parquet floor. Dr Janssen peeled open the front door and an officer and four soldiers, one injured, were ushered hastily and discreetly into his house. After glancing up and down the road, the doctor closed the door quickly behind him.

In the attic room above, Sophie Janssen, Jack, Ted, Jim and Agathe hid. They could hear scurrying feet below and the hushed sound of voices; the new arrivals were British, at least. In the background, the radio tapped in another enciphered message.

Dr Janssen beckoned to the officer and the three of the soldiers of the 2nd Parachute Battalion to go upstairs, where they could take refuge and watch from the small window that overlooked the town and the bridges they were aiming to secure. The wooden shutters were open and a pigeon cooed on the sill. Dr Janssen closed the secret door behind them and went to tend to the wounded soldier. He'd received a shrapnel injury to his upper arm. His bloodied hand held the makeshift tourniquet around it, his teeth gritted together.

Jack turned his head momentarily from the window, where his aim was on the enemy passing through the streets below.

'Sir,' he said as the officer approached the window to scan the streets. Jack kept his eye on the target and didn't salute. They had learnt in the hangar never to salute an officer on the field or – *bam!* – the enemy would have them.

'Private, what have we got here?'

'Panzergrenadiers, tanks, self-propelled guns, sir. The lot, sir – we're fucked, if you don't mind me saying.'

Lieutenant Colonel John Frost, 'Johnny' to the officers in the mess, stood and looked out. Across the street he could make out the bridge that crossed the Rhine, which was heavily under German control. He turned to the girl, Agathe. 'Resistance?' He knew immediately from her uniform it was a cover; the stitching and small alteration above the SS was incorrect, a sign to let the allies know they were in good company.

'Yes, I am.'

'Dutch?'

'Yes.'

'Escaped from where?'

Her hair was another tell-tale sign that she had been captured by the Germans and suffered the effects of their brutal, barbaric force.

'Vught concentration camp.'

'Any others?'

'No, they killed my brother and Frederik and they ra –' She stopped.

'The Wermacht field?'

She nodded.

'I'm sorry.' His hand rested on her shoulder briefly. 'I hope my men have treated you well.'

Jack's Story

'They have, sank-you.'

'Are you able to reach the British – do we have any information on ammunition? Our communication is vague, the radio messages are not reaching England.'

Sophie spoke quickly in Dutch to Agathe as another encrypted message came in.

'Major Cain of the 2nd Battalion South Staffordshire Regiment (2 South Staffs) has landed on Dutch ground. *Zere* was a problem at base, England. He is two days behind but now patrolling forward,' Agathe said. 'He is armed with PIAT and mortars. But *zat* is it.' She relayed the coded text as it came through.

'We've been watching now for a day, sir,' Jack said. 'The Germans are heavy in tank fire. We got trounced whilst patrolling, land mines on verges – our ammo is low, really low. We need more, sir. We don't stand a chance. We don't stand a fucking chance. Might as well just stand out there and let them shoot, sitting ducks, sir.'

The glint of his rifle caught in the hazy sun and flicked across towards the Germans, and the enemy took fire again. The paras fired back with all they were worth. A piece of stone from the façade of the building flew off in the firing and caught Jack, leaving an open wound. Blood trickled down the side of his face. He smeared it away, revealing a gash to his right eye.

'Send a message back – we are in need of ammo and support,' Frost said, musing on the situation.

'Ted, pass the PIAT. We've got an armoured Jeep and a tank heading south across the river. I can take 'em out,' Jack said.

Private Ted Smith sank low to the ground and handed over the PIAT. Jack cocked his weapon once and loaded it with a shell. 'Come on, come on,' he said as he lay lower with his weapon. 'Get a shell ready, Ted. I'm gonna give this son of a –' He stopped short, remembering he was in the company of two women. His eye squinted through the sight of his weapon, staying firmly on the target, his aim to be precise as it approached. There was an officer in the front seat of the Jeep – he needed him taken out of the equation. Jack dismantled and disheartened the enemy with a few well-placed shots. The Jeep skidded wildly across the bridge out of control, the driver dead too. Another shot and his target, the armoured vehicle, was annihilated, the tank still firing as a Panzergrenadier in its turret barked orders. A deadly shot that killed without warning. 'Bull's eye!' – another down, smoke pluming from the vehicle's fuel tanks. The German soldiers bailed from the burning vehicles and ran for cover, and then the mortaring started again. Walls crumbled, the air deep in fire-fighting mists, plumes of smoke, shells reducing buildings to rubble on the ground. The air blasted with deafening sounds, the constant noise of machine guns firing from behind every crook and crevice of masonry. The wails of men hit by mortars, some lying on the ground others lying still, motionless, gone.

Then silence fell across the smoky air, a greyness falling on the stillness, like a cloak of mist shielding the fallen souls. The firing ceased. The cries of a small child were the only normal sound, yet abnormal. They weren't the cries of a scolded child or a child who'd fallen and grazed their knee. They were the cries of a small child whose young world was a nightmare, a living nightmare, whose fear was as real as the bad dreams he might have in his bed at night. And then it stopped, his crying fell silent just like the mist. A woman ran from a nearby shop to reach her home safely to be with her family. The sound of her heels in the eerie stillness echoed around the walls of the buildings, and then her body crumpled to the ground as enemy fire shot her down. A civilian. An innocent woman, mother, sister, wife, with just a handful of groceries in her hands.

Jack's Story

The front door of Dr Janssen's house opened and the doctor ran hastily towards her. He turned her body gently to face him. Her eyes were closed, the blood seeping through her blouse and cardigan, staining it with a shot of red; a loaf of bread, some ham and a box of eggs smashed in her hands, their yolks as bright as the yellow tulips that would grow in the spring in his window boxes. The colour of the tulips that would sway in the spring along the canals, lining them with a simple fragrance of life.

He left her with the food. To take it would feed them – the Germans were slowly starving the Dutch – but he left it for another reason: a humane reason, a better reason, a more valued reason, a reason the enemy would never have understood. He was left free to walk back to his house with his head hung low; he was a doctor after all, and needed by the Germans to provide medical equipment and aid. To take his life would be an error of judgement for them. He would not be shot down.

He closed the door to his house and climbed the stairs to his landing, where the injured paratrooper and the small girl lay in his medical room. She was giggling on the bed that he had made up whilst the soldier played a simple game of silliness on the medical couch where he lay. Even in the worst of times, these men had a moment of spirit inside them.

He looked at them and smiled a smile that was one of sadness, despair and tiredness. The water ran in his basin and he let the red liquid wash away down the drain, watching the swirl of pinky-red water. He took the white linen towel and dried his hands and left the room. Leaving the towel to hang creased and crumpled, a little like the town he now existed in.

In the attic, the paratroopers watched from the window. Jack's eyes creased as his stare lay on the woman's body in the street. His head shook slowly and for a moment he closed his eyes. Another message came through in code from the British army: *'The 1ˢᵗ Polish Independent Parachute Brigade to be inserted in Driel under the command of Brigadier General Sosabowski.'*

Sophie Janssen as the Dutch Resistance replied.

'The 9ᵗʰ and the 10ᵗʰ SS Panzer Divisions are also near Arnhem, their military power would be hard to break. The Germans are heavy in power. You need to rethink this.'

'Ammunition arriving and supplies.' As the coded message came through, Lieutenant Colonel Frost sent a relayed message back.

'We have only a small amount of ammo. We are going to suffer heavily. We need ammunition, repeat we need ammunition, and boats. My men are down to their last. We need support. We fell directly on the waiting guns of the Germans camped out. Listen to the Dutch Resistance, they are our eyes and ears.'

The reply came back. *'Major Cain and his battalion will be with you, hold the bridges. Over and out.'*

'God damn the army – why won't they listen. Sosabowski was right when he was closed down,' Frost said out loud.

'Now what, sir?' Jim asked. 'We can't hold the Jerries off with the ammo we have. Jack's just taken out a tank and a Jeep, but how many more are going to come across that bridge? They'll sink our boats, sir. We're losing our men before we've even secured the bridges.'

'I know, but we do what we must, until we have more support. We fight them with everything we have, and we secure the bridges. God knows how but we have to secure the bridges.' He turned to Jack. 'Private ... Saunders, isn't it?'

'Yes, sir.'

Jack's Story

'Use your PIAT wisely. We will try and secure more houses as our base and watch from there. You're doing well, keep the spirit. Airborne.' His hand rested on Jack's shoulder before Lieutenant Colonel Frost left the room and went down the stairs to where Dr Janssen was treating the injured paratrooper.

'Serious?' Lieutenant Colonel Frost asked.

'I'm a paratrooper, sir,' he said, rolling down his sleeve.

'That you are. Dr Janssen ... is it serious?' Frost asked, turning from the injured soldier to face the doctor.

'Rest is required with this injury. I've stitched both the entry and exit wounds. Your man was lucky. He needs a few days at least.'

'Sir, I am fine. Just show me the way.'

'You heard the doctor – we need you fit for action. You stay and rest.' He squeezed the trooper's shoulder reassuringly and turned to leave, glancing over to the little girl, whose ankle was now mending itself in a plaster of paris cast. She was playing with her doll. He tossed her a wink and left the medical room.

The secret bookcase door closed behind him.

Chapter Fourteen

Appledaw Farm, Cowick, Exeter, early February, 1947

A chilly draft crept across the kitchen floor, as Emma pawed through the pages of *The Western Morning News*. Sitting at the table, she read the headline: *London set to welcome back refugees as Operation Pied Piper winds down.* Her fingers turned over and over again the corner of the page until a black print smudged across them. Then she turned to the bowl on the table and pushed the paper away, trying not to think about it. Instead she poured the ingredients into the basin and began to prepare the evening's meal. Aunt Emma was alone in the kitchen when the shrill sound of the phone rang from the hallway.

'Eleanor, can you answer the phone, I have my hands deep in flour.' Aunt Em called from the kitchen. Eleanor's footsteps were light on the stairs as she ran from her room to the telephone table in the hallway.

'Appledaw Farm, Cowick 6752, Eleanor speaking.'

'Good afternoon, this is the telephone exchange, telephone number London 564365. I will connect you now. Caller please go ahead.' The line remained open as the call was connected.

'Emma, darling, Emma darling sister, it's me, Charlotte.'

'Mother?'

'Eleanor! Oh my darling, yes, it's Mother. It's time to come home, my darling. How are you and the boys? I've missed you so much.'

'We're alright and we've missed you and Father too. How is Father? Harry has drawn you some pictures, so many pictures, Mother. We tell him about you and how pretty you are and how soft your skin is. It's like he forgets sometimes.' Eleanor rattled her words out, scared the line would be cut off, scared she'd forget the sound of her mother's voice, scared she'd forget to tell her everything.

'Oh, my darling, I can't wait to see you all. Is Aunt Emma there? Can I speak with her?'

'Yes, I'll get her.' Eleanor left the receiver on the table and went to the kitchen. Her heart was pounding and her head swimming with the excitement of being with her mother again. Then, as she saw Aunt Em kneading the doughy mixture, the realisation that soon she would no longer be on the farm overwhelmed her. She'd got used to the kitchen table and the warmth of the Aga, the sound of Aunt humming as she'd make their food. The way the light shone through the kitchen window and the large ceramic sink where she could watch the ducks aimlessly waddle about the yard. The huge kitchen door that would fly open with Uncle Henry beaming from ear to ear. The kitchen door still like a hug on their return from the fields, always giving that great sense of homecoming. She stood and watched and waited for a moment until the words fell out of her mouth. Words she wanted to say and yet words she wanted to keep in.

'It's for you.' Her eyes were fixed on Emma's hands in the mixture. 'It's Mother, Aunt Em.' Emma looked up from the bowl of flour and suet she was kneading. The indentation of her knuckles in the dough. She swallowed and nodded her head as if she knew.

'I'll be there.' She wiped her hands on a clean tea towel and brushed them down her apron, pressing it flat against her dress. The tea towel she folded and laid on the Aga, achieving some order in her kitchen before she left the room. She took up the receiver in the hallway and smiled a stoic smile into the mouthpiece.

'Charlotte, my darling.' Her voice carried a brave smile in it.

'Oh Emma, it's so good to hear your voice. London is safe now and the houses are liveable again.'

There was a silence on the line, and it crackled intermittently. 'Emma, are you there still?'

She exhaled, and as she did, she caught the reflection of her face in the mirror over the hall mantel. There were dustings of flour on her cheek and on the edge of her hair from where she had been making a hearty supper for her wartime family.

'I'm coming to get my children. I'm coming to finally take them home, Emma.'

Emma closed her eyes, her heart beating against her ribcage. The sound of Charlotte's words caught in her throat. Her hand pressed against her apron. The other hand across the receiver's mouthpiece, muffling the sound of her breathing. She stared at her reflection in the mirror, catching the emptiness of a face that stood in front of her. The feeling of loss being ripped from inside. Her head swam with an unwanted feeling of anger and jealousy. Her mind left bereft. She let her breathing rise from the depth of her lungs and then out of her mouth, and then she uttered the words.

'Yes of course, when will you be arriving?'

'I thought perhaps I might come at the weekend and stay for a few days with you all. Would that be alright? D'you have room?'

Emma nodded her head into the receiver, her eyes creased at the sides. She wanted to say, *No, I don't have room, it won't be alright, the children aren't ready, it's too soon.* But that would be

Jack's Story

wrong to deprive them of their mother, deny her sister's need for her children.

'Emma? Will that be alright?'

'Yes. Of course.' She stared ahead. As if ahead stretched for miles and miles through the arched window on the staircase and across the moors. 'That will be perfect.' Her eyes cast down to the address book on the table. 'Perfect,' she said again, the word just a hushed sound that came from her lips, just a sound, not a word with any meaning.

'I've already found the train times. There's a train at 7.36 from Paddington on Saturday.' Emma's eyes closed again as she heard the time, her head moving up and down nervously, like a toy dog that sits in a shop window and nods its head and wags its tail until the small child watching it with their nose smudged against the window is pulled away by a mother's hand. But the dog still nods its head and wags its tail.

'Saturday, right, of course.' Her breath held as each word blended into the next and tailed off silently.

The line closed and the crackling stopped. 'Thank you, caller,' she heard as the exchange closed the call. Emma held the receiver against her breastbone. The pendulum on the grandfather clock swung back and forth, back and forth. And for that moment in time, the walls of her house came crumbling down around her once more.

The gentle lowing of cattle from inside the barn led Eleanor to Jack. He tucked the urn of milk to the side to find Eleanor behind him, her cheeks tear-stained, her eyes bloodshot, the tip of her nose shiny and pink.

'Hey what's up?' he said as he brushed down the Red Horn's hindquarters.

'We're leaving the farm,' she cried and pushed herself straight into his chest, her sobs drenching his shirt. 'I don't want to go, Jack, I don't want to go.' She clutched the side of his shirt, her face still buried into him.

'Hey, come on. It's not that bad.'

'It is, it's worse.'

'Wait a sec'. He tossed in enough sweet hay for the cattle to feed on for the evening and then put his arm around Eleanor, guiding her into the yard, where the ducks quacked aimlessly about and the drake hissed behind his girls.

'Jack! Jack!' came the cries of the two boys as they raced across the yard from the farm's kitchen door. He stood his arms outstretched, crouching low, ready to feel the force of the boys on him. His knee on the ground, he stayed bent down, his eyes looking into Harry's. They were swimming with tears like liquid glass, until he blinked, and the tears dropped one by one and trickled down his cheek, waiting for Jack to catch each one.

'Hey, scruff, what's up?' Jack said, his arms firm around Harry.

'Mummy's coming to take us away again.'

'Hey, buddy, c'mon, that's good news.'

'No, it's not. I want to stay with you, Jack.'

Staying crouched, Jack ruffled his hair. 'It's your mum. I'd do anything to see my mum again.'

'But that's not the same.'

'Well, no, you're right, it's not the same, but my mum's not here. I'd move the world to have a hug from her again. How d'you know you're going?'

Jack's Story

'Aunt Emma just told us. She told us in the kitchen just now. She was crying too. If everyone's crying then we shouldn't be going, should we?'

'If everyone's crying then it means you have to be brave,' Jack said, pulling Harry in closer to him and perching him on his knee.

'Like you, you mean?' Harry said.

'Sure, like me, brave like a soldier. But you know what?'

'What?'

'Braveness comes from in here.' He patted Harry's heart. 'Sure, on the outside you're scared, but on the inside, you remember the good times, you see the good times, and then you're brave.'

'I want to be like you, Jack, brave like a soldier.'

'Then imagine and you will be. Now then, we'll just have to make the most of our time, won't we, and have you all smiling again.'

'Where's Beth?' Eleanor asked.

'I'm not sure,' Jack replied.

'We have to tell Beth,' the three of them said in unison.

'Yep, you do. Now why don't we go feed the chooks. C'mon, scruff.' He threw Harry under his arms like a rugby ball, his legs waggling in the air behind him and Eleanor catching them. Jack threw his other arm around Bertie for a boyish squeeze and they all sauntered over to the chicken coop, where the cockerel stood proud with the hens.

Aunt Emma watched from the window in the kitchen and a tear trickled down her cheek. The house would ache without them, as would her heart.

The door swung open and the three children stood in the kitchen with eager smiles across their faces, waiting for their hungry stomachs to be fed. Time with Jack on the farm that day had eased their feelings of woe like a plaster and soothing cream to take the stinging away. Instead, that special time with him had replaced their utter dread of leaving it all behind with their looming return to the city.

'Run and wash your hands now, dinner is almost ready.' Emma said, taking the newspaper with its unwanted headline and placing in the rack against the wall. The three skidded into the scullery and washed their hands before bundling back out into the kitchen to set about laying the table for supper. The sun had already fallen in the west and a low-lying sky pushed in around the farm, engulfing it in an early evening darkness.

The kitchen door opened and a flurry of leaves blew through the entrance, landing with a rustling sound on the tiles as they skittled across the floor. Henry pushed the door to, his face red and wind-burnt. He kicked off his boots before washing his hands. 'Last of the cold winds comin' through. Spring is pushing in, she be,' he said as he dried his hands and nuzzled his nose into Emma's neck. The aroma of beef stew and dumplings swimming in a thick gravy overtook the cold snap of wind outside and the harsh tail-end smell of winter. Henry pulled out his chair and eyed up all the children, finishing with a wink at young Harry. Emma dished up the hearty stew and placed each plate down as if taking in every moment of what she was doing, taking a picture in her head of her farmhouse kitchen table with each chair filled. Henry pulled his piled-high plate of warmth towards him. 'Smells good, Em. That'll fill me belly it will.' She stood at the head of the table, squeezed Henry's shoulder and smiled at the faces around it, her heart thumping inside her ribcage and a pang of grief beating against it. Supper was silent that night.

Emma lay in bed next to Henry.

'Summit wrong, Em?'

She turned on her side and lifted her head so that it rested on Henry's chest. She could hear the rhythm of his heart as she grazed the sheets between her fingers.

'Charlotte's coming on Saturday.'

'For the children?' His hand gently smoothed her hair.

'Yes.'

He felt her body as it sank in its heavy exhale.

'We knew this time would come.'

'I know, but I didn't realise how much I didn't want it to come.'

'I know.' He kissed her head and his hand rubbed against her skin. 'I know.'

Chapter Fifteen

Appledaw Farm, Cowick, Exeter, late February, 1947

A carpet of primroses ran along the verge of the paddocks towards the farmhouse, their delicate scent carrying in the wind. A kestrel flew ahead, soaring in the sky and then hovering, its wings splayed out whilst it waited, its beady eye pinned on a movement below until it would swoop down for its unlikely prey. Whilst the land was beginning to come alive now, food was scarce for the wild animals. A robin was becoming friendlier on the wall by the tied cottages; it chirped a little louder in song.

From the car window Charlotte watched as the primroses passed her by. The black Austin trundled up the lane, kicking up small stones and a wake of dusty soil behind its tyres. She held her handbag tightly on her lap as the hackney carriage bumped along the uneven terrain, her eyes catching the view of the land that held not a sign of war.

The cabbie pulled up outside the front door and got out. He opened her door before opening the boot to take out a small leather suitcase and hand it to her. After taking payment, he left her at the doorstep, where a wisteria twisted and turned along the stone façade, its trail of woody limbs bare of leaf or the beautiful lilac it would begin to shoot in early May. She rapped loud on the horseshoe knocker and waited. She rapped again, this time with more vigour.

'No use doing that, they're at the market,' came a voice from behind her. 'Can I help you? – you'll be waiting a while.'

Jack's Story

She turned to see a young man in brown slacks held up by braces, so they didn't slip below his waist. He wore a cap on his mop of jet-black hair and carried an empty pail in his hand. She tucked her neatly styled hair behind her ear and placed her brown case on the step beside her feet. She wore nylon stockings and heeled court shoes, her skirt tight around her hourglass figure, her tailored jacket falling to meet her nipped-in waistline, and a pretty brooch was pinned to her lapel.

'I'm Mrs Walker,' she answered, as if her name should mean something. Her eyes traced the figure in front of her.

'Jack, Jack Saunders. I work the farm with the Stephens.' He extended his hand. She cast a look at it. He rubbed it against his shirt and extended it out again.

'Charlotte Walker,' she said and allowed her hand. 'Have they been gone long?'

'An hour, I'd say. Mr Stephens is on the fields. I can get him if it's urgent.'

'No, that's fine, I can wait.'

'Well, I'll leave you here if that's alright, miss, need to get on.' He tilted his cap and left her at the door.

She watched him as he made his way over to the cowshed with the empty pail swinging in the crook of his arm. His harmonica's melody caught in the wind and fluttered past her. It reminded her of the music nights in London.

The old Fordston tractor rumbled in the distance. She sat on her suitcase and waited. She tilted her head towards the track she'd just driven up, and a figure caught her eye. It stopped at the paddock and leant over the wall. A horse walked over and butted its nose against the hand that extended out towards it. The girl patted its nose and spoke to it before it whinnied and galloped away.

Charlotte watched the girl as she skirted the edge of the stone wall and made her way towards the cowshed. A pretty girl with brown slacks snatched in at the waist by a leather belt, an oversized white cotton shirt tucked in and a pair of leather boots. The wind rippled through the shirt and the sun's glint silhouetted her body beneath it. Charlotte watched her until her nymph-like figure disappeared into the cowshed.

She got up from her suitcase and placed it next to the door before wandering toward the pond where the ducks quacked and swam. They dipped their heads below the ripples of the water, allowing only their fluffy tail ends to be seen, until they resurfaced with a bill full of algae and rich pond life. She smiled at the silliness of a duck's bottom in the air and bobbing back up. The willow swayed against the edge of the pond, giving a soft rustling noise as the wind played between its straggly fronds. She pushed them aside and walked in between the smallest of buds that clutched the dangling strands, soon to gift them with foliage, a sign that when the rain came and the sun beat down and the winds blew through, spring would awaken its canopy and another season would bestow a new awakening on the farm.

A car chugged up the track, its horn tooting as it arrived. Three children bundled out and ran towards Jack and Beth. Harry ran into him like a cannonball being released, charging straight into him. And Beth smoothed Eleanor's hair as she peered into the paper bag that had Colson & Co marked on it. Emma closed the door of the car and her eyes caught sight of a small suitcase on the step beneath the wisteria. She swallowed. She looked over to Jack and he smiled at her: he knew who Charlotte Walker was and why she was here. He nodded his head as if to confirm the truth that reality had come knocking on the door whilst they had been in town. Emma attempted a smile.

Jack's Story

The willow tree's branches parted, and Charlotte Walker stood for a while between them. Her feet frozen to the ground, her heart pounding. She watched as Jack threw Harry into the air and twizzled him around like an aeroplane in the sky, looping him up and down before landing him in a mass of dizziness, holding him steady so he didn't topple over his own feet. She watched as Bertie chattered away to Jack and took a pretend swift jab to his stomach and threw one back at Jack. She watched as Eleanor smiled and laughed with the girl she'd seen earlier with the horses. She wanted to call out to her three children, but their names caught in her throat. The sweetest of sounds she wanted to sing.

Then Jack ruffled the hair of the youngest and crouched down low and pointed toward the willow tree. And then turned the boy's small body so that he could see the beautiful view between the dangling strands of its canopy. Eleanor stopped and looked up from the bag, and Bertie turned and pushed his hair away from his eyes. The bag dropped on the floor and a small crystal mouse fell out of it.

And then she ran and then Harry ran and then Bertie ran. The dust of the yard was like a plume of smoke beneath their footsteps and the tears streamed down their faces and they ran. They ran until the arms of a woman in the curtains of a willow tree hugged them. Her soft lips on the tops of their heads, her arms tight around their bodies and the sound of their names under her breath. Each beat of her heart like a musical note escaping from an orchestra and finding a moment to sing alone. And then she stopped embracing and let her hands cup each of their faces, her nose pressed against theirs, and her hands brushed away the tears that cascaded down their soft cheeks. She drew them in and hugged them hard. Then she looked up and watched her sister as she took her case and opened the front door.

As Charlotte walked with them across the yard towards the door, she smiled at Jack as he tipped his hat. The children led her with a noise of babbling excitement until she reached the door where the wisteria hung. She pushed it open and stood in the hallway. The grandfather clock stood like a gateway to time, its pendulum swinging to and fro, to and fro, and the sun shone through the window on the staircase and at the bottom of it was her suitcase. The kettle on the Aga whistled and Emma appeared in the doorway, her hand caught in the tea towel that she twisted around them. Her eyes searched her sister's face and her lips curved into a smile despite the tears falling from her eyes.

'Come here,' she said and allowed her arms to envelop her sister. A hold so tight that not even the children could prise them apart.

'Well, young Jack said we 'ad company. 'Ow be ye, pretty maid?'

Charlotte turned her head to see Henry beaming from ear to ear. 'Ye got an 'ug for me?' She turned and let Henry throw his huge arms around her and crush her in his bear hug. 'It's good to see ye, girl. That it be. Proper job.' He kept his arm around her and led her through to the kitchen and pulled out a chair for her. Harry pressed up against her and stared into her face, not allowing his glance to leave her. 'They were right, Mother,' he said as he pressed further into her. She put her arms around him and pulled him up onto her lap.

'They were right about what, my darling?' she asked, softly brushing his fringe to the side.

'That you're so pretty and you've the softest skin.'

She brushed her face up against his and squeezed his nose. 'And you, you are my handsome boy and I have missed you every day, for every year. And my, you've grown.'

'I've drawn you lots of pictures, will you come look at them?'

'Yes, but let's have some tea first and then you can all show me everything. We have so much to catch up on.'

Emma poured the steaming water into the pot and let it sit for a while before pouring it into three cups. Henry took his and left the two women. 'I'll be back dreckly.'

'I've got a broth warming in the stove for lunch. You must be half famished after your journey. How was it?' she said, drawing up a chair and stirring the tea, the spoon scraping the bottom of the cup.

'Broth sounds wonderful and the journey was long, well, it seemed long. I was aching to get here. Half famished, yes – I am.' She laughed.

'Why don't you wash your hands, children, ready for lunch.' Emma took her cup from the table and placed it on the side by the sink. Charlotte flashed her a look. 'Sorry, it's just habit. Come on children, your mother's here now.' She took the broth from the warming oven, placed a basket of fresh cob rolls on the table and set six places. She watched from the window as Henry came back in with his empty cup and Jack and Beth made their way down the track to the tied cottages for their own lunch. The door swung open and Henry came in.

They sat around the table where an incessant amount of chatter and babbling came from the children and Charlotte laughed with every story told, aware of how much she had missed her children and the stories she was now hearing. How Jack had taught them to catch rats, collect honey and climb trees. How Beth was the prettiest girl they had ever met and could ride Storm, who nobody rode or dared ride. And how they had found – Eleanor shot Harry a glance.

'Found rats as big as a cat!' Harry blurted out, realising.

'As big as a cat, my my, that must have been some rat. I don't even think the Pied Piper was followed by a rat so large.' Charlotte tweaked his nose with adoration.

'How long are you staying?' Emma interrupted.

'We leave tomorrow.'

'Tomorrow? So soon. I thought you said a few days?' Emma rested her eyes on Charlotte.

'Yes, tomorrow. I think it's for the best, to get them back to London. You understand that, don't you?'

Emma nodded. 'Yes. Yes of course.'

'But tomorrow is so soon, Mother.' Eleanor said as she swished her spoon in her soup. 'I mean, we weren't expecting to go so soon. You've only just arrived.'

'Yes, to take you home.'

Harry banged his mug on the table. 'This is my home,' he cried. 'I'm not going, I don't want to go, I don't want to leave. I want to catch rats and climb trees. I don't want to go. I'm not going. I won't. You can't make me. I shan't go.' He pushed his chair back, so that the wooden legs scraped across the tiled floor, and he pelted past the grandfather clock and up the stairs, throwing himself onto his bed where he sobbed.

Charlotte pushed her chair back to go after him.

'Leave the bey.' Henry said, placing his hand on hers.

'He's my son.'

'That 'e be. But 'e be our bey for the last few years now. Let him cry, 'e needs to cry.'

'You think I don't know my children now?'

He shook his head and gripped her hand with a warmth that could only ever tell her that he knew her children too. His eyes

Jack's Story

lit up warmly as he smiled. His thumb grazed her skin and she sighed; she nodded her head, accepting his words against her own judgement. She didn't know her children anymore. She'd lost years of their lives. Harry had been a toddler when he left; he could barely remember her. Her sister had been his mother, not her. Her sister had shaped the children as they had grown through the war and now she, their true mother, was obsolete. They looked at life differently, they had grown up differently, and now catching rats and climbing trees had moulded them.

'May we be excused, Aunt Em?' Eleanor finally asked. Her aunt nodded. The two children left the table and went upstairs. They went upstairs to find their little brother, who would still be sobbing on his bed, with a bear and a wooden train wedged between his cheek and the pillow.

Charlotte watched as they left the room.

She drew in her cheeks and her hand rested on the cotton napkin at the side of her bowl. 'They have to come back to London. They are my children. I know this isn't easy for anyone, but neither was letting them come here. I didn't choose that. But they're my life and every day I have missed them. My boys, my girl. They're mine. War took them from me but now I have them back. I need them back. I just need my children back.' Her head dropped down onto the table and she cried – she cried the tears her own sister had cried when she lost her most precious baby. The same feeling of grief, knowing your love has been starved from you.

Emma's eyes filled with a watery liquid that would come gushing if she allowed it. She felt the pain that her sister felt, yet her sister's pain would subside and hers – well, hers would continue because she was reliving her loss. A tear fell from her eye and trickled down her cheek, landing on the back of her hand. And Henry watched her. Tenderly he placed his hand on his wife's hand and there he left it, cupping it softly, letting every feeling of knowing her grief be held by him. He knew her heart was breaking, his was too.

Chapter Sixteen

Appledaw Farm, Cowick, Exeter, late February, 1947

For weeks, months, years, Charlotte had woken in a terraced house in southwest London with only herself as company. Tim, her husband of twelve years, had enlisted with the RAF as a bomber pilot and she had worked as a secretary within the government. The decision to send her children to live in the countryside with her sister had been made for her; she was one of many families who became part of Operation Pied Piper. Daily she had caught the number 11 bus and disembarked at Parliament Square to begin her day working at the government's war office. Daily she would stare out of the window of the trolley bus and hope for an end to the war, an end to the bombs being dropped, an end to her heart aching for her husband and children to be with her again.

London had taken on a shade of dark grey and at night it was black, windows covered in blackout material, streetlamps extinguished, car headlamps only allowed to show a small slit of light in an attempt to trick the Luftwaffe and their supremacy in the London skies as buildings were bombed and terraced houses rendered unrecognisable by the nightly raids. The moon would be reflected in the silvery path of the rivers, indicating the landscape to the Germans, whose aeroplane engines droned above, taking over the skies like invading insects dropping explosives on English towns and cities below. Nobody was safe, not even the monarch. A wheeling, whizzing sound buzzed in the air as a bomber flew low and blew up the life below, innocent victims, homeless or dead beneath the rubble of their home lives. Hundreds of innocent civilians would lose their lives night after night.

Charlotte wrote in her diary: *'For fifty-seven nights we have been bombed now, will I live another fifty-seven?'* She lived for the most part of the war in underground shelters whilst the air raids sounded, their menacing blaring along the streets, the noise piercing your skull with an unwanted sound ricocheting off the walls of London, where a civilian would run for cover, hoping the protection would let them see another day break. The shelters where she huddled together with faces she had never known before now, singing songs of cheer and solidarity with faces who'd become her friends that night, until some nights those faces never arrived. She would only learn why when she'd return to the streets the next day to see the devastation of a once-loved home and a once-loved new friend.

She was unaccustomed to the quietness of country life and even more unaccustomed to its wake-up call when the sun peeped its head over the crest of the horizon and the skies took on a gentle orange and pink glow as it rose, casting its yellow light on the rolling countryside. Instead of a honking horn or the cries of the rag and bone man, she was woken by the raucous sound of the cockerel. Bleary-eyed, she rolled over from her bed and slipped her hand towards the bedside table to turn on the lamp. The room was still in semi-darkness and the only acknowledgement of the sun coming up was the unwanted alarm call from the cockerel. She stretched her arms in the air and let out an audible yawn before climbing out of bed.

She wrapped the flowery dressing gown that hung on the bedroom door around her and listened only to the gentle humming of the pipes under the floorboards, which hissed as the water rattled through. Going to the window, she drew back the curtains: a long-tailed tit flitted past her, carrying in its beak a clump of moss. She watched as it darted back and forth to the nest with tiny twigs, hopping between the entwined branches of the wisteria. She spied the cockerel who had woken her lauding himself on the roof of the coop as a handful of chickens pecked on the grain outside, their beaks bashing the metal edging of their trough before disappearing back to their perches where they'd nestle down and lay their morning eggs for the farm. The cows were ambling up the track, gently lowing, amid the calls of a young farmhand and Patch whizzing back and forth behind the herd, their girths wide, their udders low as they plodded up the track.

Charlotte let the curtain fall back a little and wrapped the belt of the dressing gown more tightly around her waist before making her way across the landing to where her children slept. The floorboards creaked a little under the soft cushioning of the sage-coloured carpet. Harry lay in his bed, one leg hanging out and his hair all ruffled. His bear and toy train were still wedged between his head and the pillow, a line of dribble running from his mouth. She sat on the side of the bed and brushed his hair with her fingers, tucking it behind his ears with each gentle stroke. He stirred in his sleep, letting out a small chomping sound from his mouth, nestling his head deeper into the feather-down pillow. She moved the wooden train, placing it on the eiderdown, and pressed her thumb against his cheek where a slight imprint of the train now lay. She smoothed it with her thumb until it disappeared. She took up his bear and held it close to her face, breathing in the soft fragrance of a small boy's love that had been given unconditionally. She could feel where the ears had been rubbed more, how every inch of this bear had been loved, right down to the stuffing inside it. How it had given her small boy comfort through the nights. It was a bear she had bought when he was born and called Rufus. She wondered if he was still called Rufus. Now it was as old as him and had been with him every night of his life. Giving him all the comfort she had ached to give him.

She leant over him and kissed his forehead. He shuffled under her, his small body snuggled in. 'Mummy.' She smiled as her nose touched his cheek and breathed in his loveliness. 'Yes, it's Mummy.'

'Mummy.' His arms wrapped around her as he snuggled her more closely. She brushed his hair with the back of her palm before leaving him to sleep.

She could see from the banister Eleanor and Bertie still fast asleep in their beds. A sight that made her heart leap with a joy only a mother could feel. She had longed for this moment and now here she was with it all. Her hand brushed along the smoothness of the banister as she made her way downstairs. The grandfather clocked ticked, chiming seven strokes. She drew up a chair in the kitchen and sat in the quietness of the farmhouse. The kitchen door swung open and Henry came in, not expecting to see Charlotte at the table.

'Ye be up early, me lover,' he said as he put the kettle on the Aga to heat. 'Ye sleep well?'

'I guess I am, Henry. The cockerel woke me.'

'Tea?'

'Love one.'

Henry took down four mugs that hung on small hooks on the dresser.

'Thirsty?' Charlotte smiled as she took one of the mugs of freshly poured tea.

Henry chortled. 'Jack and young maid, Beth, be working. Milkin' they be.'

'Of course, I met Jack yesterday. He sounded Australian?'

'Don't let 'im 'ear ye say that. He's a New Zealand bey. Fought in the war, a paratrooper of the 1st British Airborne Division. The children love 'im they do.'

'And the girl?'

'Pretty maid she be, Beth. Good worker she be. Eleanor loves 'er. Taken a proper shine she 'as.'

'Right. This isn't going to be easy for anyone, Henry. I know that.'

'Dare say it is. Go easy on Emma.'

'Meaning?'

'She's loved 'em like 'er own, she 'as. Stay another night.' He squeezed her shoulder and took up the mugs of tea, leaving Charlotte alone in the kitchen. She sat at the table and sighed into her tea before taking it up to her room. Was she about to turn their worlds upside down? Would they despise her forever if she took them away today? Was London no longer their home? Perhaps she would stay one more night.

Chapter Seventeen

Arnhem, Holland, late September, 1944

On the morning of the 20th September, the sun began to break through the clouds and cast a murky light over the small town of Arnhem. For three days now the British Airborne division had fought off enemy fire. From the attic room Jack, Ted and Jim watched the southern side of the river where the 9th and 10th SS Panzer Division patrolled the roads. Their military Jeeps tracked down the streets in the direction of the houses they had occupied for their own comfort.

The German commander stood in a Jeep that halted in the street, barking harsh, officious orders, his arm pointing toward a row of houses as he ordered his men to seize the properties and remove the occupants. The residents of those homes were taken under German orders regardless of their age, regardless of whether they were Jewish or Dutch. They were just to be taken as prisoners of war. Children cried as they were led away from their parents. The words *'mama, papa'* rang out as they were dragged away from the arms of the person who would protect them, who would tell them they were just playing hide and seek and all would be well, with a smile and shake of their head, reassuring them to go quietly, to not cause any fuss, to be brave. Only knowing that they wouldn't be playing hide and seek and their smile might be the last they'd see. The touch of their fingers as they were pulled from their mothers' arms. The horrid evilness that they would take with fearful courage, knowing that being brave was the only way to survive, obeying the orders barked

Jack's Story

at them because the British would come – the paratroopers were landing and they would be saved, the paratroopers, the men who jumped into combat, were coming to save them.

A small boy watched as the butt of a gun smashed the cheek of his dear papa because he dared to speak up and shout in defiance, to grab his child. The sight of an old man, a grandfather, falling to his knees and begging that they take him and leave his family: he'd had a good life, to let them be, to have mercy, to have kindness, to do right, *'de mensheid'*. A young SS soldier stopped and put out his hand. An order was barked at him and instead he cracked his rifle against the back of the old man's head, his feeble body hitting the ground. His face smashing the concrete, his blood running down his temple and his cheek, staining the shirt he wore. The hands of an old man, veins prominent veins under his paper-thin skin as he shakily pushed his frail body up to a standing position with dignity. His eyes stared into the young SS soldier's, allowing him the time to see his face, to see the lines on his face that had come from war, the stories of dark, dank trenches riddled with rats, the comradeship on Christmas Day when they exchanged cigarettes with an enemy who just like them was fighting for life, and the exchange of stories and laughter and cheer for a brief moment. For a brief moment, the bombs, the mortaring, the killing stopped. On Christmas Day it stopped. He too had been a soldier, in the First World War; he understood war and soldiers and commands. He also understood respect, even with the enemy. *'De mensheid,'* he said again.

The Dutch civilians were shoved into troop carriers with canvas coverings and driven away. They drove for about half an hour before the vehicle stopped in an area of farmland. They were ordered to descend and relieve themselves, stretch their legs in the fresh air of the farmer's crops, and then – the crack of a gun loading. In the silence, a machine gun pierced the air, echoing through the eerie hush of a farmer's field where the heads of barley blew in the wind like the golden rippling of the waves. Orders were barked in German as the SS vehicles pulled away, driven by cold-blooded murderers leaving the scene of a barbaric act, innocent lives taken, their bodies lying riddled with enemy bullets in a field of barley. The only sound now was the mellifluous swishing of the golden crops, crushed in places by the bodies of children, parents and a grandfather who had survived his time as a soldier in a previous world war. They lay on a farm that would become their resting ground, and when the rain fell and washed the bloodstained clothes, and the fear that lay in their still eyes, the farmer would come with his wife and bury the innocent souls.

Lieutenant Colonel John Frost's men watched from the attic window of Dr Janssen's house. Agathe and Sophie Janssen deciphered the messages that came through from the British. The south side of the river was swarming with German troops. In order to take the bridge at Arnhem they would need to push forward at night – it was their best chance, their only chance. Lieutenant Colonel Frost mulled over the information given. They hadn't the ammunition to forge ahead until XXX Corps reinforced their might.

Jack crouched at the window, his eye on the target through his PIAT. He observed as two empty troop carriers drove back up the street across from the river. It pulled up outside the house where a flag bearing a swastika was now erected. Three SS soldiers climbed out of their vehicles. They high-fived each other and laughed as they re-enacted the mass killing before they lit a cigarette. In the cab of the troop carrier, a fourth German soldier still sat, his head in his hands. It was the same soldier who under order had cracked an old man across the back of his head with the butt of a rifle. The same soldier who had put out his hand but chose the other way when given an order by a Nazi officer.

Jack watched as he got out of the vehicle and walked across the bridge to where paratroopers were hiding out. He walked unarmed to his own death, a death he gave freely. How could he tell his children and grandchildren in later years he had cracked an old man across his head because he had said the word 'humanity' – *'de menshield'*? His last word spoken. How could he live with the guilt, knowing he had aided the genocide of innocent people and an old man who fought in a previous war and now lived to tell the tales of right from wrong. Jack watched as the German soldier fell from the wall of the bridge and, as he did, he made the sign of the cross. That day, that moment was the day Jack understood respect.

Jack moved away from the window to the table where Agathe and Sophie sat huddled over their telegraph sounder. Dr Janssen had brought some tea up to the attic room for the men of Airborne Division, their officer, his wife and Agathe. Jack took his cup and his hand brushed against Agathe's, their skin touched. Jack cast his eyes down to her and moved his hand away, his eyes still fixed on hers. She glanced back to the decoder. Her hand twisted itself on her neck and then she looked at him. His touch had been smooth and warm on her and she wanted to feel it again. She wanted to feel his skin against hers again, the softness, the warmth, the closeness. Just for a brief moment the normality. He moved back to his position at the window. She felt the eyes of Sophie Janssen on her as she reverted back to the telegraph sounder as a message came through.

'Sir,' Jack said, 'the troop carriers – should we take them out?'

'Not yet, we need to reserve the ammunition. We take them out when they have German troops in them and the commander.'

'The Dutch residents, will they be prisoners of war?' Ted asked. Before Frost had a chance to answer, Agathe interjected.

'Along the south side of the river the verges are pitted with landmines. To cross at night may be too dangerous, the Resistance on the south side have said. The SS 9th and 10th have a ground force superiority, so many of the residents are now prisoners of war. But some are not. The German is strong in defence, they have the low-life criminals, is that how you say – the bad Dutch who have failed to enlist for their country, and it is better for them now to become German allies.'

'We will wait until the Polish Independent arrive,' Frost said, 'and then we will cross the river and take the bridges. We also need the brute force and ammunition of the XXX Corps. Until they arrive, though, the armoured vehicles we take out as a *'coup de main'*. He dabbed his forehead. 'Damn this.'

'Jack,' Agathe said her voice low. 'I need to cross the river to reach the Dutch Resistance on the other side.'

'You can't, it won't be safe,' he said, his eye still on his target where the swastika flew.

'I have to, it is my duty. These are my people too. The Resistance needs to spread out, not just stay in one place.'

'You're not a soldier, Agathe.'

'Maybe not, but I have a right. I have just fought from the barn to here. I am alive still.' There was more to Agathe than just a woman they had found in the barn, weak and scared. She had seen death, she had stood against the men who had raped her, she had fought against death.

'Lieutenant Frost, isn't it?' She turned to Frost, who drew in a deep breath as he looked at her.

'You are not part of my battalion,' he responded.

Jack's Story

'So that's it – because I am not a soldier, because I do not wear your uniform, or fight like a man? I am part of the Resistance, I am informing your British men, I am needed on the other side of the river. You have no ammunition, poor communication, we will all die because the Germans are stronger. What is it you do not see? You are sending men out to their death.'

Frost tapped his fingers on the back of a painting that lay upright on the floor, pursing his lips. She was right. They were running out of ammunition and their radios simply didn't work. When the Polish paras arrived, they would float through the sky like sitting ducks. There was no way of warning them.

'Alright, Jim, Agathe is your number two. We are down a soldier here in this house. She will stay with us to reach the south side of the river.'

'Sank you,' she said. She cast a look at Jack.

In the dead of night, the men of the 1st British Parachute Division moved slowly in between the shadows of the buildings that lined the small streets of Arnhem. They were nimble on their feet as they made their way towards the river, where on the bridge the voices of SS Panzer division could be heard. The smell of tobacco floated in the air as two German soldiers paced the bridge. They stopped on the bridge and lit another cigarette, the match fizzing in the cold air. The smell of sulphur and then the sweet smell of tobacco smoke funnelled up and blew downwind, travelling above the blackness of the lower Rhine, where plant life swayed in the direction of the current. An enciphered message had come through: *boats are on the banks, the Canadians and Polish Independent are with you. Secure the bridge.* Below the bridge, on the shore, the 2nd Battalion waited. They waited until the footsteps moved away and the smoke from the cigarette diminished. The paratroopers began to wade through the river.

'Shein das licht dort!' the officer commanded. The glare of a spotlight threw its beam across the rushing water of the river, illuminating the ribbon of blackness rippling through the reeds and rocks as the current swept through.

'Da ist nichts,' he replied, moving the light away from the river and onto the other side of the bridge. The light broke through the surface of the water and lit the cold depths of the lower Rhine, where the reeds snaked around the legs and bodies of the soldiers submerged. The airborne troops held their breath below the water, waiting for the light to move away from them. The rain pelted down, illuminated on the black liquid like shards of glass. Their heads came up slowly, gasping for air in silence. They waited until the Panzer's footsteps had moved on and their voices were no longer audible. The enemy had moved back to the southern side of the river.

Jack threw a small pebble towards the bank to alert the 1st Polish Independent Parachute Brigade who had now reached the river bank to start to move and for the Canadians to advance in their stormboats down the bank, slowly, staying close to the edge of the bridge to remain hidden in the dark. The first grenade was thrown by the British troops to disguise the sound of the motor-powered boats that the Canadian troops were equipped with. Jack lay low on the northern beach with Ted whilst they fired shells at the enemy. As the sky lit up like an explosion of fireworks, Jack could make out two German snipers active on the south side.

'Shell, Ted,' he bellowed across the booming sound of artillery fire. 'Another, two snipers on the south, you see 'em.' They hunkered down low whilst the rain lashed down and the bitter wind howled, and groans and wails came from men falling out of their boats as the mortar shells obliterated them,

Jack kept his watch on them. They were too far for him to blow from their point. Together the two paratroopers took up their weapons, scrambling amidst the firing of machine guns. They ran against the artillery barrage as a snowball fight with grenades ensued toward their boat.

Battlefield noise drowned out the powerboats. One made it only halfway before a mortar split it in half and killed all the crew. The airborne troops' boats were simple assault boats – no motors – and just required brute force paddling.

The three paras and Agathe sank low in the water whilst the Polish Independent lifted the boat across the pebbles, trying not to make a sound. It bobbed on the water until Jack grabbed the rope of the dinghy and pulled it towards them, pushing it diagonally against the current, pushing them further into the river. They lost their footing several times. The current was too strong for Agathe and she stumbled over a rock and fell, the water carrying her away from the men, her body still weak from her time in the Vught concentration camp at the hands of the Wermacht field. Jack sank into a dip in the bed of the river, the rope wrapped around his arm, his weapon above his head. He lunged his body forward and grabbed Agathe by her clothing, pulling her weight towards him. She coughed and spluttered, gasping for air as her body sank beneath the water again. Jack wrapped one arm under her and pulled her up towards him as he waded, his weapon still above his head, his hand hooked under her chin, keeping her afloat and alive. The men pushed the boat further along until the glare from the starlight came again. The rain was camouflaging them for all it was worth. Jack threw his weapon into the boat.

'*Shein das licht dort,*' a German officer shouted as the three men pushed their boat against the current, away from the starlight's beam. Jim hauled himself into the boat while Ted and Jack held it steady.

'Jesus Christ,' Jim said as his hand gripped Agathe's to pull her into the boat, avoiding the light. The enemy's machine-gun fire ricocheted around the boat, the water splashing up. Agathe screamed. Her hand lost Jim's and she fell back in beneath the black coldness, her body falling deeper and deeper until Jack's hand grabbed her, his hold tight on her wrist as he pulled her up next to him, manoeuvring the boat with Ted under the arch of the bridge away from the starlight's glaring beam. Jim leant back in as the light came around and grabbed her wrist to drag her into the boat, snatching at her sodden clothes to hoist her in from the cold river. Jack and Ted pushed the boat out further, wading through the freezing water before they scrambled into it and began to paddle close to the line of the bridge, staying in the shadows. The current pushed their boat away from the safety of the bridge's edge. They paddled hard against it in a diagonal fashion. Around them soldiers were swimming and crying out loud as their boats were shot down and sunk. Jim pulled those who were alive still into their boat, the paddles striking those who had not survived.

Trembling with fear and cold, Ted paddled hard, then passed the paddle to another soldier so he could take up his weapon and shoot at the enemy, trying to take out as many Germans as he could whilst the others paddled in sheer panic and tiredness. Machine guns set on fixed lines swept the river and beaches from both sides. The men cowered, protecting their heads with their arms as cold water showered them and bullets pummelled the lower Rhine river like frenzied skimming stones. Still they paddled furiously against the current until the sound of shingle on the hull and their paddles scraping against stone forced them to fall out of the boat and drag it up on to the southern shore. The light came again and shone directly at them, blinding them.

'Take cover!' Jim hollered. Agathe's body was weak and her lungs still clogged with water. Jack and Ted lay low on the ground and fired their weapons. Looking down the sight of his PIAT, Jack attempted to take out the tank that fired in the dark. His vision was poor at night. His aim was hampered by enemy fire and the driving rain that came sideways on through the wind and lashed at their faces like razors.

'Snipers, Ted, pass the ammo.'

He lay low, his eye creased as he looked down the sight of his PIAT. *Boom*. Liquidated. He turned his PIAT toward the second sniper, and the blast shot him out of the ground. Picking up his weapon, he and Ted belly-crawled up the shore. He took Agathe's hand and dragged her with him across the wet, stony terrain. 'We need to get to shelter – we're going to get killed here.' As the men scrambled up the beach, toward a nearby clump of trees, the lights from the enemy's beam shone straight at them and the firing came. The earth smashing up as they ran, dodging fire.

'Keep going!' Jack hollered. 'To the trees.' He held back and lobbed another grenade whilst Jim took Agathe, firing his weapon as he ran. And then it happened. Jim fell, his body blown from the back, a blast through his neck. Her body shrank to the ground as his fell over her, shielding her from the blasts. The black sky was awash with sparks from explosions, the force of the mortars tearing through his flesh. A scream from Jack as he ran in almost slow motion – and then another shell came, throwing Ted into the ground, the sand and pebbles spraying and blinding Jack momentarily. Ted stumbled then scrabbled up; he was alright. 'Thank God, Ted,' Jack said. And as he stood the machine guns fired and Ted's body crumpled to the ground, blood spewing from his neck. 'No!' Jack hollered. 'Fucking no!'

His face blackened with swamp-like mud, Jack's boots stuck in the ground as he tried in vain to reach Jim first. Jim's body lay over Agathe, protecting her from enemy fire, taking the force on his own. His chest was open and pulsating, and from his inside pocket he took a photograph, his blood-drenched hands holding a picture of his Peggy.

'Tell Peggy, Jack, tell her I love ...' Silence. Jack's head sank into his bloodstained uniform and the sound of the machine guns blurred into a noise that was unrecognisable.

From beneath the lifeless body of his comrade, his mucka, his brother in arms, he took Agathe in his arms and ran and stumbled until he reached the shelter of the trees. Settling her on the ground, he ran back to the beach where Ted lay, his neck spewing blood. His gasping cries, knowing he was dying, choking on his own warm blood, the fear in his eyes knowing he would not see his family again. Jack took him up and threw him over his shoulder and ran with his weight pushing him down. 'You stay with me, d'you hear. You stay alive, Ted, d'you hear. Don't you go giving up. You stay with me.' He slumped Ted down against the trunk and went back to Jim. His eyes stared out with a stillness that only comes when life has been taken. Jack brushed his fingers against his lids and closed them.

And then he cried and shouted out into the night. 'Fuck! Fuck! Fucking hell. You fucking evil fuckers.'

Chapter Eighteen

Appledaw Farm, Cowick, Exeter, late February, 1947

The next morning, Emma was preparing breakfast, but the peace of the day was broken by a scream.

'Eleanor, Eleanor!' Her cries became more frantic. 'Bertie, Harry! They have to be somewhere. They can't have just disappeared.' Charlotte screamed through tears as she raced down the stairs and into the kitchen where Emma was laying the table for breakfast.

'Where are they, Emma?' Charlotte's voice was raised in a wobble of hysteria. 'Where are my children?' She shrieked like a mad woman.

'Stop, Charlotte, just stop,' Emma said, grabbing Charlotte by the arms, gripping her tightly. 'They'll be hiding in their rooms, that's all. They always play hide and seek. Or they'll be in the bathroom washing their faces and hands before breakfast, I'll get them.'

Emma left Charlotte in the kitchen and went straight to their rooms, her feet swift on each stair's tread. She swung Harry's door open. His room looked how it always looked: his bed was made, and his curtains were still drawn. His fort was nestled on the ground between a rocking horse and a wooden chair, all the soldiers strewn around it. His toy train lay on the plump untouched pillow and his bear was gone. She exhaled before throwing open the doors of the wardrobe and pushing back the clothes in the hope of finding a small boy cuddling his bear behind the long winter coats. The hangers rattled on the pole as she swished them back. The base of the wardrobe was empty other than some hat boxes and shoes, stacked along one side.

She turned on her heels and walked quickly across the landing, checking the bathroom. Bertie's room was much the same: the bed was still made, and his curtains drawn. She wiped her hand through her hair, a bead of sweat forming on her brow, and made her way swiftly to Eleanor's room. It was no different. *Oh my God* she said in her head, over and over again.

She drew the curtains and looked across the yard. The chickens were out and pecking at the dusty ground. The pigs wallowed in mud, knocking their snouts against their swill. The willow swayed in the breeze and the ducks swam in circles around the pond. 'Where are you, children?' she said under her breath. She swallowed and felt a clamminess on her neck. She pushed the curtains further back and let her eyes scan the land that enveloped the farm until it fell into the sky on the horizon. Letting the curtain fall back, she exhaled. She had to stay calm for her sister.

Emma hurried down the stairs, her hand swinging around the newel as she reached the bottom. Her steps quickened along the hallway as she passed the grandfather clock. Its pendulum swung calmly back and forth, to and fro, belying the frenzied panic that was whirring up inside Emma and snatching at her throat as she tried to think where the children might be, where they could hide for hours in the games of hide and seek. And how now seeking wasn't fun. She felt a sickness in the pit of her stomach. She felt how the Earl and Countess of Devon might be feeling with the loss of their youngest daughter, Constance. She felt the gossip in her ears of the ladies in the community – *not only had Emma Stephens failed to have her own child, she had failed to keep safe her sister's*. Emma knew she needed to speak calmly to Charlotte when she reached the kitchen. She could not look distressed or desperate. She knew her farm and she knew how the children played. And now the walls came crashing down around her once more because she didn't know where they were, and she felt as sick as she'd felt the day she'd lost her own baby. She didn't know anything, least of all where the children were, and in her head the words *I've lost the children* came surfacing like an acidic burn in her throat from indigestion.

'They're not hiding upstairs, are they?' Charlotte said, her voice breaking as she said the words.

'No, they're not, but they'll be here somewhere. Stay in the kitchen, so at least somebody is here for them. I'll go and find them.'

'If I hadn't –'

'If you hadn't what, Charlotte, entrusted me with your children? If you hadn't let them stay here through the war, they'd still be with you? Is that it? If you hadn't what, Charlotte. Is this my fault? Is that what you're saying?'

'If I hadn't stayed another night, we'd be in London now. They wouldn't be missing.'

'And why aren't they here, Charlotte, why?'

'They're my children.'

Emma turned from the kitchen door that led out to the yard. She turned for a moment and looked at her sister, her eyes glazed with a liquid she could not let fall. She wanted to scream: *I know they're your children, you've reminded me enough times. But I have loved them like my own for the last six years. I have watched them grow, but I know they are yours. I don't have my own. Remember that.* But instead she said, 'I know they are. I'll find them. Just stay here.'

Emma went outdoors and cried, 'Eleanor!', her voice more frantic as she ran across the yard. 'Eleanor!' Her cry now a howling scream. She stood still, her eyes scanning the vastness of the farm. *They could be anywhere,* she thought. She'd forgotten after the first couple of years they'd spent on the farm that she was a bereaved woman, a sensible down-to-earth farmer's wife who had focused on three beautiful children, who had lessened the sinking feeling of abandoning the thought of ever being a mother, and now the breeze seemed colder and goose bumps prickled her skin. It wasn't cold and neither was the breeze. 'Eleanor!' she screamed again. She ran to the cowshed where Jack was clearing the empty pails with Beth.

'Everything alright?' Jack asked as he swilled out water from a pail.

Emma stood ashen-faced in front of him. The fear of not knowing where the children were was engulfing her. 'No. No, everything's not alright, Jack.' Each word seemed to take an age to form, as if the sentence had stopped in mid-flow and the world had gone silent, her words just falling to the ground, unheard.

'Have you seen the children, Jack?' Her eyes flooded with tears, her voice trembled as she uttered the words – *they're missing*. Words she never thought would be said, words she couldn't cope with hearing herself. Words that threw her into a mess in her head, made her picture a sister who would hate her forever.

'Missing? Since when?' Jack said, his eyes searching Emma's face.

'I don't know. Charlotte's in the house now. I've searched their rooms, through the wardrobes, under the beds. They haven't been here all night. Their beds are still made, and Harry's bear is gone from his pillow. I haven't told Charlotte that bit. Why would I tell her that bit?' The words *that bit* fell from her lips as they trembled, and her bottom lip dropped and quivered with an unstoppable movement. 'Why would I admit I've lost her children?'

As if time clicked into another era, another picture, another moment, Jack looked at Emma. He knew how to search, what to look for – to find hides, to follow tracks – in that moment he became Private Jack Saunders. His head switched from the Jack who played his harmonica on the farm and talked to the cattle and had a way about him that the children loved, to a man who knew how to search the terrain, who knew how to accomplish a plan, who understood strategy, who knew to never give up, who was a veteran paratrooper from the 1st British Parachute Division.

'I don't even know where to start. And the night would have been cold for them, what if, what if …'

'Stop.' He clutched her shoulders hard. 'What time did you last see them?'

'Just before bed. I said goodnight to them and let them go upstairs.' She shook her head, trying to remember everything and their last movements. 'I thought Charlotte had tucked them in – I didn't check, I always check on them and I didn't.' The tears began to stream down her face.

'So, they'd eaten dinner? Go back inside and check the larder for any missing food, simple things like bread, scones, ham, cheese. A flask. Look for missing linen, a blanket perhaps.'

'You think they've gone far, don't you?'

'I'm thinking like a soldier, Emma. They'll be hungry and cold.'

'Is everything alright?' Beth appeared beside them with a pail to fill with feed for the hens.

'The children are missing,' Jack replied.

'Oh my – I'll help look. Since when, breakfast?'

'Since last night. Beth, search the hay barn and loft. Emma, look in the milk barn and all the farm buildings, the hides where they've made dens, I'll track the farm. Once we've searched the farm, then I'll go further. I'll saddle up the horses. Beth and I will ride out.'

'Go further?'

'The moors, Emma.'

'Oh my God ... please Jack, please don't let this be true, please find them and bring them home safely. Please don't let them be on the moors, they'll never survive out there alone. Oh, my poor children.' Her body fell to the floor. Beth crouched down to her and swept the strands of her hair from her face. She saw the fear in her eyes, she saw a woman breaking, her insides caving in. She knew how frightened the children would be on the moors. She knew only too well. Should she reassure Emma? 'We'll find them, don't worry. We'll find them. Stay with your sister, I'll search the outbuildings with Jack.' Beth led her back to the kitchen where Charlotte sat at the table.

'Make some sweet tea,' Beth said as she squeezed her arm reassuringly. She left the two sisters alone and closed the door behind her, then ran across the yard back to Jack.

'Now what?' she asked.

'Go and check the buildings and hayloft, Beth. I'll search the yard and hiding places.'

Jack ran toward the weeping willow and pushed the strands of branches aside, tilting his head back to check no children were high up in the boughs. He swiftly moved to the back of the farmhouse where the private garden surrounded the family home. He raced toward the huge rhododendron bush that made a brilliant hide for Harry when he played soldiers. He scrambled down onto his belly and crawled under the foliage, pushing back the small branches that made dark tunnels through it, calling out their names as he went. His feet pushing his body though, his elbows being grazed. The sunlight struck him as he came to the end of the labyrinth of branches and pushed himself up. He ran to the soldier's watch he'd built in the line of pine trees at the back of the house, where Harry would lob small pinecones like grenades, pretending to be a soldier just like Jack. Pulling himself up the knotted rope to the platform, he surveyed the garden; there was no sign of them. He shouted their names. His voice echoed around but no child returned an *I'm here*. Taking the rope with skill and ease, he levered himself back to the lawn and ran to the yard, where Beth was coming out from the hay barn.

'Anything?' he asked. She shook her head. His eyes dropped to the ground. The children's footprints were dotted around but there was one set fresher than the others. He followed them toward the pasture where the cows grazed on the sweet grass.

'What is it?' Beth asked.

'The footprints here are too small to be Eleanor's and they lead down the track, look. They're not on the farm, which means –'

'They're on the moors.' Beth finished his sentence.

'I'll saddle the horses. Whilst I do, go back to the cottage. In the wooden box on the mantelpiece is my brass compass and whistle, can you get them? And come straight back.'

He went to the stable and took down the bridle and saddles and threw them over the wall around the meadow. Taking the first saddle, he walked down to the meadow where he clicked the side of his mouth and waited for Storm to walk over. The horse butted Jack's arm. Once he was saddled up, he led him out of the meadow and up the track, where he tethered him to the cowshed gate. He took the second saddle to Brandy and then led her back.

From the kitchen window Emma watched, her heart in her throat.

Beth returned carrying Jack's compass and whistle. He grazed his thumb across the smoothness of it and exhaled.

'It means something, doesn't it?' she said.

He nodded. 'Airborne. Follow me, Beth.'

Leaving the horses tethered, he went back to the farmhouse, where Emma opened the door for him.

'They're not on the farm, are they?'

Jack shook his head. 'We're going to head up to the moors. Have you got a map of the area?'

'Yes, in the bureau – wait, I'll get it.' She left Jack and Beth alone in the kitchen with Charlotte, who stared dead ahead. The rattling of a drawer opening could be heard and then hurried footsteps across the hall floor.

'Here.' She handed the map to Jack. Laying it across the table, he pointed to where he thought they were. The terrain was vast but he knew how to patrol forward to a rally point, and his rally point was now three children. He traced his fingers across the map and the fragmented lines like arteries running from a main vein. Ribbon-like strands running down the sheet of paper, portraying the rivers that flowed along the moors, meeting at a south-westerly point, Hartland Point, a notorious spot for ships hitting low rocks, sandbanks and unnoticed outcrops. Jack trailed his finger down, thinking like a soldier, thinking how a child would think when not scared of the darkness. 'Brooks Pond,' he said out loud.

'They can't swim.' Charlotte muttered.

'They can – Jack taught them,' Emma replied.

'Right.' She snorted. 'So, they can swim.' Her stare still fixed on a nothingness.

'Due east there's Grays House Farm, outbuildings to shelter in. They may follow the brook along, here, d'you see?' His finger trailed along Star Barton brook. 'To the west of that is the castle and north of that Pikefell Falls.'

'Parkforton?' Beth questioned.

'Yes.' Emma looked up at Beth. Beth felt Emma's stare on her.

'Parkforton runs down toward the coastline,' Jack said. Beth said nothing. Emma looked back at her, her stare drilling to the back of her skull. Her own heart was breaking at the thought of the children running away and now she had never confronted Beth. She had battled with her loyalties, between keeping Beth safe and not allowing her parents closure on losing their daughter. Another parent's heartbreak and anguish allowed for her own happiness, but not just her happiness, also the children's and Jack's. Jack was falling in love with her, she could see that as plain as day, and he deserved his own happy, ever, after, God knows he did. She had been like Beth once, and now – and now all she felt was guilt. Maybe a baby would have come later in Orchard Cottage, a small family, where she could have given the love of a surrogate aunt. Once more the walls around Emma came crumbling down. Jack broke her thoughts.

'We'll take the horses across out to Willow Point. They can't have gone far – they'll be tired and hungry.'

'They've taken food,' Emma said, 'and tea.'

'Emma, call the police station, we need to widen the search. You need to bring Henry in; he's working on the west fields.'

'What do I tell them?'

'The truth: that the children are missing, have been since early yesterday evening. Tell the police we have searched the farm and will now head out across the farmland west of Cowick Lane. We'll patrol out towards Star Barton Brook and Grays House Farm. I have my whistle. One continuous blow will mean to call off the search and that we have found them and that they are safe.'

'And if not continuous, what other one?' Charlotte asked, angrily. She threw a glare at her sister.

'There won't be another one,' Jack responded, folding the map and tucking it into his pocket.

'How can you be so sure?' Her voice was scathing.

'Because, miss, I am a paratrooper of the 1st British Airborne Division and I have fought in a war and rescued bodies from far worse than this. I have crossed the lower River Rhine at nightfall in lashing rain and have tracked terrains with my oppo on my shoulder, half dead. I have carried a Dutch Resistance woman across the bloodbath of a beach to safety. So that is how I can be so sure that there will be only a continuous whistle sound.' He tipped his cap and left the kitchen with Beth.

Charlotte sucked in her cheeks. Emma glared at her and left the kitchen to call the police station.

'You ready?' Jack said as he mounted his horse.

'Sure.' Beth latched her foot into the stirrup and threw her body over into the saddle. She clicked her mouth and dug her

Jack's Story

heels into Storm's side. Stones skittled across the track as they walked the horses down, Jack's eyes skimming the ground as they went. He pulled the reins in and looked at the verge. The carpet of yellow primroses had been de-headed and crushed, and by the stone wall that ran between the fields and the lane, the long grass was bent over and broken; it had been stomped down underfoot. He climbed down from his horse and walked over to the wall. He leant over it and looked at the harrowed earth below. Footprints ran in a trail over the trenched soil.

'They've crossed the land. They've stayed in the open. They would have been too scared to take the bridle path.' He latched his foot into the stirrup and mounted his horse. 'You ready, Beth?'

'Sure!' She heeled into Storm's girth, and rather than carrying on down the lane, they turned back on themselves and then heeled into the horses' sides. 'Yah,' Jack said as he rode hard and fast, jumping the stone wall. Beth lifted her body forward, holding the reins close to Storm's mane, and whispered in his ear. 'Come on boy.' Storm took the wall with Beth on his back, the power in his body as he strode across the stone wall with Beth holding him. Together they rode hard across the ploughed land, the crows taking flight as the heels of the horses kicked up the earth. They cantered past the scarecrow that stood alone. Jack pulled hard on the reins to slow his horse's pace. Beth followed suit until they stood in the depth of the fields, the horses' hooves dancing on the ground as they waited for their direction.

'Which way, Jack?'

He dismounted and knelt down on the ground, rubbing his hands through the earth, which was pitted with footprints. Then came a larger indentation and what appeared to be handprints. 'They've taken a straight line from the scarecrow, one of them has fallen here. Maybe Harry – it's too small to be the others.' He took out his compass and its pointer hovered until it found its bearings. 'We'll head due east. They will have followed the sun's light and walked towards the horizon. That'll take us down toward the brook.' He mounted his horse again, and she danced on the broken soil. 'Yah,' he said. As they reached the brow of the harrowed field, the sun's rays fell across the land, which seemed to undulate beneath the early spring warmth.

'They could be anywhere,' Beth said.

'They could, but my instinct says they'll follow the sun and go towards the water. Harry, at least, will want to.'

'Toward Parkforton Castle – it leads down to the coves. As a child I played there a lot.' Beth's eyes remained fixed on his face – *he knew,* she thought – he had to know. He knew her story, as did Emma; she had felt her look on her at the kitchen table. Just like she had heard hushed voices at the door of Jack's cottage months before and had watched the rear lights of Emma's car disappear up the track to the farm. Jack knew where she was from. Yet he'd never said. She swallowed and finally said, 'I came across the moors, I slept for one night under the tree.'

'The tree?' Jack's look was quizzical.

'The tree where we sat on our ride, the tree that is simply a skeleton of its former self, the tree that never bears any leaves but stands against the bleak winters on the moors.'

'Stag's Creek, you mean.'

'Yes,' Beth said, turning Storm to steady his restlessness.

Jack pulled his reins around. 'Come on,' he said. He clicked his mouth and kicked the side of his horse and rode it across the fields until they reached the barren land of the moors. The bracken and fern broke beneath the hooves of the horses. They crossed Star Barton brook, which meandered through the heathland, until they rounded up at Stag's Creek. The

Jack's Story

tree stood unflinching, its gnarly branches stretched out like antlers. Its grey bark never changing in colour, cracked and weather-beaten, but it still stood firm, old and needed. Jack climbed down from his horse and let it drink from the brook, and Beth did the same. He kicked at the fern and bracken, trying to see if anything had been left. He bent down: a toffee paper was scrunched in the tightest of balls. At the base of the tree were three crushed patches of bracken where three bottoms had rested, maybe slept for a while. He scanned the ground, looking for something else. A pathway of ferns was broken over in a trail heading east. He took out his map. If they stayed on a straight path, that would lead them to Pikefell Falls and the coves of Parkforton. Mounting their horses, they rode on.

The sky was the bluest of blues and the clouds buffered through the expanse of clear air. As if nature was allowing them to be safe and warm. The moors were not always so kind. The rushing sound of water through the falls became music to their ears as they cantered on.

And then, like that wondrous sight of a Christmas tree twinkling on the eve of Christmas, and that barn in Arnhem through the smoky grey haze amidst the shells of mortaring and an open grave of fallen men, they saw it: a small boy lay between the rocks of the glistening falls and, a little further, another lay huddled in the arms of a girl. The children of Appledaw Farm lay untouched by the beast of the moors. Jack's instinct had been right: they'd headed to the water, just as in the stories of Tom Sawyer and his adventures.

Jack and Beth dismounted their horses and led them to the water's edge to drink. Bending down at Bertie's side, Jack ruffled his hands through his hair, softly saying, 'Hey.' Bertie stirred from his sleep. 'Been on an adventure,' Jack said, scooping him up from the ground and sitting him on his horse as she drank at the water's edge. He held Bertie's hands tightly for a moment until he turned and made his way over to Eleanor. He squatted down and gently shook her shoulders. Although the sun was now high in the sky, the night had been cold.

'Jack?'

'Elle.' Taking Harry from her arms, he helped her stand and led her to Storm. He lifted her onto the back of the saddle, where she would hold Beth's waist and be ridden home. Harry, now scooped up in his arms, opened his eyes and shut them again, resting his head on Jack's shoulder.

'Block your ears, scruff.' And with that he gave one continuous whistle that pierced the quiet of the moors, that echoed through the hides of the Pikefell Falls, that caused the fish to jump in the falls and allowed a clattering of wings from the rocky pools to take flight. He lifted Harry onto the front of his horse, the boy's head dropping and his eyes slowly closing and opening as he fell in and out of his sleepy tiredness. Jack rode the boys with him, his arms safely around Harry and Bertie's clasped around his waist. Jack pulled Harry close to his chest as he rode.

They rode all afternoon through the rugged terrain of the moors, the hooves of the horses splashing through the brooks they had jumped earlier. Jack took out his harmonica and whilst he rode the dulcet tunes of *the blues* echoed around. In the distance the purple heads of the heather lay in a deep violet haze, and there they rode, their bodies lolling from side to side as the horses walked on and the sound of Jack's harmonica appeased the tiredness of the children. As they neared the farm, he blew again, one continuous whistle.

Charlotte and Emma looked up from table.

'He's found them.' The prickles on Emma's skin shot up her spine.

Chapter Nineteen

Appledaw Farm, Cowick, Exeter, mid-June, 1947

There was a quiet about the farm, the gentle drone of the tractor's engine across the fields as the dry easterly winds blew through the valleys, not racing but ambling through, bringing a midsummer warmth through their dance. The trees around the farm were now heavy in leaf and the hedgerows dripping in foliage and berries. The weeping willow swished as if whispering secrets in the breeze that rippled through its strands, and the ducks circled in the pond, dipping their heads before coming up with a bill full of slime-green goodness.

Jack stood at the pond, refilling it with fresh water. The spring had seen little rain and the water level was lower than previous years. A grass snake slid from the reeds and snaked its way into the pond, swimming across it, then twisting itself out and disappearing through the tall grasses. Hawks screamed and circled in the skies overhead, guarding their nests from swooping predators or humans that went too close to their young. Two dragonflies – delicate yet robust, independent yet together – hovered and darted above the water, lured by the sound of trickling from the hose. They danced between the splashes, a moment of playful blue before their silvery transparent wings took them away. Their iridescent playfulness breathing the smallest of joys into the midsummer's day.

Turning off the outside tap and looping up the hose, Jack left it by the side of the farmhouse. The cattle were now out in the meadows, chomping on the sweet green grass, the pigs snorting around their swill and the hens walking freely around the yard, scraping up the ground with their talons. He moseyed around to the back of the house, kicking the pinecones beneath the trees that stood high. Slouching down, he let his cap drop over his eyes, his back against the tree's trunk. The sound of the melody he played caught in the gentle breeze and drifted around to where Beth was.

'Penny for them,' she said, handing him a mid-morning tea and sitting next to him, her shoulder brushing his as she did. He took the harmonica from his mouth and placed the mug of tea beside him.

'Just thinking.'

He slouched a little more and bent his knee up, taking a pinecone and rolling in it his hands before lobbing it in a way he knew, as if it were a grenade letting off a smokescreen.

'You miss them, don't you?'

'Yeah, I do. I built this watch for Harry, so he could play soldiers and throw pinecones.' He sighed deeply.

'They'll be back. Eleanor was hoping to come to the farmers' dance, it's only a month away. She was looking forward to it.' Although there was a part of her that knew that perhaps they wouldn't return again.

'I guess.' He threw the dregs of tea across the lawn and pushed himself up, extending his hand to Beth.

'I'll catch you up,' she said. He left her under the canopy of the pine tree where the dappled light fell through. She watched him as he disappeared around the corner of the house and back toward the farmyard. She picked a daisy that smiled in amongst the blades of green, the tips of its petals tinged with the palest blush of raspberry pink. She twizzled it in her hands. It bestowed a happiness between her fingers. It had been three months since the children had left the farm. And although farm life continued, and had carried the Stephens and Jack through the months, their hearts were heavy with the loss of laughter from the children. Nobody really talked about it, as if mentioning their names might reignite the sense of loss and heartbreak that day had brought. Their leaving had been rushed and there had been an unwanted atmosphere between the two sisters.

Beth let her memory drift back to the day they left. The morning after the children had been found by the falls, a taxi had pulled up outside the front door of Appledaw Farm. The children had clung to Emma's waist, despite Charlotte's attempts to prise them away and get them into the waiting taxi. Her attempts were in vain; instead they ran into the arms of Henry, where his bear hug held them all. At last he gently eased them away and opened his arms to Charlotte. Her discomfort was evident as she loosely put her arms around him.

And then Harry spotted Jack and ran at full pelt at him, Jack crouched low to take the little soldier in his arms, Harry's feet leaving the ground as he was held in a tight embrace. The tears that came were unstoppable as the realisation hit this little boy that he was losing Jack, who was the bravest soldier he knew, who held him like a rugby ball across the yard, who dangled him upside down above a water barrel, who lay in wait between the rhododendron bushes whilst Harry's small body would lie above in the watch from the pine trees that Jack had built to lob pinecone grenades. And when Jack would scramble to the watch, rolling out of the way of prickly grenades, he would hold Harry as he'd level his body down the rope to the ground. For all the grenades thrown, he would get to wear the maroon beret and become a brave soldier like Jack. The words 'just imagine hard enough and you'll find me in your heart' – the last words he'd say to Harry as he patted his heart: 'I'm in there, scruff.'

The hold of Eleanor and Bertie as they hugged Jack hard, and how he ruffled Bertie's hair and allowed him to cry, pulling him in tighter. And the tight grasp of Eleanor's hands on his shirt as she sobbed into him, and the gentle run of her hair, and the kiss on the top of her head. And then it was Beth's turn, Eleanor's arms enveloping her as if she was a sister who'd taught her about coming of age and read to her extracts from her book – *A Tree Grows in Brooklyn* – a book she'd now finished and given to Eleanor. The secret they all held about her nights in the hayloft, and the day they had found her whilst playing hide and seek, would be taken down the farm track in a country taxi and back to the bright city lights of London. The unwanted hug between Emma and her sister only reminded Beth of her own family life and the sister she cared not to have.

The tooting of the horn as the taxi drove down the track, leaving a billow of dust in its wake, and through that billow of dust three children turned in the window to wave between their tears while their mother looked ahead and gave the instructions: 'Exeter St David's, please.'

Beth brushed her hands above the clump of daisies before getting up and leaving them smiling in the grass.

She went straight to the hens and opened the lid to the nesting box, where a plump hen sat, her feathers fluffed around her. 'Come on off those eggs, Henny.' She gently pushed the broody hen away and took eight warm eggs from the straw; they were ready to be sold. She carried them in the basket that hung on the side of the coop, taking them to the kitchen, where she retrieved another tray of eggs from the kitchen counter. Emma appeared from the larder, carrying a piece of ham.

'I'll take a couple of eggs before you leave them at the milk stand,' she said. 'I'm making a cold ham pie for the church meeting and bridge.'

Jack's Story

Beth left two eggs on the side and took the full trays of eggs to sell.

'I thought you might like to come to the meeting this evening, Beth. We'll be discussing the farmers' dance.'

Beth held the kitchen doorknob. She could feel it slip in her palm and her breathing caught for a moment. She turned from the door.

'I promised Jack I'd help harvest the salads this evening. Maybe another time.'

'Of course.' Emma smiled and went back to filling the pastry she'd rolled for the ham filling. The kitchen door closed behind Beth and she carried the tray of eggs down to the milk stand.

Jack was already back at the cottage and the table was set for their evening meal when Beth returned from the farm.

'The farmers' dance – who organises it?' Beth asked as they ate.

'Not entirely sure. I've only been to one, last year. Before that I was away at war.'

'Emma gets involved, though, doesn't she. She asked if I'd go tonight.'

'They use the barn for the dance, that's why. So, you're going?'

'No, I said I was helping you.'

'Helping me? With what exactly?' He laughed out loud and rocked back in his chair. 'You shirking community spirit?'

'I just don't want to be there, so I said we were salad picking. Can we salad pick?'

'Sure.' He winked at Beth and took up the empty plates from their dinner. 'Best get to it.'

'Ladies, ladies, welcome to this evening's meeting. In front of you you'll find the briefing of what's to be discussed. Namely the farmers' dance,' Reverend Holbrooke announced. 'Again, my thanks to those who have furnished this table with a delightful array of refreshments throughout the evening. Most kind and generous of you all. And Emma Stephens, again our thanks for allowing the community to use the barn, most kind. Perhaps I could allow the Chair to take over.'

Prudence Hubbard sat upright in her chair and drew the agenda and her notebook close to her. 'Thank you, Reverend, and of course thank you, Emma. As you know, the community is now back to a more normal way of life. As billeting officer, I have overseen the safe return of every one of our evacuees to their families in the cities. We should feel immensely proud of ourselves during that period of welcoming them into our homes.' There was a ripple of agreement throughout the hall. 'It leads me onto the sadder news that Lady Constance, the youngest daughter of the Earl and Countess of Devon, has not been found. The family believe her to be in London. She has been missing for over nine months now and, with a heavy heart, the family have accepted that she will not return home. They do not believe any harm has come to her.'

Emma Stephens cast her look to the window, where the sun dropped in the sky, throwing a reddish hue across it. She rubbed her lip with her finger as she let the words *she will not return home now* buzz around her head. She thought of how Beth had turned down the offer to come to the evening's meeting in favour of helping Jack harvest the lettuces, a job that required one person and would take seconds in his garden. She thought of how Beth had gone quiet when she'd uttered the words *Parkforton Castle*, when Jack traced the map of the moors where the children had gone missing. And then she thought of the children.

The evening drew to a close and Emma Stephens drove home along the winding lane, the sun a red glow in the sky. Her head was whirring with everything. She sat cupping a mug of warmed milk at the kitchen table, casting her mind back. When Enid had said all those months ago, *'Come on, Emma, surely you see it.'* She'd been right – Beth was Lady Constance, she knew that. But Emma too loved having Beth on the farm. She'd grown to love her like her own daughter; she wasn't just a hand to work the farm with Henry and Jack. And as Reverend Holbrooke had said, 'The Lord works in mysterious ways.' His sound words were right, they were right for Emma; maybe this was for her, to heal the heartache she'd borne. Beth made Jack's heart sing, she made all their hearts sing. It gave light to a new beginning for Emma. The children would go home, leaving a gaping hole in her heart, and Beth like a Christmas tree twinkling on the eve of Christmas morning would be a wondrous sight for her and for Henry. Over the months she had watched as Jack and Beth fell in love, the warmth and kindness they had for each other. Emma hoped that maybe one day Beth would be Mrs Jack Saunders of Orchard Cottage and the wonder of a Christmas tree would bring laughter and the beautiful sound of a new baby, a baby she could love as much as her own who lay sleeping in an angel's bed where Esther would now look over him. And she in return would be like a mother to Beth, a grandmother to what could be her surrogate family. A family that would bring laughter and an abundance of love back to the farm.

She turned down the lamp, her hand brushing along the banister as she took the stairs to where Henry slept, the grandfather clock's pendulum sweeping back and forth, back and forth. She stopped on the landing, the doors to the children's bedrooms now all closed, shutting away the empty beds behind them, shutting away the memories of happiness.

Chapter Twenty

Arnhem, Holland, late September, 1944

Jack held his fingers across Ted's neck as the blood seeped between them and trickled down. 'You stay with me, d'you hear,' he kept saying over and over again. 'I said I'd get you home, I promised you I'd get you home.' Ted's head lolled to the side, his eyes opening and closing as he tried to hear Jack's words. His breathing shallow as he gasped, choking on the blood that swam down his windpipe.

'Mum ... Dad ...' He exhaled through laboured breath. Jack rubbed away the blood that ran from the corner of his mouth. 'Ronnie ...' His eyes opened and closed. 'Penny ...' His head dropped forward again and Jack pushed it back up, holding him against his shoulder, one hand bunging the gaping hole, the other cupping his forehead. 'The sky's bright, d'you see, Jack. The light of the sky.' His head rolled forward again, and he spluttered out a mouthful of blood.

'I see it, Ted, I see it, bright like a star.' Jack looked at the blackness, the smoky screen of grey. The burnt-out smell of mortar shells, the boats of men that hadn't made it, their bodies bashing up against the river's shingle shore.

'It's bright in my eyes, Jack, can you see?'

'I can see it, buddy. Come on buddy, keep seeing the light.'

'It doesn't hurt anymore, y'know. I'm not scared anymore, y'know.' His head fell forward. 'You see that light, straight ahead.'

'I see it, Ted. You stay with me, d'you hear.' His words swam through tears, and saliva fell from his mouth in a long trail of dribble as he held his oppo. He pressed his head against Ted's as he drifted in and out of consciousness. His mouth brushed up against the boy's head, his own tears falling down his face. The slime from his nose dribbled down across his mouth. 'You stay with me, Ted. You stay with me.'

'Ronnie, you see the light,' Ted murmured between breathing that wouldn't give up but wanted to.

'You stay with me, Ted, don't you go anywhere, buddy.'

And then Jack saw it: the beam of light flickering in the haze of grey. He blinked several times. Intermittent through the smokescreen that swept across the beach of the river, the light flickered, bright then dull, bright then dull. Footsteps neared, boots on the pebbled ground.

'The light's so bright, Jack. Mum, Dad, the light's –'

'Over here!' Jack hollered, his voice breaking between joy and fear and tears and sadness. 'Over here.' The torch glimmered through the lifting smoke until four paratroopers stood with a stretcher. 'You hear that? You hear that, Ted? We're gonna get out of here.'

The torch's beam dazzled Jack.

'Over here,' the para said. 'Three more here.' They crouched by Jack's side.

'Lift him on, son,' one of them said.

'His neck, you need to bung up his neck,' Jack said as moved his hand away. Ted's neck gaped open, a vein or something pulsating inside. Throbbing, pushing, blood spurting.

'The girl?' the second para said.

Jack shook his head.

Jack's Story

'I saw the light, Jack. I said I saw the light,' Ted spluttered. His eyes closed.

'You did, buddy. You did, you saw the light.' Jack held his hand and let his lips touch his forehead. 'You did, buddy. Man, you did, drive forward, d'you hear me. We're gonna go home together.' He watched as the four paras became silhouettes on the riverbank, carrying between them on a canvas stretcher the body of his oppo, his mucka, his Number Twelve, Private Ted Smith of the 1st British Airborne Division, son of Ernest and Shirley Smith, older brother of Ronnie and Penny, hailing from Bow, East London. His brother in arms.

He turned to Agathe. She lay still on the ground, her white porcelain skin muddied with grit. She looked peaceful lying there, her eyes closed. He sat with her all night until the Canadians arrived. Until the Canadians came to help move the paratroopers out of Arnhem. To fly them out of Holland one day and leave behind the Dutch, who they had not been able to save, and leave behind his brothers in arms on the beach and the bravest of women who slept in peace.

The moon cast a silvery glow on the river, transforming it to a liquid black ribbon. Alone with only the moonlight, Jack dug two shallow graves with his entrenching tool. At first light he left the beach, carrying only the maroon beret of Private Jim Brown and a photograph of Peggy Arthur, the woman he was betrothed to. He stood on the crest of the bank, looking down. Beneath him, on the north shore of the lower River Rhine, lay sleeping eternally below the mounds of earth Private Jim Brown of the 1st British Airborne Division. His rifle stood as a post in the ground and by his side lay the most beautiful body of a woman whose soul sang now and walked with her ancestors. The rifle of Jim's oppo, which she had used on the battlefields of Arnhem, stood firm in the ground, leaning toward Jim's rifle to make a criss-cross. On top of it his helmet rested, rocking slightly when the breeze whistled through the trees. Jack stood and saluted, holding close to his chest the beret of his brother in arms.

Chapter Twenty-One

Appledaw Farm, Cowick, Exeter, late June, 1947

The subdued heat of the day still lay cloaked in black around the tied cottages, the stars high in the sky dotted around like the whitest of diamonds. The latch on the window rattled as much-needed cool night air blew into the room. Covered only by a white cotton sheet, she lay in bed and listened to the animals as they screeched in the night, a fox calling to his mate. The moon, like a warm milky glow in the sky, rested in the blackness. She turned to open the window wider and watched as the night clouds blew past it. An owl hooted overhead. She'd become accustomed to the night sounds as she lay in bed, the sounds of stillness in the cottage – the scratching in the eaves of scurrying feet, the distant, pretty chimes of the mantel clock, the gurgling of the boiler in the back kitchen.

And then his cries came. His cries of anguish, torment, nightmares.

'Get her, pull her in. Jesus Christ. The current's taking her. I can see the light. No! Fuck No! You evil fucking ... No!'

She tiptoed into his room. 'Jack.'

He sat bolt upright in bed. 'Stay with me, buddy. I see the light, stay with me. Plug his neck. Her parents are dead, her ankle is broken. Stay with me, buddy. No! No! You evil fucking –'

'Jack.' She sat at his bedside, the white cotton shirt catching on her knee as she pushed herself up to him, holding his arms. The inking on his arm of the parachute regiment.

'Agathe. Is it you?'

'Jack, you're dreaming, it's me, Beth. Can you hear me? Can you see me?'

He brushed her hair away from her face with the tip of his finger, lightly touching her temple as he did. 'Agathe.'

'No, it's me.'

She took the cuff of her sleeve and dabbed away the beads of sweat that formed on his brow. He held it against his brow. Their eyes caught. Trying to fill the silence, she continued, 'You were having a bad dream.' Her thumb grazed the inking on his bicep. 'D'you want some water?' He shook his head and closed his eyes, and when he opened them again, she was still sitting there like a mirage, an angel. The soft glow from the lamp shone through the white cotton of her shirt. She held his hand close to her cheek. She bent forward across his naked chest and let the pillows down a little so he could lie back down again. She felt his hand on her lower back as she leant across his chest, his torso strong, his chest defined. She felt his breath on her neck, the scent of his body close to her.

'There,' she said. 'Lie back down, I'm here.' She brushed her hands through his hair until his eyes closed and he slept. She pulled the sheet up over his chest and turned out the light. Standing in the doorway of his room, she watched before leaving him and returning to her bed.

What had just happened, she thought. Her mind flooded with him, his hand and his touch on her temple. His hand pressed against her back as she leant across him, the touch of his breath on her neck. A feeling she hadn't felt for months – as if her heart was being warmed and she had no control of how to deal with it; she wanted to run but couldn't. He said another girl's name, but he'd touched her face. He'd breathed her in. She lay in her bed, wishing – wishing what? Wishing that he'd sleep with no nightmares, wishing that she had left him alone to scream out in the night, wishing that – wishing that her name was Agathe. She closed her eyes, willing the feeling to leave her.

Voices below her window woke her. She pushed back the curtain to see Henry at the milk stand with Jack. She had no idea of the time, but it had to be close to seven for the milk to be placed at the end of the track for Ambrosia Dairy. Rubbing her bleary eyes, she pushed the sheet away from her and made her way to the bathroom. She splashed cold water on her face; the night had been warm, and her body was sticky and hot. She ran a tepid bath and climbed in, submerging herself below the water, scrubbing the farm smells from her hair until the fragrance that clung to her skin and hair was that of wild rose. As she climbed out of the bath, a small pool of water formed around her bare feet on the wooden floor. She wrapped the towel around herself before letting the water swirl away down the drain. Leaving a trail of wet footprints on the floorboards, she went to her bedroom to dress.

Jack was still outside by the time she came downstairs. She went through to the kitchen and poured a cup of tea from the pot. She pushed the small curtain along; it caught on the wire and she tugged it, knocking the cutlery into the sink. Storm was frisking about the meadow, perhaps she might ride him later. Today was Saturday and she and Jack weren't working on the farm for the weekend. Hearing the voices below her window and seeing Henry at the gate had reminded her of that, and how she was ready for some free time. She left the kitchen, taking her tea with her to the garden.

'Mornin' me pretty maid.'

'Morning, Henry.'

'We be watchin' the swallow nestin' in the old apple tree.'

'Really, a swallow.' She made her way over to the gnarly old tree, stunted in growth, whose branches lay like tired limbs resting on the stone wall. The green leaves formed a canopy above the small lawn and the champagne blossom was opening like a book, a book where the inking runs along the petals, forming a soft blush on the prettiest of flowers. Beth walked to the tree and bent her head as she stood beneath the leaves that threw a dappled light on her.

'It be in the hollow, ye see it.'

Beth peered a little closer until she could hear the faint chirpings of the newly born chicks. 'It's inside the trunk,' she said wistfully, moving back a low-hanging branch to get even closer.

'It be cuckoo's hole no doubt. She be dartin' in and out most of the mornin'. Pretty little thing it be.'

'That's nice.' Trailing her hand on the tree's trunk, she walked around it before standing back near the wigwam, which smelt of the sweetest fragrance, dripping with delicate green leaves on a vine that wove its way to the point of the canes with a waterfall of pink petals flowing from it.

Jack watched Beth as he leant against the wall. The daintiness of her dress fell along the soft lines of her figure and she'd caught her hair up at the sides with a pretty clip. Her feet were bare on the lush green blades of grass.

'Well, I best be going, Em will 'ave me breakfast dreckly and they cows won't milk 'emselves.' Henry climbed back up onto the cart and drove the work horse up the track, leaving the churns of milk for Ambrosia Dairy to collect.

'You're up early,' Jack said, opening the gate to the cottage.

Jack's Story

'I heard your voices below and the sunlight woke me too.'

'Breakfast?'

'Sounds lovely, shall we have it outside?' He brushed past her, and the scent of wild roses caught in the air beneath his nose. 'Jack.'

'I'm listening,' he said as he continued his walk back into the house.

'I thought I might take Storm for a ride up to Pikefell Falls.'

'Alone.'

'Yes, unless you wanted to come too.'

'I'll saddle the horses after breakfast – we can ride out together.'

A violet haze rippled through the ground as the horses took speed across the moors. Jack and Beth rode fast, taking each brook or trickling stream with a pounding leap. The sun beat down on them from the blue skies as they cantered toward Pikefell Falls. The sound of the water falling through the glistening craggy rocks as they approached.

They slowed their pace and walked the last few metres before dismounting and leading the horses to the water's edge, where they let them dip their noses in to drink. The sweat from their ride shimmered across their velvety coats. Jack threw down the crochet blanket beneath a tree that shaded them from the sun's intensity. He took from his shoulder his leather satchel and slumped himself against the tree's trunk. Beth held her slip of a dress as she did the same. The water cascaded down, forming a white frothiness as it rushed over the rocks that gleamed as they caught the sun's light. Small fish danced and jumped as they flipped themselves out of the water.

'I love it here,' Beth said, taking the soda from the bag and pouring two cups full. She took a sip and the bubbles tickled the tip of her nose. Jack pulled at a blade of long grass and chewed on it.

'Yeah, it's nice here. Reminds me of home.'

'Home – you mean New Zealand?'

He sighed. 'Probably what I miss the most: the waterfalls, lagoons, places to be free and swim. Days like these.'

'What's kept you here?'

'Not sure … the farm. Henry and Emma have been good to me and my late ma. Not sure my life would be any different back home. Maybe run my own sheep farm. But there's nothing there, family I mean. What about you – where's home for you, Beth?'

'Some place.' She pushed herself up from the blanket and ambled over with bare feet to the water, dipping her toe in.

'It's so fresh,' she said. She felt him behind her. He pulled off his white cotton shirt and undid the leather belt around his waist, his trousers sliding to the ground. Moving away from her and swimming into the churning white froth of the tumbling water below, submerging himself fully. She watched until he came back up for air. He smoothed his hair back from his face, his biceps strong, the water trickling down his toned chest.

'You coming in?' He smiled a smile that made her cheeks flush with an immediate warmth.

'I don't have anything to wear.' She crouched down and swished her hands over the surface of the water.

'Neither did I – I'm in my boxer shorts. They'll dry in this heat and if they don't, well, I'll ride home wet.'

Jack's Story

She stood up from the water and creased her eyes, cocking her head to one side. He was right, she would dry off in no time, and once upon a time she would have thought nothing of rushing into the coves half dressed. But today seemed different. Being here alone with Jack, she felt different. He turned his back to her and she could see the strength in his shoulder blades, and an ugly scar across his lower back. She watched as he dived once more into the water and vanished below the surface.

She undid the tie of ribbon that caught around her waist, the bow of the loop unfolding and falling loose. The delicate fabric of her dress fell to the ground and she stood in a pale cream camisole top and underwear. Her body submerged itself into the water and she tilted her head back, allowing her face to go under. Then she pushed her body up and gasped for air, brushing her hair away from her face. He stood near her; she looked away for a moment. Strands of hair caught against her cheeks. He moved closer to her, his eyes dropping down to her figure and then back to her face. She drew her arms up in front of her, shielding herself from the coldness on her camisole top that clung to her waiflike figure. He tucked his finger around the strands of hair and brushed them away. Her heart was beating hard against her ribcage, her stomach churning like a knotted ball inside her.

'Ever dived? Come on,' he said, pointing to the waterfall. He took her hand and waded across the pebbled bed of the river. She bit her lip, knowing that the feelings inside her were like an intoxicating feeling of pleasure, and yet he didn't touch her in the way she thought he would. Instead he took her hand and held it lightly as they waded through the fresh, cold water. She stumbled on a small rock and he caught her in his arms, his biceps flexing as he held her. She dropped her look and he lifted her chin with his finger, his body bent down to her height. 'You alright?' She nodded. He took her hand once more, this time his grip harder in hers as he led her slowly across the current, pushing his body diagonally against it, the spray of the fall hitting their bodies. He let go of her hand, the cold ripples of water flowing around her. She crossed her arms against her body, her hands clutching at her shoulders. He levered his body onto the first rock and extended his hand to her, pulling her up to each rock until they stood at the ledge of a cove within the fall.

They stood behind the falling water, the grey slate of the rock glistening in the sun's beams, the smell of icy cold water surrounding them on the hard face. Without warning, his feet left the edge and his body fell like a spear into the froth of white below. She held her breath until he surfaced, his smile reaching from one side of his face to the other. 'Come on, it's amazing.'

She stood at the edge, her camisole top clinging to her body, and shivered. Her arms and legs prickled with goosebumps. Her heart raced. 'Come on, Beth!' His voice echoed around the waterfall. The tips of her toes teetered over the edge, and then, like a falling angel, her body left the side: like a darting arrow arching in the sky, she fell gracefully into the water.

As she came up for air, the water trickling down her face, he pulled her in closer to him. 'Told you,' he said, his hands firmly holding her waist, her hands resting on his shoulders, a droplet of water trickling down her nose and onto her lips. He took her hand and led her out of the water and back to the blanket. The horses were still close by, grazing on the heath's flowers.

Together they ate a simple lunch of Scotch eggs and ham pie, and drank soda. He watched her as she took up her dress and wrapped it around her body, tying the ribbon tie in a bow at the side of her waist. The sunlight was being driven down by huge grey clouds as they rolled in across the once-blue sky.

Jack's Story

'It looks like a thunderstorm is coming in – it needs to break this heat,' Jack said, drawing up the blanket and shaking it off. He took up his slacks and pulled them up, buckling his belt and pulling on his cotton shirt and then boots. The air became colder as the clouds moved in from the south. Spits of rain fell in the wind as the heathers and ferns swayed. Storm pinned back his ears and danced his hooves on the ground. Beth took up his rein to calm his agitation. A thick crack of thunder splintered through the air. Storm whinnied and stood back on his hind legs.

'We need to go,' Jack said, taking the horses' reins. 'We can't outride a thunderstorm.' He took his brass compass from his pocket and waited whilst the pointer hovered. 'We'll ride north to Grays House Farm before storm rages through.' Taking Beth in his arms, he lifted her onto Storm. She turned him around, his hooves dancing and frisking on the ground, agitated by the change in atmosphere. 'Yah,' she said as she galloped behind Jack. A crack of thunder and fork of lightning jagged across the sky. The horses' hooves beat against the ground as the rain began to fall like sheets of glass. Drenched to their bones, they rode until the vague outline of Grays House Farm could be seen.

The barn stood alone on the moor, a brown timber frame that was weathered and battered from the changing weathers on the moors. A few hundred yards away, a stone cottage nestled on the barren land with a few goats grazing on the thistles and heather. Jack jumped down from his horse and lifted Beth as she took her leg out from the stirrup and over. Her arms were cold from the wind and rain. It lashed down around them, unrelenting, as another fork of lightning ricocheted through the skies, lighting it up like a hotwire.

He prised open the barn door and stood in the emptiness of the space. A rat scurried across the ground and disappeared through a chink in the timber. He closed his eyes for a moment. In the corner, hay bales lay on the ground, and he swallowed as he stared at them, his mind spinning with the familiar smell of a barn in barren land in lashing rain. He shook his head as the words spun around his thoughts: *'Ik ben niet de vijand – ik ben Nederlands."* He stood while the words drifted around his head and the rain lashed down around the barn until her voice, soft like an angel's, said his name.

'Jack.'

The barn was split into sections. There was an area where animals could shelter in the bleak winter months. It had a bay where iron rings hung from the timber wall and an iron trough was screwed in place to hold hay for the cattle. Jack turned and went back to the horses. He led them in and took the reins over their heads and tethered them to the rings. He unbuckled their saddles and swung them over the timber divide of the bay, then filled a pail of water from the well outside and brought it in for them to drink from. Beth watched on as he kicked the hay about the second bay and took the blanket from his satchel and threw it onto the bales in the corner. Her skin prickled with goosebumps and she shivered. Her dress clung to her body, wet through from the storm.

'You're cold,' he said, taking her hand and leading her to the corner. 'We'll stay here until the storm's passed and we can patrol on.'

'Patrol on?' She looked at him quizzically. She hadn't heard this way of talking before and didn't understand it.

'Sorry, I mean we'll rest here until the storm has passed.'

'Right,' she said, bracing her back against the wooden frame of the barn. Her lips began to quiver as she shook with cold.

'Here.' He opened his arm and pulled her in to his body. She could feel the warmth of his chest on her as she pressed into him, his hand gently rubbing her arm, the touch of his skin on hers, smoothing away the cold. He took from his pocket his harmonica and played a melody that dulled the storm outside and the wind that whipped around the barn. A melody that kept her in his arms.

Chapter Twenty-Two

Dartmoor, early July, 1947

Beth raised her head from the hay, the blanket still wrapped around her body. She squinted, trying to make out her whereabouts. She pushed herself up from the bales, her arm imprinted by the strands of hay.

'Ouch,' she said as a piece of straw stabbed into her elbow. Her neck felt tight and knotted after her night away from the comfort of her bed and soft feather-down pillow. She rolled it in a circular motion, pressing the palm of her hands on it as she did, trying to loosen the discomfort and tightness. She turned back to see if Jack was still sleeping. He wasn't about, but both horses stood snorting in the bay, still tethered. She smiled at Storm as he hoof-clipped the floor and he tossed his head as if to wish her welcome and good morning.

'Good morning, Storm.' She yawned.

Light flooded in from the barn door as it swung open and Jack stood beaming in the entrance with a bucket of fresh water from the well. 'Ah, you're awake. Morning.'

'Morning,' she said, pulling the blanket over her legs a little more.

'Sleep well?'

She closed an eye and screwed up her face, stretching her body. 'I think so.'

His eyes fell onto her figure as she stretched her arms out. Her dress gaped open a little, revealing a glimpse of the champagne camisole that fell softly onto the curves of her body. She blushed and pulled her dress across, adjusting the bow more tightly around her waist. 'Did you?' she asked, finding the loose clip dangling in her hair and clipping it back. She had no idea what she looked like and could only think a bedraggled mess: her dress was still damp and creased, her arms bore imprints of straw on them, and her hair probably resembled that of the scarecrow that stood alone near Stag Creek. She smoothed it down with the flat of her palm and hoped that she looked alright.

'I did, apart from you snoring.' He winked at her and a broad beam stretched across his face.

'Snoring? I don't snore. Do I?' A slight smile flicked across her face, unsure whether he was teasing her or not.

'How do you know? You're asleep.' He discarded the old water out of the open barn door and replaced it with the fresh bucket he'd brought in.

'Because I know I don't snore. At least, I hope I don't.'

'Is that so.' Jack chuckled.

'I wasn't snoring, was I?' Now she really was unsure and pushed hesitantly for an answer.

He winked. 'Nope. Just the horses snorting.'

She smiled at him as he brushed down the horses with his hands. There was something about Jack that had captured her heart from the moment she'd met him. There was a warmth to his smile that left a glow inside her. 'So, are we riding back now?' she asked a little hesitantly. 'I mean, has the storm passed now?'

'Sure has – the sky is blue as blue can be out there. I'll saddle the horses up.'

She got up from the hay bales and brushed away the strands that stuck to her skin, leaving small creases. Taking up the blanket, she shook it out, particles of dust dancing in the air as they caught in the sun's beams. She folded it neatly and handed it to Jack for his satchel. His hand touched hers as she did so, and stayed touching hers for a few seconds. She drew it back swiftly, her eyes catching his. He winked at her again and smiled. She looked curiously at him, her brows knitted, and then she left to go outside.

She rubbed her fingers across where he had touched her hand and pressed it up against her cheek. Her heart racing, she placed the palm of her hands against her chest, feeling it pulsate, a rhythmic beat. *Could he hear it?* She sighed a little loudly and walked a few yards away. He was right: the sky was the bluest of blues and the clouds gently buffered about in the light breeze, like huge cotton-wool balls floating aimlessly past. She bent down and picked a lavender stem and twizzled it under her nose. Crouching back down, she picked a few more stems until she'd formed a small, delicate bouquet of fragrant purple heads. She tied it with a twiggy stem and went back to the barn where Jack was finishing saddling up the horses.

He led them out and lifted her onto Storm, taking the rein over the horse's head and handing it to Beth. He mounted Brandy and, holding the reins in one hand, he took his compass from his pocket and waited until the pointer settled on north. They rode on across the moors, back to the tied cottages of Appledaw Farm.

It was good to see the familiar farm track and hear the droning sound of the tractor on the fields. The gentle lowing of the cattle in the cowshed, patiently waiting to be milked. Jack lifted Beth down from Storm, unsaddled the horses and led them with Beth back down to the meadow, to graze on the sweet grass and frisk about. Beth watched a while whilst

Jack's Story

Storm whinnied and galloped in the meadow, bucking his back legs in some kind of freedom dance. Then she walked back down the track to the cottage with Jack.

The cottage was cool inside, and the mantel clock rang eight pretty chimes.

'I'm going to have a bath,' she said as she inched off her shoes and left them at the front door. Barefoot, she went upstairs, leaving Jack in the main room. He could hear the water flowing into the bath and the bathroom door lock as he took the compass from his pocket and placed it in the wooden box on the mantel piece. He stoked the fire in the range. The remnants of yesterday's fire lay on the grid, now just a thick carpet of ash Jack added a few lumps of coal and bent his body low to blow beneath the coals, allowing for a small flickering flame to rise up and catch. The coals began to smoke around the heat and slowly the flames took hold, giving enough heat to warm the range and allow for a kettle to slowly boil. He went down into the kitchen and added more coals to the fire beneath the boiler; it was still burning, and the water was piping hot. He took the tea from the caddy and spooned it into the pot ready.

Upstairs, as he reached the landing, the key in the bathroom lock turned and the door opened. Beth stood there, a towel wrapped around her naked wet body, her hair dripping down her back, smelling of the sweetest wild rose. She caught his eyes on her and she held her towel a little closer to her.

'Sorry,' she said, 'I guess you'll want to freshen up too.' She brushed past him and closed her bedroom door behind her. She drew her curtains and sat on the edge of the bed. Lifting her pillow, she took from under it her diary and pen. She tipped the pillowcase up higher, expecting her book to fall out, and then she remembered she'd given it to Eleanor to read – she remembered being her age once. She opened her diary and clicked the lid off her ink pen. A drop of black ink fell like a teardrop on the page.

Pushing up her pillow, she drew her legs up on the bed and leant her diary against them.

Dear Diary

How do I begin? I'm not sure. I spent the night on the moors with Jack in a barn near Pikefell Fall. The thunderstorm drove us in there for shelter and I feel I should wish that we rode home, but I willed the storm to ravage the skies, to not leave. I wanted to stay with him, to feel him close to me. And yet I feel like perhaps I am the only one who feels this way, and I want to ask why, but how can I ask that question? He loves another girl – her name is Agathe and I want to be her, I wish I was her. But then me being her is no different than what I have run from. A deceit, a lie, a betrayal. I want him to hold me and yet I feel his look, his glance, his faintest touch – but it's not for me and I want it to be for me. I don't ever think it will be for me and so I need to leave. A secret I will tell only you and I know it will be kept, but I will pack my bag and leave because I fear my heart will break. I've fallen in love with a man who loves another.

She closed the lid of her pen and slid her journal back into her pillowcase. Then she towel-dried her hair and dressed before leaving her bedroom to go downstairs. The kettle whistled on the range and she poured the water into the pot. Jack appeared at the steps to the back kitchen in a crisp white cotton shirt and slacks, his mop of black hair still wet from his bath.

'Ah, you've made tea.'

'Yes, here.' She handed him a freshly brewed cup.

'I said I'd help Henry hang the bunting in the barn later, for the farmers' dance in two weeks' time.'

'Oh, of course, the farmers' dance. It sounds like a fun evening.'

'It is – lots of cider and local ale and a hog on the spit, dancing, laughter, a few raised eyebrows from the Women's Institute on the antics of some of the younger farmers. You're coming, right?'

She shook her head. 'No, I can't. I have to be somewhere else.' She took her tea and left the kitchen, brushing past him as she did.

'Somewhere else? Like where, Beth?'

'It doesn't matter,' she said, wrapping the palm of her hand around the newel of the staircase to go back upstairs.

'Alright, but it doesn't make much sense.'

'Maybe not but it does to me.' Each tread on the staircase creaked as she walked back upstairs barefoot. She'd never noticed them creak before, and yet today it was as if they creaked before she'd even placed her foot down on them. She closed her bedroom door behind her, placing her tea on the bedside table, and then she lay on her bed and cried. Cried tears she should have cried months ago, in a cold hayloft, and yet she never did. Now she cried tears that she wished she never had to cry, because this time she was falling in love and the man she was falling in love with would only ever love one girl, Agathe. As long as she stayed at the cottage, he could never be with the woman he truly loved, a woman whose name he'd call out in the night, a woman whom he mistook her for when she sat on his bed and soothed the bad dreams that were flooding his mind. She could never be that girl, and whilst she was living at the cottage, that girl would never come to stay. Her only choice was to leave.

She opened the drawer at the bottom of her wardrobe and took from it the money that she'd earned over her months of working at the farm. She counted it out: she had enough to get the train to London and find work there, and whilst she looked, she could rent some lodgings, too. *A Tree Grows in Brooklyn* had taught her many things and coming of age was one of them. She was old enough to work and fly the nest, and she had learnt so many new life experiences that had made her into the woman she now was. She knew how to work hard and give the best she could. Living with Jack had given her the independence she needed in life, an independence she would never have got in her former world. She had learnt how to master her own feelings, too, and know when it was the right time to move on and to let go. Jack would understand that she needed to find her own place in life, and he had given her that start to find it. For that she would be eternally grateful.

Each day on the farm seemed to move so quickly. Emma Stephens busied herself at the community meetings and Jack came home later and later as he helped with the preparations for the dance. One of the pigs was slaughtered and hung in the cold store, ready for the event for which the WI were vigorously selling bundles of tickets. Enid Postlethwaite had made a beautiful hamper with an abundance of gifts donated for the grand raffles. And Deller's Café had gone all out on producing some Victoria sandwich cakes that were oozing with dollops of fresh cream supplied by Ambrosia Dairy and freshly made strawberry jam. It would be the event of the year, and the funds raised would certainly replace the church roof with a little left over to repair the north-facing stained-glass window, which had seen better days. There was a hive of activity amongst the women of the church as cakes and bread buns were baked, side dishes of potato salads made and fresh salads dug up from the allotments. Wooden barrels of ale and cider were delivered by horse and cart, ready for Jack and Henry to set up under a tarpaulin of canvas and bunting. Paper chains and bunting were cut, coloured and hung across the barn in a criss-cross fashion. Jack made a raised platform from hay bales and old pallets for the band to accompany the Gay Gordon and reels. An evening of merriment was upon the community and not a drop of ale would be wasted.

As cars trundled up the track and the farm's horse went back and forth, pulling a cart with bales of hay for seating, the barn began to fill with laughter and chatter. Mr Potter, the finest butcher in Heavitree, stood proudly at the pig turning on its spit, ready to fill buns with the pulled pork and apple chutney that Emma had made from last season's apples.

With all the fuss and noise, and coming and going of cars and horse-carts, nobody noticed the figure of a girl closing the door of the tied cottages. Nobody thought anything of seeing a girl standing at the stone wall of the paddock where Storm stood grazing. Nobody heard her click the side of her mouth to call him over. Nobody noticed her stand and pat his nose and stroke him as he bumped her arm for more attention, and not a soul heard Storm whinny as he stood on his hind legs and cantered across the meadow, his head hung low and his heels high. Whilst nobody – least of all Jack – knew she had left Appledaw Farm and walked in the direction of Exeter for a train to London Paddington. Nobody would ever know where she had gone or even that she had left. She took one last look behind her, breathing in the sight of a farm that had brought her so much joy and love and a feeling of being accepted. She felt her eyes sting with tears, but she had to do this – there was no other way.

Exhaling deeply, she began her journey alone. With London as her final destination, she just needed to get there, and when she did she would be busy finding work and would have little time to think of him.

She followed the lane. Each time a car trundled past, her stomach tightened and the fear was so fierce inside that she would be seen. She kept walking until the land opened up and she could see the river running ahead of her. The early evening sun made it shimmer in the evening glow. A soft breeze caught beneath her hair and cooled her neck. She left the lane and walked carefully down a pathway, tilting her body back in the sharp descent. It led to the towpath of the river, which would take her to the centre of town.

The soft breeze whispered through the reeds of the bank and small fish occasionally jumped as it gently flowed. As she walked, her stride more powerful with more conviction, she thought of the faces she had once run from, the faces that had driven her across the moors and to the safety of a hayloft. The kind, warm faces of three children who had helped her and never did tell their aunt or uncle that she was a little like them – an evacuee of her own making.

And then she saw his face, the face that filled her heart with a glow that was as warming as the cup of Horlicks he had made her when he carried her to his cottage. Carried her up the stairs because she was too weak. She saw the face that smiled back at her when he dived from a waterfall and came up for air with his face close to hers. The face that had caught a glimpse of her body cold from the water but with a satin camisole clinging to her frame and shielding her soft skin. Her heart skipped a beat as she thought of him and her stomach twisted as if a small army of butterflies were flitting about. It somersaulted with pangs of wanting when she remembered how his touch had felt on her lower back when she'd been sitting on the edge of his bed. The feeling that bubbled up inside, like an intoxicating wanting for a man. A man she wanted to touch her skin and his fingers against her temple.

She quickened her pace, pushing away the face in her head she needed to forget. A water vole ran across her path and through the reeds and into the river. She took in a breath. A shadow seemed to throw itself in front of her own in the hazy summer sun. Her footsteps became faster – she was sure she could hear something behind her – she turned swiftly and looked, edging her bag back onto her shoulder. There was nobody there. A bead of perspiration formed on her upper lip, and she smudged it away with the edge of her finger. She lifted her hair off her neck, forming a ponytail briefly with her hand; it felt cooler. The sun was hot that day, the late afternoon balmy in its heat. She brushed her clammy hands down her side and hoisted once more onto her shoulder the cotton bags she had stuffed with her belongings, with her pillowcase holding her ink pen and diary. A small stone slipped inside her shoe, so she stopped and wobbled whilst she shook it out. She turned back again to see behind her. She carried on walking.

As she reached the second bridge, she stopped for a moment. Was she making the right choice? Should she turn back and learn how to live with the feelings she was running from? She had run once, but this was different, she kept telling herself. Her skin prickled as she went under the bridge, her footsteps echoing. It felt cold and damp underneath. Green slime like moss clung to its edges and water trickled down the arches at the side. A pool of water lay at the exit, where drops of condensation dripped perpetually. She hopped over it.

As she came back out into the sunlight, she looked up at the openness of the bridge. The cars trundled along it and a black Colson & Co store vehicle tooted its horn, giving a klaxon-style sound. She knew she had reached the city centre.

A run of stone steps brought her to the pavement, where she was surrounded by what seemed to be a million people, brushing past her. Their faces were uninterested in her or where she was going. She stopped and waited until she made out the high street and the string of black Colson & Co vehicles outside the department store. The cathedral's steeple towered behind on the green, its stained-glass windows shining for all to admire. She could see the huge cream canopies inscribed in black swirled writing overhanging the pavement, a throng of people coming and going from the fashionable department store. She smiled as she thought of her time with Eleanor there and how Eleanor had danced and cavorted around the beautiful evening gowns, wanting to be a princess, wondering what it might be like to wear a dress that was so elegantly stunning. Her heart raced, knowing she was now back on the high street where Prudence Hubbard had fixed such a stare on her as they left the grand department store. She walked with her head low so that she wouldn't be seen, hurrying past the entrance of the store. She darted down the alleyway that led toward the station, turning again to see behind her – she was certain there was still someone there. But there was only a woman, trotting along with a small dog on a lead.

She crossed the road and walked through the huge open wooden doors beneath a sign that read Exeter St David's. At the small wooden kiosk, she bought a single ticket to London Paddington.

'What time's the next train?'

'At half past four, miss. From platform one.'

'Thank you.' She tucked her ticket into her bag and made her way onto the platform. She sat on the wooden bench by a door with a brass sign on it that read waiting room. She'd never got a train alone before and she'd always had a first-class ticket. A man in brown slacks and jacket meandered down the platform and sat next to her.

'D'you mind if I smoke, miss?'

'No, not at all.' She sidled her bottom up the bench a little.

'You going far, miss?'

'Just to London.'

'Fancy place for a pretty maid like ye.'

Jack's Story

'Perhaps.' She gave a gentle smile then turned her body a little to look down the track. A man in uniform with a flag in his hand stood back from the platform's edge and dropped his flag to his side. The shunting, grating sound of the London Paddington train drew into the station.

'Have a safe journey, miss,' the man next to her said as she stood up.

'Thank you.' She smiled and walked towards the edge of the platform. A passenger leant out of the window and pulled the heavy handle down on the door and swung it open. With the door still open, Beth climbed the two steps onto the train. She took one more look behind her. The man on the bench tipped his hat and she smiled. The last of the passengers boarded and the rail guard walked up the platform, slamming all the doors closed. He blew hard on his whistle – one long, continuous sound – and raised his flag. Beth leant out of the window and watched friends, family, loved ones wave from the platform. The man on the bench had gone.

The guard blew on his whistle again and the train slowly pulled out of the station. Its wheels ground on the steel track, shunting back and forth with jerky movements. She watched from the window until she could no longer see the figures in the station. Then she heaved the window shut and walked down the carriageway until she found a compartment to sit in. She fell into the seat and the brown squidgy leather sighed as she rested in it. She sat alone with her cotton bags full of all that she had, her head full of memories. The fields moved past like a patchwork of green. She let her head sink back into the headrest and let her eyes close on it all.

Chapter Twenty-Three

Paddington, London, mid-July, 1947

In the rafters of the station, pigeons cooed, swooping around the great steel girders. The station's vastness left her feeling unsure of which way to go. A couple sat together on a leather trunk, holding hands and leaning into each other. A momentary wistful thought fluttered in her head. A signpost pointed to the underground station, another to a black hackney cab area and another to trolleybuses and trams. She stared at them all, bewildered by the choice and how it all worked.

A newspaper-stand for *The Evening Standard* stood at the double doors of the station, and a chap in black slacks, a white cotton shirt, charcoal waistcoat and a black cap shouted as London folk milled about or dashed to catch the tram in the direction of Shepherd's Bush and Ealing.

'Read all about it, read all about it,' he hollered in a broad cockney accent. 'Come'n'get the latest news. Princess Elizabeth to wed Mountbatten.'

Beth stopped and took out some change to buy a copy of the paper.

'Don't need your pennies, miss, they're free.'

He swiftly folded a copy and handed her it. 'Good evening to ya, miss.' He winked and tipped his cap. 'Read all about it, royal wedding to celebrate. Come'n'get your paper.' She waited until he finished shouting the headlines.

Jack's Story

'Um, sorry, I don't suppose you know if there's a hotel nearby?' she asked, taking the paper and pushing it into her bag.

'Depends what you want, miss. But if it's just for a bed for the night, you could try the Paddington Park Hotel. It's a left out of 'ere and you'll want to catch the tram to the end of Marylebone. Ask the gent in the whistle'n'flute in a red cap badge with London Transport just there, luv, by the apple'n'pears. He'll point you the right way. You can't miss the big white beauty. Me'n'my Shirl will stay one night.'

'Right, thank you.' She smiled and walked to the main doors of the station. Behind her, he carried on shouting the headlines.

'London news: the Exodus to ship Jews back. Read all about it!'

She had no idea quite what to look for and scanned the station for a fruit stall and busker playing a flute or some kind of penny whistle. There was nothing to suggest any apples or pears or musicians.

'Oh my,' she said out loud, looking utterly lost and confused. She felt all alone in a city that seemed to be moving at a pace she couldn't quite keep up with.

A string of horse-drawn hackney carriages and motor-driven cabs lined the pavement outside. A tram trollied past, tooting as it went. London people seemed to walk so quickly and in a bustling kind of way, she thought as she watched. She stood back and took in a deep breath. Turn left, she said in her head, that's what he said – *turn left, miss.*

She turned left outside the station, passing by the hackney carriages, and walked a little further along. Passers-by jostled her as she tried to remember the name of the hotel. She practised in her head the word *Marylebone* over and over again, and repeated *Paddington Park Hotel*. She stopped and asked a gentleman in a bowler hat and tailored suit carrying *The Telegraph* broadsheet tucked under his arm. He looked similar to someone she once knew – perhaps somebody who worked in the City, a financier maybe.

'Excuse me, sir. Could you tell me where I might catch a tram to Paddington Park Hotel?'

'Yes, of course. Jump on this tram coming along now and it's two stops along, just by the Regent's Park.'

'Thank you.'

'My pleasure, good day, madam.' He tipped his hat and strutted away.

He spoke in a desirable way – a little like the king, she thought. A little like her own father. For a moment she saw her mother's face smiling as she lounged in her striped deck chair, intermittently looking up from reading her *Vogue* magazine as she played with her sister on the beaches of Budleigh Salterton, collecting pebbles. She remembered watching from her window her father shake the hand of the groom's man who had delivered the Arabian horse to their estate. Her Silver Sixpence who stood, hooves dancing on the gravel. The man with a desirable voice who spoke a little like the king reminded her of her own life and her parents. A klaxon horn sounded and passers-by hopped out of its path.

As the tram neared, she was about to hop on at the back where a cheery conductor stretched out his hand – but a voice caught in the breeze behind her.

'Beth!'

She froze. Had she heard correctly?

'Beth!' The sound of her name came again, only louder. Then a whistle came, the sort of whistle that would call a sheepdog

Jack's Story

through two fingers, a whistle she'd only ever heard on the farm. She stopped and turned back. A man flagged a cab and clambered in. It was a mistake – she hadn't heard anything, just her imagination playing tricks on her.

Then her name came again, followed by another whistle, a loud, shrill, ear-piercing whistle with one continuous blow. Her eyes filled with tears she had to hold back. She knew that whistle: it was different to the one used by the guardsman at Exeter St David's. It was the whistle she had held once and given to him to find the children, it was the whistle that was brass and matched a compass that was beautifully engraved with the words *Private Jack Saunders* and below *Airborne*.

'Beth, stop!' She felt a lump in her throat. She closed her eyes for a brief moment and then opened them again. 'Beth.' The sound of her name behind her, the closeness of his breath on her neck. She clenched her hands together tightly and waited. Maybe she'd dreamt it. She went to step up to the tram.

'Hop on, love.' The cheery conductor took her hand. Her other hand went to hold the pole to embark – then came the feeling of his hand cupping hers. He stood on the step behind, hovering, one leg off the tram.

'You left without saying goodbye.' Her heart raced, pounding against her ribcage. She went to take a step forward but found his hand still taking hers, stopping her from going any further. 'You left without saying goodbye.' She turned, and there, standing in front of her on the tram's wooden step, searching her face for an answer, for some kind of reason, was Jack.

Her eyes filled with a watery liquid that she couldn't hold back. The tears fell uncontrollably down her cheeks and he brushed them away. He bent his body down to her level and tilted his head to one side. 'You left without saying goodbye,' he said again.

The tram pulled away. 'Where to, love?' the conductor asked.

'Paddington Park Hotel, please, two tickets.'

'That's tuppence, love.'

Beth handed him tuppence and took two tickets from him.

They stood together without a word between them. The tram tootled along, passing the green grass and botanical gardens of the Regent's Park, its wrought iron railings topping a cream Georgian stone wall.

'Paddington Park Hotel, love.' He dinged his bell and the tram halted whilst Jack and Beth hopped down and a few Londoners jumped on.

The newspaper seller was right: it was a magnificent white-buff building with great sash windows on a terrace that was in the shape of a crescent. Women in fashionable outfits sashayed in a unique way along the broad pavements. Men in tailored suits from Savile Row sauntered through, their black polished shoes clipping the stone pavements that ran along the Nash terraces of the Regent's Park. The terraces had been badly bombed and left a sad picture of London, even two years after the war. Together they walked across the road and wandered into the park, where they sat beneath a huge elm tree that shaded them from the early evening sun.

'How did you know I was here?' Beth asked, looking straight ahead at a water fountain where small children dipped their hands in a playful manner.

'I followed you.'

'I didn't see you. I thought I heard someone.'

'I'm a soldier, Beth.'

'I daresay.'

'Why have you left? Why not come to the farmers' dance?'

'Because – because I couldn't. I'm not who you think I am, Jack.'

'I know who you are.'

'To you I'm Beth.'

'No ... to me, yes, you're Beth, but you're also the daughter of the Earl and Countess of Devon. You're Lady Constance, who went missing last year.'

'How d'you know that?'

'Something Elle said. Mrs Hubbard had gossiped about Lady Constance running away with a carpenter.'

'A carpenter?'

'The tittle-tattle of the grapevine.'

'So, Eleanor knew too?'

'Maybe.'

'I don't want to be that person. I needed to escape. There was no carpenter – that would have made my life easier. I was to be married. At least I thought I was.' She twisted her hands in front of her and the tears fell down her face. He turned to face her and cupped her hands in his.

'And? What happened?'

'I saw him, the man who dresses like these men here.' She waved her hand at the well-heeled passers-by. 'In tailored suits from Savile Row, owned by my uncle's estate, the Earl of Burlington. I saw him – a man just like these, who stroll by with an air and grace that I want none of. Tarquin, his name was Tarquin, a Viscount. One night, when he'd come to stay for the weekend with friends – society people – his attention was drawn to my sister. I went into the garden and I could see the shadows of two figures in the summerhouse. And as I got closer, I saw my sister laughing as her neck was caressed.

I smiled at first because I thought she was with one of the friends who'd come down from London. And then, as he lifted her dress and drew her up closer to him, I saw his face. Tarquin Crawford, the man who weeks earlier had asked for my hand in marriage. Something I never want to see again, that image of the two of them. A betrayal I can never forgive. Is it wrong of me to run? How can a person be so highly educated – the finest schools, the finest colleges, a title – and yet to be able to simply care and love was not even part of his make-up?'

'I'm sorry, Beth. I'm sorry that a man did this to you. But you have to learn to forgive. Or it will eat you up inside. War teaches you forgiveness; it teaches you to respect the enemy, and you don't see that until the enemy realises his own mistakes. I watched a German soldier take his own life on the bridge of Arnhem because the guilt he carried was too much to bear. That day I learnt to respect the enemy. Some of them were bad, but some were like me, just soldiers. You can't keep running, Beth. You have to face your fears and respect them.'

'But I can't stay at the cottage, it's just too much.'

'Why?'

'Because I hear you in the night. I hear your screams, your anguish, and then, and then –'

'And then what?'

'You call her name. You were having a bad dream the other night and I went into your room and I sat on the edge of your bed and you thought I was her. The girl you love. I will be never that girl and I can't be there, or she will never come back to you.'

'Girl – what girl?'

Jack's Story

'You called me *Agathe*. And it's too hard for me. Because I wish …' A tear fell down her cheek. 'I wish I was her. But I'm not and I never will be.'

'Agathe?' he questioned. 'Agathe is a girl I rescued from the barn in Arnhem when we landed as paratroopers. I found her with Ted, my oppo. She was from the Dutch Resistance. One of the bravest women I have ever known. She fought alongside us, was raped by the SS, escaped from the Germans. But she is dead. She died in my arms on the pebbled shores of the River Rhine. I was unable to save her. I buried her with one of my brothers in arms on the shores of Arnhem. Her soul rests there in Holland, alongside one of the bravest soldiers I have fought with. The cries you hear in the night are the dreams I have of my time at war, the men I left behind, the haunting sounds of death, the fear, the cold, the pride. They'll never go, and finding you in the hayloft was like finding Agathe again. You were cold and thin and hungry and frightened. You were running from your own nightmare. Maybe one day you'll learn to forget it all and live a life that's happy and fulfilled, and where you can be the person you want to be. But I didn't want you to leave. I've never wanted you to leave. I knew you had to be Lady Constance – the way you rode Storm told me as much.'

She felt his hand gently brush away her hair from the side of her face and tuck it behind her ear. He lifted her chin with the crook of his finger.

'Beth, I saw you at the edge of my bed like an angel. When I rode with you to the waterfall and swam with you in the water, I wanted to hold you tight to me, to never let you go. When you lay in my arms in the barn, all that flooded my mind was you. D'you get what I'm saying to you?' She stared into his eyes, her gaze unflinching. 'I love you.'

'But …'

'There are no buts. I love you.' He cupped her face and she felt his lips on hers. Soft and warm and the feeling that she wanted. Her heart filled with a warmth that encompassed her. His hands were still tenderly cupping her face as he helped her gently to her feet and pressed her against the solid trunk of the tree, and there he kissed her whilst the water trickled in the fountain and dappled shade fell upon them.

Epilogue

As they walked through the park, the sun began to dip in the London sky, its pale baby blue heavily marbled with silvery clouds floating by. Young lovers meandered hand in hand through the walkways and ornate arbours where roses climbed, their scent drifting with the evening breeze, and couples paused at the water fountains or the benches for a romantic embrace. Jack took his harmonica from his pocket and, with one arm around Beth, he strolled along the flower walk, playing Louis Armstrong's *Before Long*. He pulled Beth closer in to him and she nestled her head against his chest as they walked together, falling perfectly in love in a London park on the west side of a city that harboured memories of a war, where birds sat on the low branches of the trees and chirped their evensong almost in time to Jack's melodic playing, like a Valentine's serenade.

A few paces behind, a figure walked unnoticed by the two lovers. His steps quickened as the music drifted towards him, his shadow falling ahead of him as the sun threw its cast from the west.

'Twelve go!' he shouted and paused, waiting for a reaction, his hands in his pockets, his fingers twisting the felt fabric within. 'Thirteen go!'

Jack stopped dead in his tracks. He knew that voice, he knew those numbers. The hair on the back of his neck prickled. He took the harmonica away from his mouth.

'Twelve go, Thirteen go. Go on, buddy, I'm right behind you.' The figure called out louder, his voice carrying a cockney accent, chipper and merry. Jack turned and there behind him was a soldier whose smile cracked across his face. A beam that stretched from ear to ear. And from his pocket he took the felt material, a maroon felt beret, that only the paratroopers wore.

Jack's arm dropped from around Beth and he walked towards the figure that came towards him, his smile as large as a Cheshire cat's grin. With a rush of elated feeling, he took from his pocket his own maroon beret. Arms outstretched, they took each other's hands, their grip strong and firm, and then Jack pulled the man into his chest with an embrace and a bear hug that could break ribs. Jack held his face. 'Ted – man, it's good to see you. God, it's good to see you.'

'You too, Jack. I heard your tunes and thought, it can't be. It has to be. It can only be. You got me home, Jack. You got me home, buddy.'

'I said I would, Ted. Oh man, come here.'

He pulled Ted back in, holding him tightly in his arms, and from a distance Beth watched as the two paratroopers became brothers in arms once more, a friendship forged from the moment they sat shoulder to shoulder in a hangar somewhere in England, from the moment they sat shoulder to shoulder on a Dakota C47 and from the moment they fell through the sky together, like giant mushrooms drifting in the slipstream. Their time in Arnhem, where their memories lay with their brothers who had lost their fight, and Agathe, who'd been a woman of the Resistance and fought to the bitter end.

Now reunited, Jack and Ted walked together, their arms around each other in a manly embrace. With Beth held close at Jack's side, the three of them walked past the fountains, past the line of elms and out of the gates on the west side, where a flower girl stood calling for passers-by to buy her flowers.

Jack's Story

The sweet scent of her blooms and bouquets perfuming the air with a fragrance of life.

'Bunch a'roses, sir, for ya pretty miss. Tuppence a bunch.'

The three of them stopped. Both he and Ted smiled at the sweetness of the flowers and the sentiment that some would carry from war.

'Pink or red roses, sir. Such a pretty bunch for a pretty miss like yours,' the girl said, wiping her hands on her apron.

He cast his eyes across the myriad colours and the rows of pails with flowers overflowing from them. And there his eyes rested on one particular bucket of water, its blooms drooping a little, the curve in their petals soft and delicate and the palest of yellows.

'I'll take those, miss,' he said, holding his beret in one hand and delving into his pocket for tuppence.

Wrapped in a string bow, the five tulips she handed him were as yellow as the sun that fell in the sky and as fragrant as the ones that would line the waterways of Holland and the window boxes of a doctor's house in Arnhem. Five tulips that signified the lives that survived and the losses of those in Arnhem – their comrade and brother in arms who'd sacrificed his life, their Jim. And Agathe, a woman who had the courage and determination to fight against wrong and that made her soul beautiful. Ted, who came home injured but got to be with his mum and dad and younger sister, Penny, and little brother, Ronnie, in the East End of London again. And a little Dutch girl, Marta, who was dug from the rubble of a broken home and survived – whose ankle was fixed and who would now be nine years old.

The final tulip was for Jack, who hailed from Christchurch, New Zealand and was a paratrooper who had jumped into the slipstream with his brother in arms and carried Ted on his shoulders across the shore of the lower River Rhine, who in his arms carried Agathe to the shelter of the trees where she died in his arms. Who with his entrenching tool laid to rest both the bravest of women and the bravest of soldiers, with their rifles and Jim's helmet marking their resting place, and had carried a small girl to the safety of a kind doctor's house. Who had gone on to work as a farmhand and was idolised by three children evacuated from London, and had fallen in love with Beth, a girl found hiding in the hayloft. Private Jack Saunders, a paratrooper from the 1st British Airborne Division who came back from Arnhem and had a story to tell.

"Airborne"